*Yasmina Khadra*

# THE SIRENS OF BAGHDAD

Yasmina Khadra is the nom de plume of the former Algerian army officer Mohammed Moulessehoul. He is the author of six books published in English, among them *The Swallows of Kabul* and *The Attack*, for which he was awarded the Prix des Libraires and was shortlisted for the Prix Goncourt, Prix Femina, and Prix Renaudot. He lives in Aix-en-Provence, France.

# THE

❖

# SIRENS

❖

# OF

❖

# BAGHDAD

❖

ANCHOR BOOKS

A DIVISION OF RANDOM HOUSE, INC.

NEW YORK

THE

•

SIRENS

•

OF

•

BAGHDAD

•

*a novel*

•

YASMINA KHADRA

*Translated from the French
by John Cullen*

FIRST ANCHOR BOOKS EDITION, MAY 2008

*English language translation copyright © 2007 by John Cullen*

All rights reserved. Published in the United States by Anchor Books, a division
of Random House, Inc., New York, and in Canada by Random House of Canada
Limited, Toronto. Originally published as *Les Sirènes de Bagdad* in France by
Éditions Julliard, Paris. Copyright © 2006 by Éditions Julliard. This translation
originally published in hardcover in the United States by Nan A. Talese, an
imprint of The Doubleday Broadway Publishing Group, a division
of Random House, Inc., New York, in 2007.

Anchor Books and colophon are registered
trademarks of Random House, Inc.

The Library of Congress has cataloged the
Nan A. Talese edition as follows:
Khadra, Yasmina.
[Sirènes de Bagdad. English]
The sirens of Baghdad / Yasmina Khadra ; translated from the
French by John Cullen. —1st ed. in the U.S. of America.
p. cm.
1. Baghdad (Iraq)—Fiction. I. Cullen, John. II. Title.
PQ3989.2.K386S513 2007
843'.914—dc22
2006101879

Anchor ISBN: 978-0-307-38616-8

*Book design by Song Hee Kim*

www.anchorbooks.com

# THE

＊

# SIRENS

＊

# OF

＊

# BAGHDAD

＊

Night veils Beirut's face again. If the tumults of the evening haven't awakened her, that just proves she's sleepwalking. According to ancestral tradition, a somnambulist is not to be interfered with, not even when he's headed for disaster.

I'd imagined a different Beirut, Arab and proud of it. I was wrong. It's just an indeterminate city, closer to its fantasies than to its history, a fickle sham as disappointing as a joke. Maybe its obstinate efforts to resemble the cities of its enemies have caused its patron saints to disown it, and that's why it's exposed to the traumas of war and the dangers of every tomorrow. It's lived through a life-size nightmare, but to what end? The more I observe the place, the less I get it. It's so trifling, it seems insolent. Its affected airs are nothing but a con. Its alleged charisma doesn't jibe with its qualms; it's like a silk cloth over an ugly stain.

I arrived here three weeks ago, more than a year after the assassination of the former prime minister, Rafik Hariri. I could feel the city's bad faith as soon as the taxi deposited me on the sidewalk. Beirut's mourning is only a facade, its memory a rusted sieve; I abhorred it at first sight.

In the mornings, when its souklike din begins again, I'm overcome with silent loathing. In the evenings, when the party animals show off their gleaming high-powered cars and crank up their stereos to full blast, the same anger rises inside me. What are they trying to prove? That they're still having a great time despite the odd assassination? That there may be some rough patches but life goes on?

This circus of theirs makes no sense.

I'm a Bedouin, born in Kafr Karam, a village lost in the sands of the Iraqi desert, a place so discreet that it often dissolves in mirages, only to emerge at sunset. Big cities have always filled me with deep distrust, but Beirut's double-dealing makes my head spin. Here, the more you think you've put your finger on something, the less certain you can be of what exactly it is. Beirut's a slapdash affair: Its martyrdom is phony; its tears are crocodile tears. I hate it with all my heart for its gutless, illogical pride, for the way it falls between two stools, sometimes Arab, sometimes Western, depending on the payoffs involved. What it sanctifies by day, it renounces at night, what it demands in the public square, it shuns on the beach, and it hurtles toward its ruin like an embittered runaway who thinks he'll find elsewhere the thing that's lying within reach of his hand. . . .

"You should go out. Stretch your legs, clear your head."

Dr. Jalal's standing behind me, practically breathing down my neck. How long has he been watching me rant to myself? I didn't hear him come out here, and it's irritating to find him hovering over my thoughts like a bird of prey.

He senses my discomfort and points his chin in the direction of the avenue. "It's a wonderful evening," he says. "The weather's lovely, the cafés are packed, the streets are full of people. You should enjoy yourself, instead of staying here and brooding over your problems."

"I don't have any problems."

"Well, what *are* you doing here, then?"

"I don't like crowds, and I detest this city."

The doctor jerks his head back as though a fist has struck him. He frowns. "You're mistaking your enemy, young man. Nobody detests Beirut."

"I detest it."

"You're wrong. Beirut has suffered a lot. It's touched bottom. But it's been miraculously cured. Although it seemed to be on its last legs not so long ago, now it's starting to recover. Still groggy and feverish, but hanging on. I find it admirable. What's to criticize? What don't you like about it?"

"Everything."

"That's pretty vague."

"Not to me. I don't like this city. Period."

The doctor doesn't insist. "Well, to each his own. Cigarette?"

He holds the packet toward me.

"I don't smoke."

He offers me a can. "Would you like a beer?"

"I don't drink."

Dr. Jalal places the beer can on a little wicker table and leans on the parapet wall. We stand there shoulder-to-shoulder. His alcoholic breath strangles me. I don't remember ever having seen him sober. In his early fifties, he's already a wreck, with a purplish complexion and a concave mouth furrowed at the corners. This evening, he's wearing a tracksuit stamped with the colors of Lebanon's national soccer team. The top is open, revealing a bloodred sweat-shirt, and the laces on his new sneakers are undone. He looks as though he just got out of bed after a long nap. His movements are languid, and his eyes, usually lively and pas-sionate, are barely visible through puffy lids.

With a weary gesture, he pats his hair into place on the top of his skull, camouflaging his bald spot. He asks, "Am I disturbing you?"

I say nothing.

"I was getting bored in my room. Nothing ever happens in this hotel—no banquets, no weddings. It's like an old folks' home."

He raises the can of beer to his lips and takes a long pull. His prominent Adam's apple makes each swallow visible. I notice, for the first time, a nasty scar running all the way across his throat.

My frown doesn't escape him. He stops drinking and wipes his mouth with the back of his hand. Then, nodding his head, he turns toward the hysterical lights of the boule-vard below us.

"Once, a long time ago, I tried to hang myself," he says, leaning out over the parapet. "With a length of hempen twine. I was barely eighteen."

He takes another swallow and continues: "I had just caught my mother with a man."

His words are disconcerting, but his eyes hold mine fast. I must admit that Dr. Jalal has often taken me by surprise. I never know what to make of his frankness; I'm not used to confessions of this sort. In Kafr Karam, such revelations would be fatal. I've never heard anyone speak like this about his mother, and the doctor's casual way of spreading out his dirty linen confounds me.

"Such things happen," he adds.

"I agree," I say, hoping the conversation will move on.

"Agree with what?"

I'm embarrassed. I don't know what he's getting at, and it's tiresome to have nothing to say.

Dr. Jalal drops the subject. We're not cut from the same cloth, he and I, and when he talks to someone like me, it must be like addressing a wall. Nevertheless, solitude weighs on him, and a bit of a chat, however inane, will serve at least to keep him from sinking into an alcoholic coma. When Dr. Jalal's not talking, he's drinking. He's a fairly serene drunk, but he doesn't trust the world he's fallen into. No matter how often he tells himself he's in good hands, he's never convinced it's the truth. Aren't those the same hands that fire weapons in the dark, slit throats, strangle people, and place explosive devices under selected chairs? It's true that there haven't been any punitive operations since he landed in Beirut, but his hosts have a record of bloodbaths, and what he reads in their eyes is unmistakable: They're death on the march. One false step, one indiscretion, and he won't even have time to understand what's happening to him. Two weeks ago, Imad, a young fellow assigned to taking care of me, was found in the middle of a square, squelching around in his own excrement. According to the police, Imad died of an overdose— and it's better that way. His comrades, who executed him with the help of an infected syringe, didn't go to his funeral; they pretended they didn't know him. Since then, the doctor checks under his bed twice before slipping between the sheets.

"You were talking to yourself just now," he says.

"I do that sometimes."

"What was the topic of your conversation?"

"I can't remember."

He nods and goes back to contemplating the city. We're on the hotel terrace, a sort of glass alcove overlooking the main thoroughfare in this part of town. There are a few wicker chairs and two low tables; in one corner, there's a sofa, and behind it shelves with books and brochures.

"Don't ask yourself too many questions," the doctor says.

"I no longer ask myself questions."

"A man who isolates himself often has unresolved issues."

"Not me."

Dr. Jalal had a long career as a teacher in European universities. He made regular appearances in television studios, bearing witness against the "criminal deviationism" of his coreligionists. Neither the fatwas decreed against him nor the various attempts to abduct him sufficed to silence his virulent attacks. He was well on his way to becoming a leading figure among those who castigated the doctrines of armed jihad. And then, without any warning, he found himself in an ideal position for the fundamentalist Imamate. Profoundly disappointed by his Western colleagues, aware that his status as useful raghead was outrageously supplanting any recognition of his scholarly accomplishments, he wrote a tremendous indictment of the intellectual racism rampant among respectable coteries in the West and performed some incredible pirouettes in order to gain admittance to Islamist circles. At first, he was sus-

pected of being a double agent, but then the Imamate reha-
bilitated him, made him their representative, and gave him
a mission. Today, he travels to Arab and Muslim countries
to lend his oratorical talent and his formidable intelligence
to jihadist directives.

"There's a whorehouse not far from here," he proposes.
"Feel like dropping in and getting laid?"

I'm flabbergasted.

"It's not really a whorehouse, Madame Rachak's place,
not like the others. It serves a very restricted, very classy
clientele. When you're there, you're in distinguished company. You drink together and pass joints, but nothing ever
gets out of hand, if you see what I mean. Then you take your
leave. All very discreet. As for the girls, they're beautiful and
inventive, real professionals. If you're inhibited for one reason or another, they'll straighten you out in no time."

"That's not for me."

"How can you say that? At your age, I never passed up a
piece of ass."

His crudeness flusters me. I can't believe an educated
man of his stature is capable of such crass vulgarity.

Dr. Jalal's about thirty years my senior. In my village, the
idea of having this sort of conversation with an older person is unimaginable and has been so since the dawn of
time. I remember a single occasion, in Baghdad, when I was
out for a walk with a young uncle of mine, and someone
cursed as we passed. At that instant, if the earth had
opened under my feet, I wouldn't have hesitated to jump in
and hide myself.

"So what do you say?"

"I say no."

Dr. Jalal feels sorry for me. He hangs over the wrought-iron railing and flicks his cigarette out into the void. Both of us watch the red tip tumble past one floor after another until it hits the ground and scatters in a thousand sparks.

"Do you think they'll join us one day?" I ask him, hoping to change the subject.

"Who?"

"Our intellectuals."

Dr. Jalal gives me an oblique look. "You're a virgin, is that it? I'm talking to you about a whorehouse not far from here—"

"And I'm talking to you about our intellectuals, Doctor," I reply, firmly enough to put him in his place.

He grasps the fact that his indecent proposals have upset me.

"Are they going to join our ranks?" I say insistently.

"Is that so important?"

"For me it is. Intellectuals give everything a sense. They'll tell our story to others. Our combat will have a memory."

"What you've gone through isn't enough for you?"

"I don't need to look behind me in order to advance. The horrors of yesterday are what's pushing me on. But the war's not limited to that."

I try to read his eyes, to see if he's following me. The doctor stares down at a shop and contents himself with wagging his chin in acquiescence.

"In Baghdad," I say, "I heard a lot of speeches and sermons. They made me mad as a rabid camel. I had only one desire: I wanted the whole planet, from the North Pole to the South Pole, to go up in smoke. And when someone like you, a learned man like you, expresses my hatred for the

West, my rage becomes my pride. I stop asking myself questions. You give me all the answers."

"What kind of questions?" he asks, raising his head.

"A lot of questions cross your mind when you're firing blind. It's not always our enemies who get taken out. Sometimes there's a cock-up, and our bullets hit the wrong targets."

"That's war, my boy."

"I know that. But war doesn't explain everything."

"There's nothing to explain. You kill, and then you die. It's been happening that way since the Stone Age."

We fall silent, both of us gazing at the city.

"It would be a good thing if our intellectuals would join our struggle. Do you think there's any possibility they'll do that?"

"Not many of them, I'm afraid," he says after a sigh. "But a certain number will, I have no doubt. We have nothing more to hope for from the West. Eventually, our intellectuals will have to face the facts. The West loves only itself and thinks only of itself. It throws us a line so it can use us as bait. It manipulates us and sets us against our own people, and then, when it's through toying with us, it files us away in its secret drawers and forgets us."

The doctor's breathing hard. He lights another cigarette. His hand trembles, and for a moment his face, illuminated by the flame of his lighter, crumples up like a rag.

"But you used to be all over the television—"

"Yes, like some sort of mascot," he grumbles. "The West will never acknowledge our merits. As far as Westerners are concerned, Arabs are only good for kicking soccer balls or wailing into microphones. The more we prove the contrary, the less they're willing to admit it. If, by some chance, the Aryan inner circles feel forced to make some sort of gesture toward their homebred ragheads, they choose to anoint the worst and belittle the best. I've seen that happen close-up. I know all about it."

It's as though he were trying to consume his entire cigarette in a single drag. The glow lights up the terrace.

I hang on his words. His diatribes express my obsessions, reinforce my fixed ideas, and energize my mind.

"Others before us have learned this lesson, to their cost," he continues, his voice filled with chagrin. "They thought they'd find a homeland for their knowledge and fertile soil for their ambitions in Europe. And when they saw they weren't welcome, for some stupid reason they decided just to hold on as well as they could. Since they subscribed to Western values, they took for granted the ideals people whispered in their ears: freedom of expression, human rights, equality, justice. Bright, shining words—but how many of our geniuses have been successful? Most of them died with rage in their hearts. I'm sure regret still gnaws at them in the grave. It's clear that they strove and struggled for nothing. Their Western colleagues were never going to allow them to achieve recognition. True racism has always been intellectual. Segregation begins as soon as one of our books is opened. In the old days, it took our leading intellects forever to notice this fact, and by the time they adjusted their sights, they were off the agenda. That won't happen to us. We've been vaccinated. As the old proverb says, He who possesses not gives not. The West is nothing but an acidic lie, an insidious perversity, a siren song for people shipwrecked on their identity quest. The West calls itself 'welcoming,' but in fact it's just a falling point, and once you fall there, you can never get back up completely."

"You think we don't have a choice."

"Exactly. Peaceful coexistence is no longer possible. They don't like us, and we won't put up with their arrogance anymore. Each side has to turn its back on the other for good and live in its own way. But before we put up that great wall, we're going to make them suffer for all the evil they've done to us. Our patience has never been cowardice. It's imperative that they understand that."

"And who will win?"

"The side that has little to lose."

He throws down his cigarette butt and stamps it out as though he were crushing a serpent's head. Then his angry eyes turn to me again. He says, "I hope you're going to give it to them good and hard, those bastards."

I keep quiet. The doctor's not supposed to know the reason for my sojourn in Beirut. No one's supposed to know. Even I don't know what my mission is. All I know is, what's been planned will be *the greatest operation ever carried out on enemy territory, a thousand times more awesome than the attacks of September 11. . . .*

Realizing that he's drawing me into dangerous territory—dangerous for both of us—he crushes his beer can and tosses it into a refuse basket. "That's going to be a mighty blow, a mighty blow," he says in a low voice. "I wouldn't miss it for the world." Then he withdraws to his room.

Alone again, I turn my back on the city and reminisce about Kafr Karam . . . Kafr Karam: a miserable, ugly, backward town I wouldn't trade for a thousand festivals. It used to be a snug little spot, way out in the desert. No garlands disfigured its natural aspect; no commotion disturbed its lethargy. For generations beyond memory, we had lived shut up inside our walls of clay and straw, far from the world and its foul beasts, contenting ourselves with whatever God put on our plates and praising Him as devoutly for the new-born He confided to us as for the relative He called back to Himself. We were poor, common people, but we were at peace. Until the day when our privacy was violated, our taboos broken, our dignity dragged through mud and gore . . . until the day when brutes festooned with grenades and handcuffs burst into the gardens of Babylon, come to teach poets how to be free men . . .

KAFR KARAM

# I

＊　●　＊

Every morning, my twin sister, Bahia, brought me breakfast in bed. "Up and at 'em," she'd call out as she opened
the door to my room. "You're going to swell up like a wad
of dough." She'd place the tray on a low table at the foot of
the bed, open the window, and come back to pull my toes.
Her brusque, authoritative movements contrasted sharply
with the sweetness of her voice. Since she was my elder, if
only by a few minutes, she treated me like a child and failed
to notice that I'd grown up.

She was a frail young woman, a bit of a fussbudget, a
real stickler for order and hygiene. When I was little, she
was the one who dressed me before we went to school. Since
we weren't in the same class, I wouldn't see her again until
recess. In the schoolyard, she'd observe me from a distance,
and woe to me if I did anything that might "shame the family." Later, when I was a sickly teenager and the first few
scattered hairs began to appear on my pimply face, she
took personal charge of keeping my adolescent crisis in
check, scolding me whenever I raised my voice in front of

my other sisters or spurned a meal. Although I wasn't a difficult boy, she found my methods of negotiating puberty boorish and unacceptable. On a few occasions, my mother lost patience with her and put her in her place; Bahia would keep quiet for a week or two, and then I'd do something wrong and she'd pounce.

I never rebelled against her attempts to control me, however excessive. On the contrary, they amused me—most of the time anyway.

"You'll wear your white pants and your checked shirt," she ordered, showing me a pile of folded clothes on the Formica table that served as my desk. "I washed and ironed them last night. You ought to think about buying yourself a new pair of shoes," she added, nudging my musty old pair with the tip of her toe. "These hardly have any soles left, and they stink."

She plunged her hand into her blouse and extracted some banknotes. "There's enough here for you to get something better than vulgar sandals. Buy yourself some cologne, too. Because if you keep on smelling so bad, we won't need any more insecticide for the cockroaches."

Before I had time to prop myself up on my elbow, she put the money on my pillow and left the room.

My sister didn't work. Obliged to quit school at sixteen in order to become betrothed to a cousin who ultimately died of tuberculosis six months before the wedding, she was fading away at home, waiting for another suitor. My other sisters, all of them older than Bahia and I, didn't have a lot of luck, either. The eldest, Aisha, had married a rich chicken farmer and gone to live in a neighboring village, in a big house she shared with her in-laws. This cohabitation deteriorated a little more each season, until finally, refusing to bear any more abuse and humiliation, she gathered up her four children and returned to her parental home. We thought her husband would turn up and take her back, but he never appeared, not even to see his children on holidays. The next sister, Afaf, was thirty-three years old and had not a single hair on her head. A childhood disease had left her bald. Because my father was afraid her classmates would make fun of her, he'd decided it would be wise not to send her to school. Afaf lived like an invalid, shut up inside a single room; at first, she mended old clothes, and later she made dresses my mother sold all over town. When my father lost his job after suffering an accident, Afaf took charge of the family. In those days, there were times when her sewing machine was the only sound for miles around. As for Farah, who was two years younger than Afaf, she was the only one who pursued her studies at the university, despite the disapproval of the tribe, which didn't look kindly on the idea of a young girl living far from her parents and thus in proximity to temptations. Farah held out and received her diploma with flying colors. My great-uncle wanted to marry her to one of his offspring, a pious, considerate farmer; Farah categorically refused his offer and chose to work at a hospital. Her attitude caused the tribe deep consternation, and the humiliated son, followed by his mother and father, cut the lot of us. Today, Farah practices in a private clinic in Baghdad and earns a good living. It was her money that my twin sister put on my pillow from time to time.

In Kafr Karam, young men of my age had stopped pretending to be horrified when a sister or mother discreetly

slipped them a few dinars. At first, they were a little embarrassed, and to save face they promised to repay the "loan"
as quickly as possible. They all dreamed of finding a job
that would allow them to hold their heads high. But times
were hard; wars and the embargo had brought the country
to its knees, and the young people of our village were too
pious to venture into the big cities, where their ancestral
blessing had no jurisdiction, and where the devil was at
work, nimbly perverting souls. In Kafr Karam, we had
nothing to do with that sort of thing. Our people think it's
better to die than to sink into vice or thievery. The call of
the Ancients drowns out the sirens' song, no matter how
loud. We're honest by vocation.

I started attending the university in Baghdad a few
months before the American invasion. I was in heaven. My
status as a university student gave my father back his pride.
He was illiterate, a raggedy old well digger, but he was also
the father of a physician and of a future doctor of letters!
Wasn't that a fine revenge for all his setbacks? I'd promised
myself not to disappoint him. Had I ever disappointed him
in my life? I wanted to succeed for his sake; I wanted to read
in his dust-ravaged eyes what his face concealed: the happiness of seeing the seed he'd sown flourishing in body and
mind. While the other fathers were hastening to yoke their
progeny to the same laborious tasks that had made their
own lives a torment, like those of their ancestors, my father
tightened his belt to the last notch so I could pursue my
studies. It wasn't a sure thing that this process would lead
to social success for either of us, but he was convinced that
a poor educated person was less lamentable than a poor
blockhead. If a man could read his own letters and fill out

his own forms, he thought, a good part of his dignity was safe and secure.

The first time I set foot on the university campus, I chose to wear spectacles, even though I've always had excellent vision. I think they were the reason why Nawal noticed me in the first place; her face turned as red as a beet whenever our paths crossed after classes were over. Even though I had never dared address a word to her, the least of her smiles was enough to make me happy. I was just on the point of declaring myself and unveiling to her the prospect of a bright future, when strange fireworks lit up the sky over Baghdad. The sirens echoed in the silence of the night, buildings started to explode in smoke, and from one day to the next, the most passionate love affairs dissolved in tears and blood. The university was abandoned to vandals, and my dreams were destroyed, too. I went back to Kafr Karam, wild-eyed and distraught, and I didn't return to Baghdad.

I had nothing to complain about in my parents' house. I could be satisfied with little. I lived on the roof, in a remodeled laundry room. My furniture consisted of some old crates, and I put my bed together from an assortment of lumber I salvaged here and there. I was content with the little universe I'd constructed around my privacy. I didn't have a television yet, but there was a tinny radio to keep my solitude warm.

On the courtyard side of the upper floor, my parents occupied a room with a balcony; on the garden side, at the end of the hall, my sisters shared two large rooms filled with old stuff, including religious pictures picked up from traveling souks. Some of these pictures showed labyrinthine calligraphy, while others portrayed Sidna Ali manhandling demons or thrashing enemy troops, his legendary double-bladed scimitar whirling like a tornado above their impious heads. Similar pictures were all over the house—in the other rooms, in the entrance hall, above doorways and windows. They were displayed not for decorative reasons, but for their talismanic powers; they preserved the house from the evil eye. One day, I kicked a soccer ball and knocked one of them off the wall. It was a lovely picture, verses from the Qur'an embroidered in yellow thread on a black background. It shattered like a mirror. My mother almost had a stroke. I can still see her, one hand against her chest, her eyes bulging, her face as white as a block of chalk. The prospect of seven years of bad luck would not have turned her so thoroughly pale.

The kitchen was on the ground floor, across from a closetlike space that served Afaf as a workshop, two larger rooms for guests, and a huge living room with French windows opening onto a vegetable garden.

As soon as I had put my things away, I went downstairs to say hello to my mother, a sturdy, open-faced woman whom neither household chores nor the weight of the passing years could ever discourage. A kiss on her cheek transferred a good dose of her energy to me. We understood each other completely.

My father was sitting cross-legged in the courtyard, in the shade of an indefinable tree. After the Fajr prayer, which he dutifully performed at the mosque each morning, he would return home to finger his beads in the patio, one arm hanging useless under the folds of his long robe; the collapse of a well he was scraping out had crippled him. My father had suddenly turned into an old man. His village-elder aura had vanished; his look of command had no more vigor and no more range. In days gone by, he'd sometimes join a group of relatives and friends and exchange views on some subject or other. Then, when malicious gossip started overtaking good manners, he'd withdraw. Now, he left the mosque right after the morning prayer, and before the town was fully awake, he was already installed under his tree, a cup of coffee within reach of his hand, listening intently to the ambient sounds, as though he hoped to decipher their meaning. My dad was a decent man, a Bedouin of modest means who didn't always have enough to eat, but he was nonetheless *my father*, and he remained the object of my greatest respect. Every time I saw him at the foot of his tree, I couldn't help feeling enormous compassion for him. He was certainly a brave and worthy person, but his unhappiness torpedoed the appearances he tried so hard to keep up. I think he'd never gotten over the loss of his arm, and the thought that he was living off his daughters was driving him further down.

I don't remember having been close to him or ever nestling against his chest; nevertheless, I was convinced that if I should make the first move, he wouldn't push me away. But how could I take such a risk? Immutable as a totem, my father let none of his emotions show. When I was a child, he was a sort of ghost to me. I'd hear him at dawn, tying up the bundle he carried to his workplace, but before I could reach him, he'd already left the house, and he wouldn't be back until late at night. I don't know whether or not he was a good father. Too reserved or too poor to give us toys, he seemed to attach little importance either to our childish tumults or to our sudden lulls. I wondered if he were capable of love, if his stature as begetter wasn't going to transform him into a pillar of salt. In Kafr Karam, fathers were convinced that familiarity would detract from their authority, and so they had to keep their distance from their progeny. On occasion, I thought I caught a glimpse of a sparkle in my father's austere eyes; then, suddenly, he'd pull himself together and clear his throat, signaling me to get lost.

That morning, although my father, sitting under his tree, cleared his throat when I solemnly placed my lips on the crown of his head, he didn't pull his hand back when I seized and kissed it, so I understood that my company wouldn't annoy him. But we couldn't even look each other in the face. Once, some time previously, I had sat down beside him, but during the course of two hours, neither of us had managed to pronounce a syllable. He contented himself with fingering his beads; I couldn't stop fiddling with a corner of his mat. Had my mother not come to send me on an errand, we would have stayed like that until nightfall.

I said, "I'm going out for a bit. Do you need anything?"

He shook his head.

I seized the chance to take my leave.

　　　　❖　　●　　❖

Kafr Karam was always a well-ordered little town. We didn't have to go elsewhere to provide for our basic needs. We had our parade ground, our playgrounds (vacant lots, for the most part), our mosque (you had to get up early on Friday morning if you wanted a choice spot), our grocery stores, two cafés (the Safir, frequented by the young, and El

Hilal), a fabulous automobile mechanic capable of fixing any engine, provided it was a diesel, a master blacksmith who occasionally doubled as a plumber, a tooth-puller (an herbalist by vocation and a bone-setter in his spare time), a placid, distracted barber who looked like a carnival strong man and took longer to shave someone's head than a drunk trying to thread a needle, a photographer as somber as his studio, and a postal worker. At one time, we also had a cheap eating place, but seeing that no pilgrim ever deigned to stop in Kafr Karam, the restaurateur transformed himself into a cobbler.

For many people, our village was nothing but a hamlet sprawled beside the road like roadkill—by the time they caught a glimpse of it, it had already disappeared—but we were proud of it. We'd always been wary of strangers. As long as they made wide detours to avoid us, we were safe, and if sandstorms occasionally obliged them to take refuge in Kafr Karam, we received them in accordance with the recommendations of the Prophet, but we never tried to hold them back when they started packing their bags. We had too many bad memories.

Most of the inhabitants of Kafr Karam were related by blood. The rest had lived there for several generations. Of course, we had our little idiosyncrasies, but our quarrels never degenerated into anything worse. Whenever trouble loomed, our village elders would intervene and calm everyone down. If the injured parties deemed an affront irreversible, they stopped speaking to one another, and the matter was closed. Aside from that sort of thing, we liked meeting in the square or the mosque, shuffling along our dusty streets, or basking in the sun beside our mud-plaster walls, which were disfigured here and there by an expanse of chipped, bare cinder blocks. It wasn't paradise, but—since penury resides in the mind, not the heart—we were able to laugh aloud at every jest and to draw from one another's eyes whatever we needed to cope with the nuisances of life.

Of all my cousins, Kadem was my best friend. In the morning, when I left my house, I always headed in his direction. I invariably found him behind a low wall on the corner of the butcher's street, his behind glued to a large rock and his chin in his hand; he and the rock were one. He was the most disgusted creature I knew. As soon as he saw me coming, he'd pull out a packet of cigarettes and hold it out to me. He knew I didn't smoke, but he couldn't help making the same welcoming gesture every time. At length, just to be polite, I accepted his offer and put a cigarette in my mouth. He presented his lighter immediately and then indulged in a little silent laughter when the first puffs made me cough. After that, he went back into his shell, his eyes staring into space, his features impenetrable. Everything, from evenings spent in the company of friends to wakes, made him tired. Discussions with him tended to veer off in unexpected directions, sometimes ending in absurd rages whose secret he alone knew.

"I have to buy myself a new pair of shoes."

He shot a quick glance at my footwear and went back to studying the horizon.

I tried to find some common ground, some topic we might develop; he wasn't having any.

Kadem was a virtuoso lutenist. He made a living by playing at weddings. At one point, he had an idea of organizing an orchestra, but fate shattered his prospects. His first wife, a girl from our village, died in the hospital from a banal case of pneumonia. At the time, the UN "oil for food" program was foundering, and there was a shortage of basic medications, even on the black market. Kadem suffered a great deal from the premature loss of his young spouse. In the hope of assuaging his grief, Kadem's father forced him to take a second wife. Eighteen months after the wedding, a virulent attack of meningitis made him a widower once again. As a result, Kadem lost his faith.

I was one of the few persons who could approach him without immediately making him uncomfortable.

I crouched down beside him.

In front of us stood the Party's community antenna, inaugurated amid fanfare thirty years previously and fallen into disrepair for lack of ideological conviction. Now the building was sealed, and behind it, two convalescing palm trees tried to look their best. They had been there, it seemed to me, since the beginning of time, their silhouettes twisted, practically grotesque, and their branches dangling and withered. Except for dogs who stopped beside them, lifting their legs, and a few birds of passage looking for a vacant perch, no one paid any attention to those palms. They intrigued me when I was a little boy. I never understood why they didn't sneak away under cover of darkness and disappear forever. An itinerant charlatan told a story about them; he said the two trees were actually the product of an immemorial collective hallucination that the mirage forgot to carry off when it faded away.

"Did you hear the radio this morning? It looks like the Italians are packing it in."

"Fat lot of good that'll do us," he growled.

"In my opinion—"

"Weren't you on your way to buy a pair of shoes?"

I raised my arms to the level of my chest in a gesture of surrender. "You're right. I need to stretch my legs."

He finally deigned to turn toward me. "Don't take it like that. These news stories give me a headache."

"I understand."

"You shouldn't hold it against me. I spend my days boring myself to death and my nights losing my mind."

I got up. Just when I reached the end of the wall, he said, "I think I have a pair of shoes at home. Pass by the house in a little while. If they fit you, they're yours."

"All right. See you later."

He was already ignoring me.

# 2

* • *

In a square transformed into a soccer pitch, a bunch of boys shrieked as they kicked a well-worn ball. Their attacks were chaotic, their fouls breathtaking. They looked like a flock of sparrows fighting over a kernel of corn. All at once, a little runt managed to extract himself from the melee and took off like a grown man in the direction of his opponents' goal. He dribbled around one adversary, blew past another, swerved toward the sideline, and sent a no-look pass to a teammate behind him, who charged the goal at full speed and fired a lamentably wide shot before falling on the sharp gravel and cutting his behind. Without warning, an abnormally tall boy who'd been quietly squatting against a wall sprang to his feet, ran for the ball, picked it up, and sprinted away as fast as he could. Puzzled at first, the soccer players quickly realized that the intruder was stealing their ball and set off en masse in pursuit, calling him names.

"They didn't want him on their teams," the blacksmith

explained, sitting with his apprentice on the doorstep of his workshop. "So he's playing the spoilsport."

The blacksmith smiled tenderly and his apprentice looked distracted as the three of us watched the tall boy disappear behind a block of houses, with the others on his heels.

"Have you heard the latest news?" the blacksmith asked me. "The Italians are leaving."

"They haven't said when."

"The important thing is they're getting out," he said, and then he launched into a long analysis that soon branched off into some imprecise theories about the renewal of the country, freedom, et cetera. His apprentice, a puny fellow as dark and dry as a nail, listened to him with the pathetic docility of a dazed boxer between rounds, nodding at his trainer's instructions while his eyes are lost in space.

The blacksmith was a courteous man. When called upon at impossible hours to repair a small leak in a tank or an ordinary crack in some scaffolding, he always came without grumbling. Tall, strapping, heavy-boned, he had bruises all over his arms and a face like a knife blade. His eyes sparkled with metallic glints identical to the sparks he sent flying from the tip of his blowtorch. Jokers pretended to wear a welding mask when they gazed upon his countenance. Actually, his eyes were damaged and watery, and his vision had been growing increasingly cloudy for some time. The father of half a dozen children, he used his workshop much more as a refuge from the pandemonium that reigned in his home than as a place for tinkering with metal. His oldest son, Sulayman, a boy nearly my age, was mentally retarded; he could remain in a corner without budging for days on end, and then, without warning, he'd throw a fit and start running and careen along until he passed out. No one knew what it was that came over him. Sulayman didn't talk, didn't complain, was never aggressive; he lived entrenched in his world and ignored ours totally. Then, all at once, he'd give a cry—always the same cry—and take off across the desert without looking back. In the beginning, we'd watch him scamper off into the blazing heat, his father charging after him. As time passed, however, people realized that those headlong dashes were bad for Sulayman's heart and that the poor devil was in increasing danger of dropping dead from a coronary. So the villagers organized a sort of rapid-response system designed to intercept him as soon as the alarm was given. When he was caught, Sulayman didn't struggle; offering no resistance, he let himself be overcome and brought back home, his mouth open in a lifeless smile, his eyes rolled back in his head.

"How's that boy doing?"

"He's as good as gold," the blacksmith said. "He's been good for weeks. You'd think he was completely cured. And how's your father?"

"Still under his tree . . . I have to buy a new pair of shoes. Is anyone going to town today?"

The blacksmith scratched the top of his head. "I thought I saw a van on the trail an hour ago, but I couldn't say if the driver was going to town or not. You have to wait until after the prayer. In any case, it's getting harder and harder to move around, what with all these checkpoints and the hassles that go with them. Have you talked to the cobbler?"

"My shoes are beyond repair. I need new ones."

"But the cobbler's got more to sell than just soles and glue."

"His merchandise is old-fashioned. The shoes I want have to be soft and stylish."

"You think they'll be a hit with your audience here?"

"That's not a reason not to get them. I wish someone could give me a ride to town. I want to get a nice shirt, too."

"In my opinion, you're going to wait a long time. Khaled's taxi's out of commission, and the bus stopped coming here a month ago, after a helicopter nearly wasted it."

The kids had got their ball back and were returning in triumph.

"Our practical joker didn't get very far," the blacksmith observed.

"He's too big to outrun them."

The two teams reoccupied the pitch, lined up as before, and continued the game at the point where it had been interrupted. Right away, the shrieking began again.

I took a seat on a piece of cinder block and followed the match with interest. When it was over, I noticed that the blacksmith and his apprentice had disappeared and the workshop had closed. By now, the sun was beating down with both fists. I got to my feet and walked up the street in the direction of the mosque.

There was a crowd in the barbershop. As a rule, on Fridays, after the Great Prayer, the old men of Kafr Karam met there. They came to watch one of their number submit to the clippers wielded by the barber, an elephantine individual draped in a calf butcher's apron. Before, when discussing things, they used to avoid certain subjects. Saddam's spies were always on the alert. One inappropriate word, and your whole family would be deported; mass graves and gallows appeared everywhere. But ever since the tyrant had been caught in one rat hole and shut up in another, tongues had loosened, and the men of Kafr Karam—at least those with nothing to do—had discovered in themselves a stunning volubility. That morning, all the village sages were gathered in the barbershop, and since the discussion promised to be a lively one, there were also several young men standing outside. I identified Jabir, known as "Doc," a grouchy septuagenarian who had taught philosophy in a prep school in Basra two decades ago and then spent three years languishing in Baathist prisons because of some obscure etymological controversy. When he left the dungeons, the Party informed him that he was forbidden to work as a teacher anywhere in Iraq and that the Mukhabarat had him in their sights. Realizing that his life was in danger, Doc returned to his natal village and played dead until the statues of the Rais were removed from the public squares. Doc was tall and looked rather lordly, even hieratic, in his immaculately clean blue djellaba. Next to him, hunched on a bench, Bashir the Falcon was holding forth at some length. He was a former highway robber who had scoured the region at the head of an elusive band before taking refuge in Kafr Karam, where his booty made him respectable. He wasn't a member of the tribe, but the elders preferred giving him hospitality to suffering his raids. Facing him were the Issam brothers, two formidable old fellows, who were trying to destroy everyone else's arguments; they had contradiction in their blood and were capable of totally rejecting an idea they'd advanced twenty-four hours previously should an undesirable ally adopt it. Beyond them, immovable in his corner, sat the eldest of the tribe; his distance from the others was a demonstration of his prominence. The wicker chair he occupied was carried by his supporters wherever he went, while he fingered his imposing beads with one hand and with the other grasped the pipe of his narghile. He never intervened in debates, preferring to voice his opinions only at the end, unwilling to let anyone usurp his right to the last word.

"They got rid of Saddam for us, all the same," protested Issam two.

"We never asked them to," the Falcon grumbled.

"Who could have done that?" asked Issam one.

"Exactly right," his brother added. "Who could even spit without risking his hide? Without being arrested on the spot for an affront to the Rais and hanged from a crane?"

"If Saddam tyrannized us, it was because of our cowardice, large and small," the Falcon insisted contemptuously. "People have the kings they deserve."

"I can't agree with you," said a quavering voice. The speaker was an old man sitting on the Falcon's right.

"You can't even agree with yourself."

"Why do you say that?"

"Because it's the truth. One day you're on one side, and the next day you're on the other. Always. I've never heard you defend the same opinion two days in a row. The truth is, you don't have an opinion. You climb on the bandwagon, and when another bandwagon shows up, you jump on that one without knowing where it's going."

The old man took refuge behind a look of grim outrage.

"I don't mean to offend you, my friend," the Falcon said in a conciliatory tone. "If I were disrespectful to you, I wouldn't forgive myself. But I can't let you unload our faults onto Saddam's shoulders. He was a monster, yes, but he was our monster. He came from among us, he shared our blood, and we all contributed to consolidating his megalomania. Do you prefer infidels from the other side of the world, troops sent here to roll over us? The GIs are nothing but brutes and wild beasts; they drive their big machines past our widows and orphans and have no qualms about dropping their bombs on our health clinics. Look at what they've made of our country: hell on earth."

"Saddam made it a mass grave," Issam two reminded him.

"It wasn't Saddam; it was our fear. If we had shown a minimum of courage and solidarity, that cur would never have dared become such a tyrant."

"You're right," said the man under the barber's clippers, addressing the Falcon in the mirror. "We let ourselves be pushed around, and he took advantage of the situation. But you won't make me change my mind: The Americans freed us from an ogre who threatened to devour us raw, all of us, one after the other."

"Why do you think they're here, the Americans?" the Falcon went on obstinately. "Is it Christian charity? They're businessmen, we're commodities, and they're ready to trade. Yesterday, it was oil for food. Today, it's Saddam for oil. And what do we get out of all this? If the Americans had an ounce of human kindness, they wouldn't treat their blacks and their Latinos like subhumans. Instead of crossing oceans to come to the aid of some poor, emasculated ragheads, they'd do better to put their own house in order. They could do something about the Indians they've got rotting away on their reservations, kept out of sight like people with some shameful disease."

"Absolutely!" the quavering old man cried out. "Can you imagine American GIs getting themselves blown up thousands of kilometers from home out of Christian charity? Not very likely."

Eventually, Jabir's voice made itself heard. "May I say a word?" he asked.

A respectful silence filled the shop. When Doc Jabir prepared to speak, it was always a solemn moment. The former philosophy professor, whom Saddam's jails had elevated to the status of a hero, seldom joined the debates, but his rare interventions always served to put things in their proper place. His voice was loud, his gestures precise, and his arguments irrefutable.

"I have a question," he intoned gravely. "Why did Bush attack our country?"

The question passed around the room without finding a taker; the others figured it was a trap, and no one wanted to be the subject of ridicule.

Doc Jabir coughed into his fist, certain that he had everyone's attention. His ferrety eyes searched his audience for a hostile look; then, finding none, he began:

"Because they wished to rid us of a despot, their former flunky, but now a compromising figure? Because our sufferings had finally touched the hearts of the vultures in Washington? If you believe that fairy tale for one second, then you're irredeemably screwed. The USA was extremely worried about two things that might interfere with its hegemonic projects. One: Our country was very close to acquiring full sovereignty—that is, a nuclear weapon. In the new world order, only nations that have a nuclear arsenal are sovereign; the others may be potential hotbeds of tension or providential sources of raw materials for the great powers, but from now on, that's all. The world is run by the forces of international finance, for which peace is equivalent to layoffs. It's all a matter of living space. The second thing the USA knew was that Iraq was the only military force in the region capable of standing up to Israel. Bringing Iraq to its knees would make it possible for Israel to dominate the Middle East. Those are the two real reasons that led to the occupation of our country. Saddam was nothing but an excuse. If he seems to give the Americans' aggression legitimacy in the eyes of public opinion, that doesn't mean using him is any less of a diabolical ploy. Their trick is to create a diversion in order to conceal the essential objectives of the exercise, which are to prevent an Arab country from acquiring the means of its strategic defense and therefore from protecting its integrity, and, at the same time, to help Israel establish definitive authority over this part of the world."

The conclusions landed like sudden blows, and Doc's audience sat openmouthed. Satisfied, he savored for a moment the effect produced by the pertinence of his arguments; then, confident that he'd scored a knockout, he cleared his throat arrogantly and rose to his feet. "Gentlemen," he declared, "in the hope of seeing you again tomorrow, enlightened and improved, I leave you to ponder my words."

Whereupon he dramatically smoothed the front of his djellaba and, with exaggerated hauteur, left the barbershop.

The barber, who had paid no attention, eventually noticed the silence that had fallen around him. He raised an eyebrow, but then, incurious, he returned to cutting his customer's hair.

Now that Doc Jabir had withdrawn, all eyes turned toward the eldest. He moved about in his wicker chair, smacked his lips, and said, "That's one possible way of looking at things." Then, after a long moment of silence, he added, "It's true that we're reaping what we sowed: the fruit of our broken oaths. We've failed. In the past, we were ourselves, good, virtuous Arabs with just enough vanity to give us a bit of guts. Instead of improving over time, we've degenerated."

"And where have we gone wrong?" the Falcon asked testily.

"In our faith. We've lost it, and we've lost face along with it."

"As far as I know, our mosques are full."

"Yes, but what's become of the believers? They go to prayers mechanically, and then, as soon as the service is over, they return to the world of illusions. That's not faith."

A supporter of the eldest handed him a glass of water. The old man took several sips, and the sound of his swallowing resounded in the shop.

"Fifty years ago, when I was in Jordan at the head of my uncle's caravan—about a hundred camels in all—I stopped in a village near Amman. It was the time of prayer. I went to a mosque with a group of my men, and we set about performing our ritual ablutions in a little paved courtyard. The imam, an imposing personage dressed in a flaming red tunic, came up to us and asked, 'Young men, what are you doing here?' 'We're washing ourselves for the prayer,' I replied. He inquired further: 'Do you think your goatskins will suffice to cleanse you?' I pointed out to him that it was our duty to perform our ablutions before entering the prayer hall. He took a fine fresh fig from his pocket and washed it meticulously in a glass of water; then he peeled it open before our eyes. Inside, the beautiful fig was crawling with maggots. The imam concluded his lesson by saying, 'It's not a question of washing your bodies, but your souls, young men. If you're rotten inside, neither rivers nor oceans will suffice to make you clean.'"

Overcome, everyone in the barbershop nodded.

"Don't try to make others wear the hat we've fashioned for ourselves with our own hands. If the Americans are here, it's our fault. By losing our faith, we've also lost our bearings and our sense of honor. We ha—"

"There we are!" the barber cried out, shaking his brush above the crimson nape of his customer's neck.

The other men in the shop froze in indignation.

Blissfully unaware that he'd just rudely interrupted the revered eldest and scandalized his listeners, the barber kept on carelessly waving his brush.

His customer gathered up his old eyeglasses, which were held together with bits of tape and wire, adjusted them on his lumpy nose, and looked at himself in the mirror facing him. "What do you call this?" he moaned. "You've sheared me like a sheep."

"You didn't have all that much hair when you came in," the barber pointed out impassively.

"Maybe not, but you've gone too far. You've practically scalped me."

"You could have stopped me."

"How? I can't see a thing without my glasses."

The barber made a slightly embarrassed face. "Sorry. I did my best."

At this moment, the two men realized that something wasn't right. They turned around and received with full force the outraged looks of everyone gathered in the shop.

"What's the matter?" said the barber in a little voice.

"The eldest was instructing us," someone told him reproachfully, "and not only were you two not listening but on top of it you start squabbling about a bad haircut. It's inexcusable."

Made aware of their boorishness, the barber and his customer both placed a hand on their mouths, like children caught saying dirty words.

The young people who'd been standing around the entrance to the shop left on tiptoe. In Kafr Karam, when sages and important men start quarreling, teenagers and bachelors must depart from the scene. For propriety's sake. I took the opportunity to pay a visit to the cobbler, whose little shop stood about a hundred meters away, nestled in the side of a ghastly building hidden behind some facades so ugly, they seemed to have been erected by djinns.

The sunlight ricocheted off the ground and hurt my eyes. Between two hovels, I caught a glimpse of my cousin Kadem, still in the spot where I'd left him, huddled on his big rock. I waved at him, he failed to notice me, and I proceeded on my way.

The cobbler's shop was closed, but in any case, the aging shoes he had for sale were suitable only for the elderly; if some of his wares had been languishing in their cardboard boxes for years on end, it wasn't because money was tight.

In front of the building's large iron door, which was painted a repulsive shade of brown, Omar the Corporal was playing with a dog. As soon as he saw me, he waved me over, simultaneously aiming a kick at the animal's hindquarters. The dog yelped and ran away. Omar turned to me and said, "I'll bet you're in heat, that's what you are. You came here looking for a stray ewe, right?"

Omar was a walking disease. The young people of the village appreciated neither his crude language nor his sick innuendos; people avoided him like the plague. His time in the army had corrupted him.

Five years previously, he'd gone off to serve in the ranks as a cook; shortly after the siege of Baghdad by the Americans, he'd returned to the village, unable to explain what had happened. One night, he said, his unit was on full alert, locked and loaded; the next day, there was no one left. Everyone had deserted, the officers first. Omar came home hugging the walls. He reacted very badly to the defection of his battalion and sought to drown his grief and shame in adulterated wine. This was probably the source of his coarseness; having lost his self-respect, he took a malicious pleasure in disgusting relatives and friends.

"There are decent people around here," I reminded him.

"What did I say that wasn't Sunnite?"

"Please . . ."

He spread out his arms. "Okay. Okay. A guy can't even fart around anymore."

Omar was eleven years my senior. He'd signed up for the army after a disappointment in love: The girl of his dreams turned out to be promised to someone else. Omar hadn't known a thing about it; neither had she, for that matter. It was only when he'd gathered up his courage and charged his aunt with soliciting his beloved's hand that his illusions had collapsed around him. He'd never recovered from that.

"I'm freaking out in this shithole," he moaned. "I've knocked on every door, and nobody wants to go to town. I wonder why they'd rather stay cooped up in their crappy shacks instead of enjoying a little stroll on a nice avenue with air-conditioned shops and flowers on the café terraces. What's there to see around here, I ask you, except lizards and dogs? At least in town, you go to a café, you sit at a table on the terrace, and you can watch the cars pass and the girls slink by. You feel that you exist, dammit! You feel you're alive. Which is not the feeling I get in Kafr Karam. Here, it's more like slow death, I swear to you. I'm suffocating. I'm dying. Shit, Khaled's taxi isn't even running, and the bus hasn't come near these parts for weeks."

Omar's torso resembled a big bundle on short legs. He was wearing a threadbare checked shirt too tight to hide his large belly, which hung down over his belt. His grease-stained pants weren't much to look at, either. Omar inevitably had black blotches on his clothes. No matter how fresh and clean they were, he always found a way to stain them with some oily substance a minute after putting them on. You'd have thought his body secreted it.

"Where are you going?" he asked.

"To the café."

"To watch some cretins play cards, like yesterday, and the day before yesterday, and tomorrow, and twenty years from now? That's a way to lose your mind. Damn! What could I have done in a former life to deserve rebirth in a dirty little dump like this?"

"It's our village, Omar. Our first fatherland."

"Fatherland, my ass. Even the goddamned crows avoid this place."

He sucked in his big belly to stick his shirt into his pants, took a deep breath, and said with a sigh, "In any case, we have no choice. The café it is."

We went back toward the square. Omar was furious. Every time we walked past a car, no matter how decrepit, he started griping. "Why do these jackasses buy these crates if they're just going to park them in front of their shacks and let them rot?"

He held himself back for a minute and then returned to the charge. "How about your cousin?" he asked, jerking his chin in the direction of Kadem, who was sitting by the low wall at the other end of the street. "How the hell can he stay in that one spot without moving, dawn to dusk? His brain's going to implode one of these days, I promise you."

"He just likes to be alone, that's all."

"There was a guy in my battalion who behaved just like that. He always stayed in a corner of the barracks, never went to the club, never hung out with friends. One morning, he was found in the latrines, hanging from a ceiling light."

"That won't ever happen to Kadem," I said as a shiver ran down my back.

"How much you want to bet?"

＊　　●　　＊

The Safir café was run by Majed, another cousin of mine, a gloomy, sickly man who seemed to be wasting away. Dressed in blue overalls so ugly they looked as though they'd been cut out of a tarpaulin, his head covered by an old military cap pulled down to his ears, he stood behind his rudimentary counter like a failed statue. Since the only reason his customers came to his place was to play cards, he no longer bothered to turn on his machines, contenting himself with making a thermos of red tea at home and bringing it to the café; often, he was obliged to drink the tea alone. His establishment was frequented by unemployed young people, all of them flat broke, who arrived in the morning and stayed until nightfall without ever having put their hands in their pockets. Majed had often dreamed about chucking it all, but then what? In Kafr Karam, the general dereliction defied belief; anyone who had anything resembling employment held on to it stubbornly so as not to risk going on the skids.

Majed gave Omar a bitter look when he saw him arrive. "Here comes trouble," he grumbled.

Unconcerned, Omar briefly considered the young men seated at tables here and there. "It's like a barracks when everyone's been consigned to quarters," he declared, scratching his behind.

He noticed the twins, Hassan and Hussein, standing in front of a window in the back of the room and watching a card game. The players were Yaseen, Doc Jabir's grandson, a brooding, irascible young man; Salah, the blacksmith's son-in-law; Adel, a tall, strapping, and rather stupid fellow; and Bilal, the son of the barber.

Omar approached the table, greeted the twins in passing, and took up a position behind Adel.

Annoyed, Adel shifted in his chair and said, "You're in my light, Corporal."

Omar took a step backward. "The real shadow's in your thick skull, my boy."

"Leave him alone," Yaseen said without taking his eyes off his cards. "Don't distract us."

Omar sniggered scornfully but held his tongue.

The four players contemplated their cards with great intensity. At the end of a lengthy mental calculation, Bilal cleared his throat. "It's your play, Adel."

Adel thrust out his lips and kept pondering his hand, indecisive, taking his time.

"Look, are you going to play?" Salah asked impatiently.

"Hey," Adel protested. "I've got to think."

"Stop exaggerating," Omar said. "You tossed away your last gram of brain when you jerked off this morning."

The atmosphere in the café turned leaden. The young men sitting near the door vanished; the others didn't know which way to turn.

Omar realized his blunder and swallowed hard, waiting for all hell to break loose.

The players at the table kept their heads bent over their cards, as though petrified, except for Yaseen, who folded his hand, delicately placed it to one side, and fixed his eyes, white with indignation, on the former corporal. "I don't know what point you think you're making with your filthy language, Omar, but this is going too far. In our village, the young, like the old, respect one another. You were raised here, and you know what I'm talking about."

"I didn't—"

"Shut up! Shut your big mouth and keep it shut," Yaseen said in a monotone that contrasted violently with the fury blazing in the eyes. "You're not in the mess; you're in Kafr Karam. We're all brothers, cousins, neighbors, and relatives here, and we watch what we do and how we act. I've told you a hundred times, Omar: no obscenity. Keep your disgusting soldier's lingo to yourself."

"Come on, I was just joking."

"Well, look around, Omar. See anyone laughing? Do you?"

The former corporal's throat quivered.

Yaseen pointed a peremptory finger at him. "From this day on, Omar, son of my uncle Fadel and my aunt Amina, I forbid you—*I forbid you*—to utter a single curse, to say a single improper word—"

"Whoa," Omar said, interrupting Yaseen, much more to save face than to chastise him. "I'm your elder by six years, and I won't let you speak to me that way."

"So stop me!"

The two men measured each other, their nostrils quivering.

Omar turned aside first. "All right," he growled, violently stuffing his shirt into his pants. Then he turned on his heels and headed for the exit. At the door, he stopped and shouted, "You know what I think?"

Yaseen cut him off. "Disinfect your mouth before you tell me."

Omar shook his head and disappeared.

*   *   •   *   *

After Omar's departure, the uneasiness in the café intensified. The twins went away first, heading in different directions. No one felt like resuming the disrupted card game.

Yaseen got up and left next, closely followed by Adel. There was nothing left for me to do but go back home.

Shut up in my room, I tried to listen to the radio, thinking it might serve to dissipate the acute embarrassment I'd felt ever since the scene in the Safir. I was doubly uncomfortable, first for Omar, and then for Yaseen. Of course, the Corporal deserved to be called to order, but he was older than Yaseen, whose severity toward him upset me, as well. The more pity I felt for the deserter, the fewer excuses I could find for his cousin. Actually, if relations in the village were turning ugly, it was because of the news coming out of Fallujah, Baghdad, Mosul, and Basra, while we floated along, light-years away from the tragedy depopulating our country. Since the beginning of hostilities, despite the hundreds of attacks and the legions of dead, not even a single helicopter had flown over our sector, not so far, nor had any patrol violated the peace of our little town. This feeling that we were excluded from history had developed into a genuine case of conscience. The older people seemed to be resigned to it, but the young men of Kafr Karam took it very hard.

The radio couldn't distract me, so I lay down on the bed and put the pillow on my face. The suffocating heat made everything worse. I didn't know what to do. The village streets distressed me; my little room baked me. I was dissolving in my displeasure. . . .

That evening, the beginnings of a breeze stirred the curtains. I got out a metal folding chair and sat in the doorway of my room. Two or three kilometers from the village, the Haitems' orchards flourished amid stones and sand, the only green patch for miles around. The trees shimmered defiantly in the haze of the sun, which was going down in a cloud of dust. Soon the horizon caught fire from one end to the other, accenting the contours of the hills and valleys in the distance. On the arid plateau that fled breathlessly southward, the dirt road recalled a dried-up riverbed. A group of youngsters was returning from the orchards, empty-handed and unsteady on their feet; apparently, the little marauders' expedition had come to a sudden end.

"Here's a package for you," my twin sister, Bahia, announced, placing a plastic bag at my feet. "I'll bring you your dinner in half an hour. Can you hold out that long?"

"No problem."

She flicked some dust off my collar. "You didn't go to town?"

"I couldn't get anyone to drive me there."

"Try again tomorrow, and be more persuasive."

"I promise. What's this package?"

"Kadem's little brother dropped it off for you a minute ago."

She went into my room to check that everything was in order and then returned to her cooking.

I opened the plastic bag and drew out a cardboard box held together with adhesive tape. Inside the box was a superb pair of brand-new black shoes and a piece of paper with a few lines written on it: "I wore them twice, once on each wedding night. They're yours. No hard feelings. Kadem."

3

A hostage to its own emptiness, Kafr Karam was unraveling a little more with each passing day.

At the barbershop, in the café, by the walls, people chewed over the same subjects. They talked a lot and did nothing at all. Their indignation grew less and less spectacular; temperamental outbursts cut some arguments short, while other debates were prolonged by soporific speeches. Little by little, people stopped listening to one another, but something unusual was nevertheless taking place. For the older villagers, the hierarchy remained inflexible, but among the young, it appeared to be undergoing a curious change. After the dressing-down Yaseen had inflicted on Omar the Corporal, the privileges of primogeniture started looking rather shaky. Of course, most people decried what had happened at the Safir, but it inspired a minority made up of hotheads and rebels-in-waiting to assert themselves.

The elders pretended to know nothing about this incident, which—even though it was not bruited about on the public thoroughfares—nonetheless made the rounds of the village. Otherwise, things followed their usual course with pathetic lethargy. The sun continued to rise when it felt like it and go down as it wished. We remained candied in our little autistic happiness, gaping wide-eyed into space or twiddling our thumbs. It seemed as though we were vegetating on another planet, cut off from the tragic events that were eroding the country. Our mornings featured trivial, routine sounds, our nights unsatisfactory sleep; dreams serve no purpose when all horizons are bare. For a long time, the shadows of our walls had held us captive. We had known the most abominable regimes and survived them, just as our livestock had survived epidemics. Sometimes, when one tyrant had been cast out by another, the new tyrant's henchmen had descended on us like hunting dogs flushing out game, hoping to get their hands on some prey that could be sacrificed in the public square as a way of bringing the rest of us back into line. Very quickly, however, they grew disenchanted and returned to their kennels, a little shamefaced, but delighted not to have to set foot again in a godforsaken hole where it was hard to distinguish the living from the ghosts that kept them company.

But as the ancestral proverb says, If you close your door on your neighbors' cries, they'll come through your windows. Likewise, when bad luck is roaming around, no one is safe. It's no use trying to avoid mentioning it, no use believing it happens only to others or thinking all you've got to do to keep it away is to stay very still in your corner; too much restraint will eventually set it off anyway, and one morning, there it is, standing on your threshold and having a look around. . . .

And what had to happen happened. Bad luck turned up among us, without any fanfare, almost on tiptoe, hiding its hand. I was having a cup of tea at the blacksmith's shop when his little daughter came running in and cried, "Sulayman! Sulayman!"

"Has he run away again?" the blacksmith asked in alarm.

"He cut his hand on the gate. . . . He doesn't have any more fingers," the little girl said between sobs.

The blacksmith leaped over the low table between us, kicking over the teapot as he passed, and ran to his house. His apprentice rushed out to overtake him, signaling to me that I should follow. A woman's voice, crying out, reached us from the end of the street. A crowd of kids was already gathering in front of the wide-open patio gate. Sulayman held his wounded hand against his chest and laughed silently, fascinated by his own bleeding.

The blacksmith commanded his wife to be quiet and to find him a piece of clean fabric. The cries stopped immediately.

"There are his fingers," the apprentice said, pointing at two bits of flesh on the ground near the gate.

With amazing composure, the blacksmith gathered up the two severed phalanges, wiped them off, and placed them in a handkerchief, which he slipped into his pocket. Then he bent over his son's wounds.

"We have to get him to the health center," he said. "If we don't, the blood's going to drain right out of him." He turned to me. "I need a car."

I nodded and rushed over to Khaled's house and burst in on him as he was fixing his little boy's toy in the courtyard.

"We need you," I announced. "Sulayman cut off two of his fingers. We have to get him to the hospital."

"I'm awfully sorry, but I'm expecting guests at noon."

"It's urgent. Sulayman's losing a lot of blood."

"I can't drive you. If you want, take my taxi. It's in the garage. I can't go with you. Some people are coming here in a few minutes to ask for my daughter's hand."

"All right, give me the keys."

He abandoned the toy and invited me to follow him into the garage, where a battered old Ford was parked.

"You know how to drive?"

"Of course."

"Help me get this crate out into the street."

He opened the garage doors, whistled to the kids lounging in the sun, and asked them to come and give us a hand. "The car's got an obstinate starter," he explained to me. "Sit behind the wheel. We're going to push you."

The kids rushed into the garage, amused and happy at having been called upon for assistance. I released the brake, put the gearshift in second, and let the enthusiasm of my bratty assistants propel me along. By the time we'd gone some fifty meters, the Ford had reached a negotiable speed. I released the clutch and, at the end of some quite impressive bucking, the engine roared to life with all its banged-up valves. Behind me, the kids raised a shout of joy identical to the one they used to greet the return of electric lights after a long power cut.

When I reached the blacksmith's patio, Sulayman's hand was already completely bound up in a terry-cloth towel, and there was a tourniquet around his wrist; his face showed no sign of pain. I found this strange. I couldn't believe that a person would show such insensibility after he'd just sliced off two of his fingers.

The blacksmith put his son in the backseat and sat beside him. Disheveled and sweating, his wife arrived on the run, looking like a desperate madwoman; she handed her husband a stack of dog-eared pages held together by a rubber band.

"It's his medical record. Someone will surely ask you for it."

"Very good. Now go back inside and try to behave. It's not the end of the world."

Tires squealing, we left the village, briefly escorted by an urchin band. Their shouts pursued us across the desert for a long time.

It was about eleven o'clock, and the sun sprinkled false oases all over the plain. A couple of birds flapped their wings against the white-hot sky. The trail proceeded in a straight line, pallid, vertiginous, and quite unusual on that stony plateau, which it bisected like a gash from one end to the other. The dilapidated old Ford bounced over the deep potholes, rearing up here and there and giving the impression that it was commanded by nothing but its own frenzy. In the backseat, the blacksmith, clutching his son tightly so he wouldn't strike his head, said nothing. He was letting me drive as best I could.

We passed an abandoned field, a disused pumping station, and then emptiness. The naked horizon spread out to infinity. Around us, as far as we could see, there was not so much as a hut, not a machine of any sort, not a living soul. The health clinic was sixty kilometers west of Kafr Karam, in a newly built village with paved roads. The new village also boasted a police station and a preparatory school, the latter—for reasons that escaped me—studiously avoided by our people.

"You think we've got enough gas?" the blacksmith asked.

"I don't know. There's not a working gauge on this dash-board."

"That's what I was afraid of. We haven't passed a single vehicle. If we break down, we're screwed."

"God won't abandon us," I told him.

Half an hour later, we saw an enormous cloud of black smoke rising in the distance. By this time, we were only a few hundred meters from the national highway, and the smoke intrigued us. After we passed a small hill, we could finally see the highway and the burning semitrailer. It lay across the road, its cabin in the ditch and its tank burst open; gigantic flames were devouring it.

"Better stop," the blacksmith advised me. "This must have been a fedayeen attack, so it can't be long before the military shows up. Go back to the access ramp and take the old trail. I don't feel like winding up in the middle of a fire-fight."

I turned around. Once we reached the old trail, I started looking out for soldiers on their way to the scene. Hundreds of meters below us, running parallel to our trail, the national highway sparkled in the sun. It reminded me of an irrigation canal, perfectly straight and terribly deserted. Soon the cloud of smoke became a grayish smudge in the distance. Every now and then, the blacksmith stuck his head out the window and scrutinized the sky for helicopters. We were the sole sign of life in the vicinity, and we might be making a mistake. The blacksmith was worried; his face grew gloomier and gloomier.

As for me, I felt rather serene; I had an injured person on board, and I was on my way to the neighboring village.

The trail made a wide swerve to avoid a crater, climbed a hill, plunged down, and leveled out after a few kilometers. Once again, we could see the national highway, still straight and still disconcertingly deserted. The trail turned toward the highway and then merged with it. As soon as the Ford's tires hit the asphalt, they changed their tone, and the engine stopped its incongruous gargling.

"We're less than ten minutes from the village, and there's not a vehicle in sight," the blacksmith said. "Very odd."

I didn't have time to reply to him. A checkpoint was blocking our route with barriers on both sides of the roadway. Two individuals dressed in bright colors were on the shoulders of the road, holding automatic weapons at the ready. Facing us, erected on a mound, a makeshift sentry box was barricaded behind barrels and sandbags.

"Stay calm," the blacksmith said, his breath hot on the nape of my neck.

"I am calm," I assured him. "We haven't done anything wrong, and one of us needs medical attention. They won't give us any trouble."

"Where are the soldiers?"

"They're hunkered down behind the embankment. I see two helmets. I think they're watching us through binoculars."

"Okay. Slow down to a crawl. And whatever they tell you to do, do it."

"Don't worry. Everything's going to be all right."

The first soldier to step out into the open was an Iraqi. He signaled to us to stop the car in front of a road sign that was standing in the center of the highway. I followed his instructions.

"Cut the engine," he ordered me in Arabic. "Then put your hands on the steering wheel and keep them there. Don't open the door, and don't get out until you're told to. Understand?"

He was standing well away from the car and pointing his rifle at my windshield.

"Understand?"

"I understand. I keep my hands on the steering wheel, and I don't do anything without authorization."

"Very good. How many are you?"

"Three. We—"

"Just answer my questions. And don't make any sudden moves. Don't make any moves at all, you hear me? Tell me where you're coming from, where you're going, and why."

"We come from Kafr Karam, and we're going to the health clinic. One of us is ill and he's cut off a couple of fingers. He's mentally ill, I mean."

The Iraqi soldier aimed his assault rifle at different parts of me, his finger on the trigger and the butt against his cheek; then he took aim at the blacksmith and his son. Two GIs approached in their turn, tense and alert, their weapons ready to transform us into sieves at the least quiver. I kept my cool. My hands remained on the steering wheel, in plain sight. Behind me, the blacksmith was breathing hard.

"Watch your son," I muttered. "Make sure he keeps still."

"Shut up!" a GI shouted at me, looming up on my left from I didn't know where. The barrel of his gun wasn't far from my temple. "What did you just say to your pal there?"

"I told him to keep—"

"*Shut your trap!* And keep it shut!"

He was a gigantic black, crouched over his assault rifle, his eyes white with rage and the corners of his mouth wet with frothy spittle. He was so enormous, he intimidated me. His orders exploded like bursts of gunfire and left me paralyzed.

"Why is he yelling like that?" the blacksmith asked in a panicky voice. "He's going to scare Sulayman."

"Zip it!" the Iraqi soldier barked. I assumed he was there as an interpreter. "At the checkpoint, you don't talk, you don't discuss orders, you don't grumble," he recited, like someone reading an amendment. "You keep quiet and you obey every order completely. Understand? *Mafhum?* You, driver, put your right hand on your window and slowly open your door with your left hand. Then put both hands behind your head and get out, very slowly."

Two more GIs appeared behind the Ford, harnessed like draft horses, wearing thick sand goggles over their helmets and bulging bulletproof vests. They approached us, aiming their rifles from their shoulders. The black soldier was hollering loudly enough to rupture a vocal cord. As soon as one of my feet touched the ground, he yanked me out of the car and forced me to kneel down. I let him manhandle me without resistance. He stepped back, pointed his rifle at the rear seat, and ordered the blacksmith to get out.

"I beg you, please don't shout. My son is mentally ill, and you're scaring him."

The black GI didn't understand very much of what the blacksmith was trying to tell him; the fact that someone would address him in a language he didn't know seemed to infuriate him, and so now he was doubly angry. His lacerating screams made my joints twitch and prickle. *"Shut up! Shut the fuck up or I'll blow your brains out! Hands behind your head!"* Around us, the impenetrable, silent soldiers kept a close eye on our slightest movements. Some of them were hidden behind sunglasses, which made them look quite formidable, while others exchanged coded looks. I was astonished as I looked down the barrels of the weapons pointed at me from all sides, like so many tunnels to hell. They seemed vast and volcanic, ready to bury us in a sea of lava and blood. I was petrified, nailed to the ground like a post, incapable of speech. The blacksmith got out of the car, his hands on his head. He was trembling like a leaf. He tried to speak to the Iraqi soldier, but a kick to the back of his knee forced him to kneel down. When the black GI leaned in for the other passenger, he noticed the blood on Sulayman's hand and shirt. *"Goddamn! He's dripping blood,"* the soldier shouted, jumping away from the car. *"This asshole's wounded."* Sulayman was terrified. He looked for his father. The soldier kept yelling, *"Hands on your head, hands on your head!"* The blacksmith cried out to the Iraqi soldier, "He's mentally ill." Sulayman slid across the seat and got out of the car in confusion. His milky eyes rolled in his bloodless face. The GI screamed out his orders as belligerently as before, reducing me another notch with every shout. You could hear nothing but him; he alone drowned out the din of all the earth. Suddenly, Sulayman gave *his* cry—penetrating, immense, recognizable among a thousand apocalyptic sounds. It was a sound so weird that it froze the American soldier. But the blacksmith had no time to hurl himself on his son or hold him back or stop his flight. Sulayman took off like an arrow, running in a straight line, so fast that the GIs were flabbergasted. *"Let him go,"* a sergeant said. *"He might be carrying a load of explosives."* All weapons were now aiming at the fugitive. "Don't shoot," the blacksmith pleaded, partly in English. "He's mentally ill. *Don't shoot. He's crazy.*" Sulayman ran and ran, his spine straight, his arms dangling, his body absurdly tilted to the left. Just from his way of running, it was evident that he wasn't normal. But in time of war, the benefit of the doubt favors blunderers over those who keep their composure; the catchall term is "legitimate defense." The first gunshots shook me from my head to my feet, like a surge of electric current. And then came the deluge. Utterly dazed, I saw puffs of dust, lots of them, bursting from Sulayman's back, marking the impact points. Every bullet that struck the fugitive pierced me through and through. An intense tingling sensation consumed my legs, rose, and convulsed my stomach. Sulayman ran and ran, barely jolted by the projectiles riddling his back. Beside me, the blacksmith was shrieking like a maniac, his face bathed in tears. *"Mike!"* the sergeant barked. *"He's wearing a bulletproof vest, the little prick. Aim for his head."* In the sentry box, Mike peered through his telescopic sight, adjusted his firing angle, held his breath, and delicately squeezed his trigger. Bull's-eye, first shot. Sulayman's head exploded like a melon; his unbridled run stopped all at once. The blacksmith clutched his temples with both hands, wild-eyed, his mouth open in a suspended cry, as he watched his son's body fold up in the distance and collapse vertically, like a falling curtain: the thighs on the calves, then the chest on the thighs, and finally the shattered head on the knees. An unearthly silence settled over the plain. My stomach rose, backed up; burning liquid flooded my gullet and spewed out through my mouth into the open air. The daylight grew hazy . . . And then, oblivion.

    ❖    ●    ❖

I regained consciousness slowly. My ears whistled. I was lying on the ground, facedown in a pool of vomit. My body had lost its power to react. I was in a heap next to the Ford's front wheel, and my hands were tied behind my back. I had just enough time to see the blacksmith shaking his son's medical record under the nose of the Iraqi soldier, who seemed embarrassed, while the other soldiers looked on in silence, holding their weapons at ease. Then I lost consciousness again.

By the time I recovered some of my faculties, the sun had reached its zenith. The rocks were humming in the broiling heat. They'd taken the plastic cuffs off my wrists and placed me in the shade of the sentry box. Still in the spot where I'd parked it, the Ford looked like a ruffled fowl; all four of its doors were open, its trunk lid hoisted high. On the ground beside it, there was a little heap consisting of the spare tire and various tools. The search had yielded nothing—no firearms, no big knives, not even a medical kit.

An ambulance with a red crescent on its side was waiting near the sentry box. The vehicle's rear doors were open, revealing a stretcher that bore what was left of Sulayman. Two pathetic feet protruded from the sheet that covered him; the right foot was missing its shoe and displayed five toes, discolored by blood and dust.

A noncommissioned officer in the Iraqi police and the blacksmith were standing a little distance away and having a conversation, while an American officer, recently arrived in his Jeep, listened to the sergeant's report. Apparently, they all realized that a mistake had been made, but they weren't going to make a big deal of it. Incidents of this kind were commonplace in Iraq. Amid the general confusion, everyone sought his own advantage. To err is human, and fate has broad shoulders.

The black GI handed me his canteen. I didn't know whether I was supposed to drink or wash my face, but in any case, I rejected his offer with a feverish hand. He put on a sorrowful expression—a vain effort, as far as I was concerned, because his new, compassionate persona seemed incompatible with his temperament. A brute is still a brute, even when he smiles; the eyes are where the soul declares its true nature.

Two male nurses, Arabs, came to comfort me; they crouched down, one on each side, and patted my shoulders. Their light taps resounded in my body like blows from a club. I wanted to be left alone; every sympathetic gesture carried me back to the source of my grief. From time to time, a sob shook me, but I did everything I could to contain it. I felt stricken by an incredible weariness; I could hear only my breath, emptying me, and in my temples the pulsing of my blood, its rhythm matching the lingering echoes of the detonations.

The blacksmith tried to claim his son's remains, but the chief of police explained to him that there was an administrative procedure that must be followed. Such an unfortunate accident as this entailed a lot of formalities. Sulayman's body had to be taken to the morgue and could not be released to his family until an investigation into the tragic error had been completed.

A police car took us back to the village. I didn't completely grasp what was happening. I was inside a sort of evanescent bubble, sometimes suspended in a void, sometimes fraying apart like a cloud of smoke. I remembered clearly the mother's unbearable cry when the blacksmith returned home. Immediately, a crowd gathered, dazed and incredulous. The old struck their hands together, devastated; the young were outraged. I reached my house in a lamentable state. The moment I stepped over the threshold and into the patio, my father, who was dozing at the foot of his indefinable tree, started in his sleep. He'd understood at once that something bad had happened. My mother didn't have the courage to ask me what the matter was; she settled for putting her hands on her cheeks. My sisters came running with kids clinging to their skirts. Outside, the first howls began, somber lamentations heavy with anger and passion. My sister Bahia took me by the arm and helped me to my rooftop room. She laid me down on my pallet, brought me a basin of water, took off my filthy, vomit-stained shirt, and started washing me from the waist up. Meanwhile, the news spread through the village, and our entire family went to condole with the blacksmith and his household. After putting me to bed for the evening, Bahia left to join them, and I fell asleep.

The next day, Bahia came back to open my windows and give me clean clothes. She told me that an American colonel, accompanied by some Iraqi military authorities, had come to the village the previous evening to offer condolences to the bereaved parents. The eldest of the tribe received them at his home, but in the courtyard, to indicate to the colonel that he was unwelcome. The old man didn't believe the colonel's version of the accident, nor would he accept any justification for firing on a simpleminded boy— that is, on a pure and innocent creature closer to the Lord than the saints. Some television teams wanted to cover the event and proposed a feature story on the blacksmith so that people could hear what he had to say about the matter. On this point as well, the eldest held firm; he categorically refused to allow strangers to disturb his grieving village.

# 4

•

Three days later, a small van from the village, dispatched by the eldest himself, brought Sulayman's body home from the morgue. It was a terrible moment. The people of Kafr Karam had never felt such gloom. The eldest insisted that the burial should take place with dignity and in strict privacy. Except for the villagers, only a delegation of elders from an allied tribe was allowed in the cemetery. After the funeral services were over, everyone returned home to ponder the blow that had robbed Kafr Karam of its purest creature, its mascot and its pentacle. That evening, old and young gathered at the blacksmith's house and chanted verses from the Qur'an until late in the night. But Yaseen and his followers, who made an open display of their indignation, saw things differently and chose to meet at Sayed's place. Sayed was Bashir the Falcon's son, a taciturn, mysterious young man said to be close to the Islamist movement and suspected of having attended school in Peshawar during the rule of the Taliban. He was a tall fellow of about thirty or so, his ascetic face beardless except for his lower lip, where a tiny tuft of wild hairs, like the beauty mark on his cheek, embellished his face. He lived in Baghdad and never came back to Kafr Karam except for special occasions. He'd arrived the previous day and attended Sulayman's funeral.

Around midnight, other young insomniacs joined the group at Sayed's. He received them all with a great deal of deference and entertained them in a large room whose floor was covered with wicker mats and cushions. While everyone else was sipping tea and digging into baskets of peanuts, Yaseen couldn't stay still. He looked like a man possessed by the devil. Trying to pick a quarrel, he stared extravagantly at the others, who were sitting or reclining here and there. As no one was paying any attention to him, he absolutely turned on his most faithful companion, Salah, the blacksmith's son-in-law.

"I saw you crying at the cemetery," Yaseen said.

"It's true," Salah admitted, ignorant of where the conversation was heading.

"Why?"

"Why what?"

"Why did you cry?"

Salah frowned. "According to you, why do people cry? I felt grief, all right? I cried because Sulayman's death caused me pain. What's so shocking about that, crying over someone you loved?"

"I understand that," Yaseen insisted. "But why the tears?"

Salah felt that things were escaping him. "I don't understand your question."

"Sulayman's death broke my heart," Yaseen said. "But I

didn't shed a single tear. I can't believe you would make such a spectacle of yourself. You cried like a woman, and that's unacceptable."

The word *woman* shook Salah. His cheeks bulged as he gritted his teeth. "Men cry, too," he pointed out to his leader. "The Prophet himself had that weakness."

"I don't give a damn!" Yaseen exploded. "You didn't have to behave like a *woman,*" he added, heavily emphasizing the last word.

Outraged, Salah rose suddenly to his feet. He stared at Yaseen with wounded eyes for a long time, then gathered up his sandals and went out into the night.

There were about twenty people gathered in the big room, and rapid looks darted in all directions. No one understood what had gotten into Yaseen or why he'd behaved so despicably to the blacksmith's son-in-law. A sense of ill-being settled over everyone there. After a long silence, Sayed, the master of the house, coughed into his fist. It was his duty, as the host, to set things straight.

He gave Yaseen a scathing look and began: "When I was a child, my father told me a story I didn't completely grasp. At that age, I didn't know that stories had a moral. This was the story of an Egyptian strongman who reigned like a satrap over the seedier districts of Cairo. He was a downright Hercules. He looked as though he'd just been cast in some ancient Greek bronze foundry. He had an enormous mustache that looked like a ram's horns, and he was a leader as hard on himself as he was on others. I don't remember his name, but the image I formed of him is intact in my memory. I thought of him as a kind of Robin Hood of the working-class suburbs, as ready to roll up his sleeves and lend a hand as to swagger around the square and lord it over porters and donkey trainers. When there was a disagreement between neighbors, they came to him and submitted to his arbitration. The decisions he made could not be appealed. However, although he was a strong man, he wasn't a silent one. He was conceited, irascible, and demanding, and since no one questioned his authority, he proclaimed himself king of the outcasts and shouted from the rooftops that there was nobody in the world who dared to look him straight in the eye. His words didn't fall on deaf ears. One evening, the chief of police summoned him to the station. No one knows what happened that night. The next day, when the strongman returned home, he was unrecognizable, his head bowed, his eyes elusive. He wasn't bearing any wounds or any traces of blows, but he had an evident mark of infamy in the form of his suddenly sunken shoulders. He shut himself up in his hovel until his neighbors began to complain about a strong odor of decomposition. When they kicked his door in, they found the strongman stretched out on his straw mattress. He'd been dead for several days. Later, a cop described the strongman's meeting with the chief of police: Before the chief could reproach him for anything at all, the strongman had thrown himself at the chief's feet to beg his pardon. And he never got up again."

"And so?" Yaseen asked, on the lookout for insinuations.

A mocking smile quickly crossed Sayed's face. "That's where my father ended the story."

"That's just rubbish," Yaseen grumbled, conscious of his limitations when it came to deciphering hidden meanings.

"That what I thought, too, at first. As time passed, I was able to find a moral in the story."

"Are you going to tell me what it is?"

"No. That moral's mine. It's up to you to find one that suits you."

With this, Sayed got up and went upstairs to his room. Seeing that the evening was over, most of the guests collected their sandals and left the house. The only people still in the room were Yaseen and his "Praetorian guard."

Yaseen was beside himself; he thought he'd been too vague, and he felt that he'd made a bad showing in front of his men. There was no way he was going to go home without getting to the bottom of this matter. He sent away his companions with a nod of his head, went upstairs, and knocked on Sayed's bedroom door.

"I don't understand," Yaseen said.

"Salah didn't understand what you were getting at, either," Sayed replied. The two of them were standing on the landing.

"I looked like a chump. You and your fucking story! I bet you made it up. I bet all that stuff about a moral was a lot of nonsense."

"You're the one who talks nonsense, Yaseen. Constantly. And you behave exactly like that strongman from Cairo."

"Well, if you don't want me to set this place on fire, you'd better enlighten me. I can't stand being talked down to, and nobody—*nobody*—is going to make a fool of me. I may not have enough education, but I've got pride to spare."

Sayed wasn't intimidated. On the contrary, his smile grew wider in direct proportion to Yaseen's raving. After a pause, he said in a monotone, "The man who feeds on others' cowardice nourishes his own; sooner or later, it devours his guts, and then his soul. You've been acting like a tyrant for some time now, Yaseen. You shake up the order of things. You no longer respect the tribal hierarchy. You rise up against your elders and offend people close to you; you even like to humiliate them in public. You shout everything you say, whether yes or no, so loudly that no one in the village can hear anything but you anymore."

"Why should I concern myself about them? They're worthless."

"You behave exactly the way they do. They stare at their navels; you stare at your biceps. It comes to the same thing. No one has any cause to envy or reproach anyone else in Kafr Karam."

"I forbid you to associate me with those imbeciles. I'm no coward."

"Prove it. Come on, what's stopping you from turning words into deeds? Iraqis have been fighting the enemy for a long time. Every day, our cities crumble a little more, blown up by car bombs and ambushes and bombardments. The prisons are filled with our brothers, and our cemeteries are gorged with our dead. And you, you lounge around your godforsaken village, you get your hackles up, and you cry out your hatred and indignation from the rooftops; then, once your spleen is vented, you go back home, slip up to your room, and turn off the light. Too easy. If you really think what you say, translate talk into action and make those goddamned Americans pay for what they've done. If not, calm down and back off."

Then, according to my twin sister, Bahia—who had the story from the very mouth of Sayed's sister, who'd heard the whole conversation through the door—Yaseen withdrew ungraciously, without uttering another word.

*　●　*

Sulayman's death threw Kafr Karam into confusion. The village didn't know what to do with the corpse it was carrying. Its last feats of arms dated back to the war with Iran, a generation earlier; eight of its sons had returned from the front in sealed caskets, which no one had the authority to open. What had the village buried back then? A few planks, a few patriots, or a part of its dignity? Sulayman's end was an entirely different matter, a horrible and vulgar accident, and people couldn't make up their minds: Was Sulayman a martyr, or just a poor bugger who had found himself in the wrong place at the wrong time? The elders of the village called for calm. No one was infallible, they said. The American colonel had demonstrated genuine sorrow. His only mistake was in broaching the subject of money with the blacksmith. In Kafr Karam, one never speaks of money to a person in mourning. No compensation can lessen the grief of a distraught father at his son's fresh grave. Had Doc Jabir not intervened, the talk of indemnity would have veered into confrontation.

The weeks passed, and little by little, the village rediscovered its gregarious soul and its routines. The violent death of a simpleminded person arouses more anger than grief, but, alas, you can't change the course of things. God's concerned about being fair, so he gives His saints no help; the devil alone takes care of those who serve him.

As a man of faith, the blacksmith adopted an attitude of fatalistic resignation. One morning, he could be seen opening his shop and taking up his blowtorch again.

The discussions in the barbershop resumed, and the

young people went back to the Safir to kill time with dominoes when the card games grew stale. Bashir the Falcon's son Sayed didn't stay among us long. Urgent business called him back to town. What business? Nobody knew. However, his lightning sojourn in Kafr Karam had made an impression; the young were seduced by his frank talk, and his charisma had compelled the respect of young and old. Our paths were to cross again later on. He would be the one to raise me in my own esteem, to train me in the basics of guerrilla warfare, and to open wide for me the gates of the supreme sacrifice.

Soon after Sayed's departure, Yaseen and his band reoccupied the square. Sullen and aggressive, they were the reason why Omar the Corporal dropped out of sight. Since the incident in the café, the deserter had become a shadow of his former self and spent most of his time shut up in his little house. When he was forced to show his face outside, he crossed the village like the wind and went to drown his shame far from provocations, only to return—generally on all fours—when the night was well advanced. Often, some kids would spot him getting sloshed in the back of the cemetery or find him in an alcoholic coma, his arms crossed and his shirt open on his giant belly. Then one day, without a sound, he slipped away and was seen no more.

After Sulayman's funeral, which I didn't attend, I stayed in my room. Memories of the awful scene tormented me without letup. As soon as I fell asleep, the black GI's screams would assail me. I dreamed of Sulayman running, his stiff spine, his dangling arms, his body leaning sometimes to one side, sometimes to the other. A multitude of minuscule geysers spurted from his back. At the moment when his head exploded, I woke up screaming. Bahia was at my bedside with a potful of wet compresses. "It's nothing," she said. "Just a nightmare. I'm here. . . ."

One afternoon, my cousin Kadem paid me a visit. He'd finally made up his mind to detach himself from his rock, and he brought me some cassette tapes. At first, he was embarrassed—he didn't want to disturb me in my condition. By way of breaking the ice, he asked me if the shoes he'd given me were my size. I told him they were still in the box.

"They're new, you know."

"I do," I said. "And more than that, I know what they mean to you. I'm deeply touched. Thanks."

If I wanted to get back to normal, he said, I shouldn't stay shut up in my room. Bahia agreed with him. I had to overcome the shock and resume a normal life. But I wasn't very eager to go out into the street; I was afraid someone would ask me for the details of what had happened at the checkpoint, and I dreaded the thought of the knife twisting in my wound. Kadem rejected this notion. "All you have to do is tell them to buzz off," he said.

He continued to visit me, and we spent hours talking about everything and nothing. It was thanks to him that one evening I screwed up my courage and agreed to leave my lair. Kadem proposed taking a walk far from the village. Halfway between Kafr Karam and the Haitems' orchards, the plateau made a sudden descent, and a vast dry riverbed strewn with little sandstone mounds and thorny bushes split the valley for several kilometers. The wind sang in that spot like a baritone.

It was a fine day, and in spite of a veil of dust hanging over the horizon, we enjoyed a superb sunset. Kadem handed me the headphones attached to his Walkman. I recognized the voice of Fairuz, the Lebanese singing star.

"Have I told you I've taken up my lute again?" he asked.

"That's excellent news."

"I'm composing something at this very moment. I'll let you hear it when it's finished."

"A love song?"

"All Arab songs are love songs," he said. "If the West could only understand our music, if it could even just listen to us sing, if it could hear our soul in the voices of Sabah Fakhri and Wadi es-Safi and Abdelwaheb and Asmahan and Umm Kulthum—if it could commune with our world—I think it would renounce its cutting-edge technology, its satellites, and its armies and follow us to the end of our art. . . ."

I enjoyed Kadem's company. He knew how to find soothing words, and his inspired voice helped me lift up my head. I was happy to see him revived. He was a magnificent fellow, one who didn't deserve to waste away sitting beside a little wall.

"I was just about to go under," he admitted. "For months and months, my head was like a funeral urn. The ashes were obscuring my vision, coming out of my nose and ears. I couldn't see any way out. But then Sulayman's death brought me back. Just like that," he added, snapping his fingers. "It opened my eyes. I don't want to die without having lived. Up until now, all I've done is put up with things. Like Sulayman, I haven't always understood what was happening to me. But there's no way I'm going to wind up like him. When I heard about his death, I asked myself, What? Sulayman's dead? Why? Did he really exist? And it's true, cousin. The poor guy was just about your age. We saw him in the streets every day, wandering around in his own world. And sometimes running after his visions. And yet, now that he's gone, I wonder if he really existed. . . . On my way back from the cemetery, I was automatically heading for the little wall and my rock, when I found myself entering my house. I went up to my room, searched the depths of the storage closet, located the trunk with the brass fittings—it looked like a sarcophagus—opened it, took my lute out of its case, and, I swear, without even tuning up, I started composing. I was carried away—it was as though I were under a spell."

"I can't wait to hear you."

"I just have to add a few finishing touches and I'll be ready."

5

Life in Kafr Karam resumed its course, empty as fasting.

When you've got nothing, that's what you make do with. It's a question of outlook.

Men are pathetic, narrow creatures, blood brothers of Sisyphus, built for suffering; their vocation is to undergo life until death ensues.

The days went their way like a phantom caravan. They came out of nowhere, early in the morning, without charm or panache, and in the evening they disappeared, surreptitiously, swallowed up by darkness. Nonetheless, children continued to be born, and death still took care of keeping things in balance. At the age of seventy-three, our neighbor became a daddy for the seventeenth time, and my great-uncle passed away in his bed, an old man surrounded by his loved ones. What the desert wind carries away, memory restores; what sandstorms erase, we redraw with our hands.

Khaled, the taxi owner, had agreed to give his daughter's hand in marriage to one of the Haitem family, whose orchards stood a few hundred meters beyond the village limits. This was a first. Some even declared it a practical joke. Usually, the Haitems—wealthy, taciturn people—sought their daughters-in-law in town, among urbane families whose girls would have good table manners and know how to receive high society. Their sudden decision to turn to us was a cause of some consternation in certain quarters, but generally it was taken as a good augury that the Haitems were returning to their roots. Although they had snubbed us for a long time, we weren't going to be coy now that one of their scions had fallen for a maiden from our village. And in any case, a prospective marriage, whether rich or poor, made everything worthwhile. At last we could look forward to a happy event that would compensate for the chronic emptiness of our daily lives!

There was an innovation at the Safir: a television set, complete with parabolic antenna. This was a gift from Sayed, who expressed the hope "that the young men of Kafr Karam would not lose sight of their country's tragic reality." Overnight, the seedy café was transformed into a veritable mess hall for unstable soldiers. It was enough to make the proprietor, Majed, tear out his hair. His business was already going down the drain; if, on top of that, his customers were going to arrive with their gargantuan snacks and their packs, the game was clearly up. As for the customers, they weren't bashful. At dawn, without having bothered even to wash their faces, they'd come knocking on his door and ask him to open the café. It was as if they were camped in the street. Once the TV was on, they'd surf through the channels—taking humanity's pulse, as it were—before moving on to Al-Jazeera and staying put. By noon, the little place was teeming with overexcited young men. The air was filled with commentary and invective. Every time the camera offered another look at the national tragedy, the protests and death threats shook the neighborhood around the café. Supporters of preventive war were hooted at, anti-Yankees were applauded, and the people hired to be members of parliament were hissed for being opportunists and flunkies for Bush. Yaseen and his band, in the best seats, seemed to be the guests of choice. Even when they came late, they always found their chairs empty. Behind them were two or three rows of sympathizers, and in the back of the room, the small fry. Majed had no idea what to do. With his chin in his hands and his thermos standing neglected on the counter, he gazed with wounded eyes at the crowd of idlers who were causing incredible commotion and wrecking his furniture.

For a while, my cousin Kadem and I were regulars at the Safir. The experience changed our ideas a bit. Sometimes a trivial remark would bring the house down, and then there was nothing better than an off-the-wall observation to raise it up again. And to see that whole damned, gaping crowd bust a gut when one of them made a fool of himself was excellent therapy, far more effective than we could have suspected. But comedy grows tiresome in the long run, and the wise guys who seized any occasion to amuse the gallery started getting on people's nerves. As might have been expected, Yaseen was obliged to set things straight.

We were all watching the news on Al-Jazeera. The announcer led us to Fallujah, the scene of ongoing battles between American troops, aided by Iraqi security forces, and the local resistance. The besieged city had sworn to die rather than surrender. Disfigured, smoke-filled Fallujah

fought on with touching combativeness. There were reports of hundreds of dead, mostly women and children. The
crowd in the café was silent and heartsick, helpless wit-
nesses to a genuine slaughter: on one side, extravagantly
equipped soldiers, supported by tanks, drones, and helicopters, and on the other side, a populace left to shift for itself,
held hostage by a group of ragged, starving "rebels," armed
with filthy rifles and rocket launchers and scampering
around in all directions. It was then that a young fellow
with a beard cried out, "These American infidels will live to
regret what they've done. God will bring the sky down on
their heads. Not a single GI will leave Iraq intact. Let them
swagger as much as they want—they'll wind up like those
old-time infidel armies the Ababil birds reduced to mince
meat. God's going to send the Ababil birds against them!"

"Bullshit!"

The bearded fellow stiffened, swallowing hard. Then he
turned to the blasphemer. "What did you say?"

"You heard me."

The man with the beard was stunned. His face was
flushed and quivering with anger. "Did you say 'bullshit'?"

"You got it! Bullshit! That's exactly what I said. Not one
syllable more, not one syllable less: BULL SHIT. Is that a
problem for you?"

Everyone in the room had turned their backs on the TV
to see just how far their two young companions were willing to go. "Do you realize what you're saying, Malik?" the
bearded one asked.

"As far as I can tell, you're the one who's talking rubbish,
Harun."

The crowd stirred. Yaseen and his band followed with interest what was happening behind them. Harun, who considered Malik's blasphemous insolence beyond all bounds of decency, seemed to be on the verge of an apoplectic fit. "Come on, I was talking about the Ababil birds," Harun whined. "They're from an important passage in the Qur'an."

"I fail to see the connection with what's going on in Fallujah," Malik said, not backing down. "What I see on that screen is a city under siege. I see Muslims buried in its ruins, I see fugitives at the mercy of a rocket or a missile, and, all around, I see faithless, lawless brutes trampling on us in our own country. And you—you talk to us about Ababil birds. Can you even get an inkling of how ridiculous that is?"

"Keep quiet," Harun warned him. "The devil's in you."

"Right," Malik said with a disdainful sneer. "When you get out of your depth, blame the devil. Wake up, Harun. The Ababil birds are as dead as the dinosaurs. We're at the dawn of the third millennium, and some foreign sons of bitches are here in our land, dragging us in the mud every day God sends. Iraq is occupied, my friend. Look at the TV. What's the TV telling you? What do you see there, right under your nose, while you so sagely stroke your little beard? Infidels subjugating Muslims, demeaning their leaders, throwing their heroes into cages where sluts in fatigues pull their ears and their testicles and pose for posterity. What's God waiting for, you think, before He falls on them? They've been here for some time now, mocking Him where He lives, in His sacred temples and in the hearts of His faithful. Why doesn't He flick His little finger, when those bastards are strafing our souks and bombing our celebrations and shooting our people down like dogs on every street corner? What's become of the Ababil birds? In the old days, when the enemy army invaded the holy land, the Ababils reduced the invaders to a pulp, so where can those birds be now? My dear Harun, I'm just back from Baghdad. I'll spare you the details. We're alone in the world. We can count on no one but ourselves. Heaven will send us no reinforcements, and no miracle's going to rescue us. God's got other fish to fry. At night, when I'm lying in my bed and I hold my breath, I can't even hear Him breathing. The night, all night, every night, belongs to them. And in the day, when I raise my eyes to heaven to implore Him, I can't see anything except their helicopters—their very own Ababil birds—burying us with their fiery droppings."

"There's no more doubt: You've sold your soul to the devil."

"I could offer it to him on a silver platter and he still wouldn't want it."

*"Astaghfirullah."*

"Exactly. At the moment, GIs are profaning our mosques, manhandling our holy men, and bottling up our prayers like flies. How much more provocation does He need, *your* God, before He loses His temper?"

"What did you expect, you imbecile?" Yaseen thundered. All eyes turned toward him. He stood with his hands on his hips, eyeing the blasphemer scornfully. "What did you expect, big mouth? Eh? You thought the Lord was going to ride down on a white horse, burnoose flying in the wind, to cross swords with these animals? *We are His wrath!*"

His outcry had the effect of an explosion inside the café. A few gulps were all that could be heard.

Malik tried to withstand Yaseen's stare but couldn't stop his cheeks from twitching.

Yaseen struck his chest with the flat of his hand. "*We* are the wrath of God," he said in cavernous tones. "We are His Ababil birds. And His thunderbolts, and His chastisements. And we're going to blow these Yankee bastards sky-high; we'll trample them until their shit comes out of their ears and their calculations spurt from their assholes. Is that clear? Now do you understand? Now do you see where God's wrath is, you little prick? It's here, it's in us. We're going to send those devils back to hell, one by one, until they're all gone. It's as true as the sun rises in the east. . . ."

Yaseen crossed the room while people feverishly got out of his path. His eyes devoured the blasphemer. He was like a python moving inexorably upon its prey. He stopped in front of Malik—they were practically nose-to-nose—and squinted a little to concentrate the fire of his gaze. Then Yaseen said, "If I ever hear you expressing the smallest doubt about our victory over those mad dogs, I swear before God and all the guys in this room, I'll tear your heart out with my bare hands."

Kadem pulled me by my shirt and signaled with his head for me to follow him outside.

"Quite a bit of electricity in the air," he said.

"Something's snapped in Yaseen's brain. I don't think ten straitjackets could hold him."

Kadem held out his pack of cigarettes.

"No, thank you," I said.

"Take one," he insisted. "You need a change of air."

When I gave in, I noticed that my hand was trembling. "He scares the shit out of me," I confessed.

Kadem flicked his lighter under my cigarette before applying the flame to his own. Then, throwing back his head, he blew his smoke out into the breeze. "Yaseen's a half-wit," he said. "As far as I know, there's nothing stopping him from jumping onto a bus and going to Baghdad to wage some war. That number he does is going to get tiresome after a while. It may even cause him some serious problems. Shall we go to my place?"

"Why not," I replied.

Kadem lived with his sickly, elderly parents in a little stone house backed up against the mosque. We climbed the stairs to his quarters on the upper floor. The room was large and well lit. There was a double bed surrounded by carpets, a "Made in Taiwan" stereo set dwarfed by two gigantic speakers, a chest of drawers flanked by an oval mirror and an overstuffed chair.

In the corner nearest the door, mounted on a stiff sheepskin, stood a lute—the noblest and most mythical of musical instruments, the king of the Oriental orchestra, the instrument that could elevate its virtuosos to the rank of divinities and transform the shadiest dive into Parnassus, abode of the Muses. I knew the fantastic history of this particular lute, which had been made by Kadem's grandfather, a peerless musician who delighted Cairo throughout the 1940s before conquering Beirut, Damascus, and Amman and becoming a living legend from the Mashriq to the Maghrib. Kadem's grandfather played for princes and sultans, warlords and tyrants; he bewitched women and children, mistresses and lovers. It was said that he was the cause of innumerable conjugal conflicts in the uppermost circles of Arab society. And indeed, it was a jealous army captain who put five bullets in his belly while he was performing under the filtered lights of the Cleopatra, Alexandria's trendiest nightclub, toward the end of the 1950s.

Facing the lute, as if committed to a permanent exchange of influences, was a picture in a carved frame, enshrined on the night table: a photograph of Faten, my cousin's first wife.

"She was beautiful, wasn't she?" Kadem asked as he hung his jacket on a nail.

"She was very beautiful," I acknowledged.

"That picture has never moved from its place. Even my second wife left it where she found it. It bothered her, that's for sure, but she proved to be very understanding about it. Only once, during the first week of our marriage, did she ever try to turn it to face the wall. She didn't dare get undressed under that immense gaze. But then, little by little, she learned to live with it. . . . Tea or coffee?"

"Tea."

"I'll go down and get some."

He made a sudden dash down the stairs.

I stepped closer to the picture. The young bride was wide-eyed and smiling while the wedding festivities went on behind her. Her radiant face outshone all the paper lanterns put together. I remembered when she was a young teenager and she'd leave her house to run errands with her mother; we youngsters would race all the way around the block just so we could watch her pass by. She was sublime.

Kadem returned with a tray. He put the teapot on the

chest of drawers and poured two steaming glasses of tea. Then, to my surprise, he said, "I loved her the first time I saw her." (In Kafr Karam, one never spoke of such things.) "I wasn't yet seven years old. But even at that age, and even though I had no real prospects, I knew we were meant for each other."

His eyes overflowed with splendid evocations as he pushed a glass in my direction. He was floating on a cloud, his brow smooth and his smile broad. "Every time I heard someone playing a lute, I thought of her. I really believe I wanted to become a musician just so I could sing about her. She was such a marvelous girl, so generous, so humble! With her at my side, I needed nothing else. She was more than I could have ever hoped for."

A tear threatened to spill out of one eye; he quickly turned his head and pretended to adjust the lid of the teapot. "Well," he said. "How about a little music?"

"Excellent idea," I said approvingly, quite relieved.

He rummaged in a drawer and fished out a cassette, which he slipped into the tape player. "Listen to this," he said.

Once again, it was Fairuz, the diva of the Arab world, performing her unforgettable song "Hand Me the Flute."

Kadem stretched out on his bed and crossed his legs, still holding the glass of tea in one hand. "Ah!" he exclaimed. "No angel could sing better than that. Her voice is like the breath of the cosmos. . . ."

We heard the cassette through to the end, each of us in his own private universe. Street noises and children's squeals failed to reach us. We flew away with the violins, far, very far from Kafr Karam, far from Yaseen and his outrages. The sun shined its blessings down on us, covering us with gold. The dead woman in the photograph smiled upon us. For a second, I thought I saw her move.

Kadem rolled himself a joint and dragged on it rapturously. He was laughing in silence, beating time with one languorous hand to the singer's unfaltering rhythm. At the beginning of a refrain, he started singing, too, thrusting out his chest. He had a magnificent voice.

After the Fairuz cassette was over, he put on others, old songs by Abdel Halim Hafez and Abdelwaheb, Ayam and Younes, Najat and other immortal glories of the *tarab al-arabi.*

Night surprised us, completely intoxicated as we were with joints and songs.

❖　●　❖

The TV that Sayed had donated to the idle youth of Kafr Karam proved to be a poisoned chalice. It brought the village nothing but turmoil and disharmony. Many families owned a television set, but at home, with the father seated on his throne and his eldest son at his right hand, young people kept their comments to themselves. Things were different in the café. You could boo, you could argue about any subject whatsoever, and you could change your mind according to your mood. Sayed had hit the bull's-eye. Hatred was as contagious as laughter, discussions got out of control, and a gap formed between those who went to the Safir to have fun and those who were there "to learn." It was the latter whose point of view prevailed. We started concentrating on the national tragedy, all of us together, every step of the way. The sieges of Fallujah and Basra and the bloody raids on other cities made the crowd seethe. The insurgent attacks might horrify us for an instant, but more often than not they aroused our enthusiasm. We applauded the successful ambushes and deplored skirmishes that went wrong. The assembly's initial delight at Saddam's fate turned to frustration. In Yaseen's view, the Rais, trapped like a rat, unrecognizable with his hobo's beard and his dazed eyes, exposed triumphantly and shamelessly to the world's cameras, represented the most grievous affront inflicted on the Iraqi people. "By humiliating him like that," Yaseen declared, "they were holding up every Arab in the world to public opprobrium."

We were at a loss as to how to assess the ongoing events; we no longer knew whether a given attack was a feat of arms or a demonstration of cowardice. An action vilified one day might be praised to the skies the next. Clashing opinions led to incredible escalations, and fistfights broke out more and more frequently.

The situation was degenerating, and the elders refused to intervene publicly; each father preferred to give his offspring a talking-to in the privacy of his home. Kafr Karam was reeling from the most serious discord in its history. The silences and submissions accumulated through many years and various despotic regimes rose like drowned corpses from a muddy river bottom, bobbing up to the surface to shock the living.

Yaseen and his band—the twins Hassan and Hussein, the blacksmith's son-in-law Salah, Adel, and Bilal, the barber's son—disappeared, and the village entered a period of relative calm. Three weeks later, persons unknown set fire to the disused pumping station, a deteriorating structure some twenty kilometers from Kafr Karam. There was a report that an attack on an Iraqi police patrol had resulted in some fatalities among the forces of order, along with two vehicles destroyed and various weapons carried off by the attackers. Rumor raised this ambush to the status of a heroic action, and in the streets people began to talk about furtive groups glimpsed here and there under cover of night, but no one ever got close enough to identify or capture any of them. A climate of tension kept us all on the alert. Every day, we awaited news from the "front," which we figured was coming soon to a neighborhood near us.

One day, for the first time since the occupation of the country by the American troops and their allies, a military helicopter made three passes over our area. Now there was no more room for doubt: Things were happening in this part of the country.

In the village, we prepared for the worst.

Ten days, twenty days, a month passed. We could see nothing on the horizon—no convoy, no suspicious movements.

When it looked as though the village was not going to be the target of a military raid, people relaxed; the elders returned to their barbershop antiphony, the young resumed their tumultuous meetings at the Safir, and the desert regained its stultifying barrenness and its infinite banality.

The order of things seemed to have been reestablished.

# 6

·

Khaled Taxi was in his mid-thirties. Wearing a pair of cheap sunglasses, his hair oiled and slicked back, he was prancing around in the street and looking impatiently at his watch. Despite the ferocious heat, he'd squeezed himself into a three-piece suit that, in a former life, had known better days. A tie fit for a clown costume—garish yellow streaked with brown—spread across his chest. Now and again, he reached inside his jacket and took out a tiny comb, which he passed through his mustache.

"Are they coming?" he shouted up to the terrace, where his fourteen-year-old son was stationed as a lookout.

"Not yet," the boy replied, keeping his hand over his eyes like a visor, even though the sun was behind him.

"What the hell are they doing? I hope they haven't changed their minds."

The boy stood on tiptoe, carefully studying the horizon to show his father how conscientious he was.

The Haitems were making them wait. They were an hour late, and still no cloud of dust was rising from the midst of their orchards. The part of the wedding procession that was due to set out from Kafr Karam was ready: Five automobiles, polished and beribboned, were parked and waiting across from the bride's patio, their doors wide open because of the heat. With an exasperated gesture, the man keeping an eye on the cars shooed away the flies that were buzzing around his head.

For the umpteenth time, Khaled looked at his watch. Disgusted at what he saw, he went up to the terrace and joined his boy.

The Haitems hadn't invited many people from Kafr Karam. They'd presented a rather short list of handpicked guests, among them the eldest of the tribe and his wives, Doc Jabir and his family, Bashir the Falcon and his daughters, and five or six other notables. My father was not eligible for this honor. Although he'd been the Haitems' official well digger for thirty years—he'd dug all the wells in their orchards, installed the motorized pumps and the rotary sprinklers, and laid out a great many irrigation channels—he had remained, in the eyes of his former employers, a mere stranger. This casual ingratitude had offended my mother, but the old man, sitting under his tree, couldn't have cared less. And in any case, it wasn't as though he owned clothes he could wear to such a party.

Evening crept up on the village. The sky was sprinkled with a thousand stars. The heat nevertheless promised to maintain its siege until late in the night. Kadem and I were on the terrace at my house, sitting on two creaking chairs, a teapot between us. Like our neighbors, we were gazing out toward the Haitems' orchards.

Swirls of dust lifted by the wind occasionally traversed the whitish trail, but no vehicle turned onto it.

Bahia appeared regularly to see if we had need of her services. I found her a bit nervous and noticed that she kept coming back upstairs to bring us biscuits or fill our glasses. Her little game intrigued me, and soon, by watching the looks she gave us, I realized that my twin sister had her eye on our cousin. She blushed violently when I caught her smiling at him through the window.

Finally, the Haitems' procession approached, and the village went into a frenzy of car horns and ululations. The streets were jammed with unruly kids; only after much supplication was the first flower-laden Mercedes allowed to pass through the crowd. The Haitems had spared no expense. The ten vehicles they sent were all luxury cars, excessively decorated; they looked like Christmas trees, with their multicolored sequins and spangles, their bright balloons and long ribbons. All the drivers wore identical black suits and white shirts with bow ties. A photographer brought in from the city immortalized the event, his video camera on his shoulder and his every step accompanied by a swarm of children; flashes went off wildly all around him.

Superb in her white dress, the bride issued forth from her family home and was greeted by bursts of celebratory rifle fire. As the procession made a small detour past the mosque before returning to the dirt road, a powerful movement rippled through the crowd in the square. Kids ran behind the vehicles, shouting at the top of their lungs, and the entire throng accompanied their virgin to the outskirts of the little town, joyously kicking stray dogs as they went.

Kadem and I were standing against the railing of the roof terrace. We watched the procession moving away—he captivated by his memories, and I amused and impressed at the same time. Off in the distance, in the growing darkness, we could glimpse the party lights amid the black mass of the orchards.

"Do you know the groom?" I asked my cousin.

"Not really. I saw him at the house of a friend, a fellow musician, about five or six years ago. We weren't introduced, but he seemed like an unpretentious guy. Not a bit like his father. I think he's a good match for her."

"I hope so. Khaled's a good man, and his daughter's adorable. Did you know that I had my eye on her?"

"I don't want to know about it. She belongs to someone else now, and you have to put such things out of your head."

"I was just saying—"

"You shouldn't have. Just thinking about it's a sin."

Bahia appeared again, her eyes glowing. "Will you stay for dinner with us, Kadem?" she chirped in a quavering voice.

"I can't, but thanks anyway. The old folks aren't well."

"But no, you're staying for dinner," I said peremptorily. "It's almost nine o'clock. Don't insult us by leaving just as we're about to sit down."

Kadem hesitated, pressing his lips together. Bahia's hands tormented each other as she awaited his response.

"All right," he said, yielding. "I haven't tasted my aunt's cooking in a long time."

"*I* did the cooking tonight," Bahia declared, crimson-faced. Then she dashed down the stairs, as happy as a child at the end of Ramadan.

We hadn't finished eating when we heard a distant explosion. Kadem and I left the table to go and have a look. Some neighbors, soon joined by the rest of their family, appeared on their terrace, too. Down in the street, someone asked what was going on. Except for the tiny lights shining through the orchards, the plateau appeared serene.

"It was a plane," someone cried out in the night. "I saw it come down."

The sound of running footsteps moved past the house in the direction of the square. Our neighbors started leaving their terrace, eager to hear the news in the street. People came out of their houses and gathered here and there. In the darkness, their silhouettes loomed together distressingly. "A plane crash," people said, passing the words around. "Ibrahim saw a burning plane crash to the ground." The square was teeming with curious villagers. The women stayed behind their patio doors, trying to gather bits of information from passersby. "A plane crashed, but very far from here," they were told reassuringly.

Suddenly, two automobile headlights emerged from the orchards and zoomed toward the trail. The car bore down on the village at top speed.

"This is bad," Kadem said, watching the vehicle bound and pitch as it hurtled toward us. "This is very bad."

He made a dash for the stairs.

The car nearly fishtailed as it bounced onto the smaller trail leading to Kafr Karam. We could hear the blasts of its horn, indistinct but disturbing. Then the headlights reached the first houses of the village, and the horn blasts catapulted pedestrians against walls. The car crossed the soccer pitch, braked in front of the mosque, and skidded a good distance before stopping in a cloud of dust. The driver leaped out while people were still running toward him. His face was distraught and his eyes white with terror. He pointed at the orchards and babbled unintelligible sounds.

Another car roared up. Without taking the trouble to get out, the driver shouted to us, "Get in, quick. We need help at the Haitems'. A missile came down on the party."

People started running off in all directions. Kadem pushed me into the backseat of the second car and jumped in beside me. Three other young men piled in around us, and two more sat up front.

"You've got to hurry," the driver shouted to the crowd. "If you can't get a ride, come on foot. Lots of people are buried under the rubble. Bring whatever you can—shovels, blankets, sheets, medicine kits. Don't dawdle. Please, please, come quick!"

He made a U-turn and gunned the car in the direction of the orchards.

"Are you sure it was a missile?" one of the passengers asked.

"I don't know," said the driver, obviously still stunned. "I don't know anything. The guests were having a good time, and then the chairs and tables blew away, like in a windstorm. It was crazy. . . . It was . . . I can't describe it. Bodies and screams, screams and bodies. If it wasn't a missile, then it must have been lightning from heaven."

A bad feeling came over me. I didn't understand what I was doing in that car, tearing along in the dark, nor was it clear why I'd accepted an opportunity to see horror up close, me, when I wasn't yet over my last awful shock. Sweat poured down my back and rolled off my forehead. I looked at the driver, at the other men in the front seat, at those with me in the back, including Kadem, who was gnawing his lips, and I couldn't believe I'd agreed to go with them. A voice inside me cried, Where are you going, you poor fool? I couldn't tell whether my body was rising in revolt or being slammed about by the ruts in the trail. I cursed myself, grinding my teeth, my fists clenched against the fear that was rising like a solid mass in my belly. Where are you running to, stupid? I asked myself. As we approached the orchards, the fear grew so large that a kind of torpor numbed my limbs and my mind.

The orchards were sunk in a malignant darkness. We raced through them. The Haitems' house looked intact. There were shadowy figures on the staircase leading to the entrance, some of them collapsed on the steps, their heads in their hands, and others leaning against the wall. The focal point of the tragedy lay a little farther on, in a garden where a building, apparently the hall the family used for parties, was burning at the center of a huge pile of smoking debris. The force of the explosion had flung chairs and wedding guests thirty meters in all directions. Survivors staggered about, their clothes in rags, holding their hands out in front of them like blind people. Some mutilated, charred bodies were lined up along the edge of a path. Cars illuminated the slaughter with their headlights, while specters thrashed about in the midst of the rubble. Then there was the howling, drawn out, interminable; the air was full of pleas and cries and wails. Mothers looking for their children called out into the confusion; the more they went unanswered, the louder they shouted. A weeping man, covered with blood, knelt beside the body of someone dear to him.

A wave of nausea cut me in half the moment my foot hit the ground; I fell on all fours and puked my insides out. Kadem tried to lift me up, but before long he left me and ran toward a group of men who were busy helping some injured people. I crept over to a tree, put my arms around my knees, and contemplated the delirium. Other vehicles arrived from the village, filled with volunteers and shovels and bundles. Anarchy added a dimension of demented activity to the rescue operation. With their bare hands, people lifted burning beams and sections of collapsed walls, searching for a sign of life. Someone dragged a dying man to a spot near me and begged him, "Don't go to sleep." When the injured person started slipping weakly into unconsciousness, the other slapped him several times to keep him from fainting. Another man came up and leaned over the body. "Come on, there's nothing more you can do for him." The other kept slapping the injured man, harder and harder. "Hold on," he said. "Hold on, I'm telling you." The third man said, "Hold on to what? Can't you see he's dead?"

I got to my feet like a sleepwalker and ran toward the fire.

I don't know how long I was there, yanking, heaving, and turning over everything around me. When I came out of my trance, my hands were bruised and my fingers lacerated and

bleeding; I sank to my knees, wretchedly sick, my lungs polluted with smoke and the stench of cremation.

※   •   ※

The sun rose on the disaster.

Wreaths of smoke from the blasted hall rose into the sky
like burnt offerings. The air was heavy with horrid exhalations. The dead—seventeen of them, mostly women and
children—lay under sheets at one side of the garden. The
injured sprawled here and there, groaning and surrounded
by medical workers and relatives. Ambulances had reached
the scene a short while before, and the stretcher-bearers
didn't know where to begin. Although the level of confusion had subsided, agitation grew as the true extent of the
tragedy became apparent. From time to time, a woman
screamed, setting off a new round of cries and wailing.
Men went around in circles, stunned and lost. The first police vehicles arrived. The officers were Iraqis, and their
leader was immediately taken to task by the survivors. The
situation degenerated; then, when people started throwing
things at the cops, they jumped back into their cars and
sped away. An hour later, they returned, reinforced by two
truckloads of soldiers. An extremely stout officer asked to
speak to a representative of the Haitem family. Someone
flung a rock at the fat officer, and the soldiers fired their
weapons into the air to calm everyone down. At that moment, some foreign television teams turned up. A grieving
father shouted at them, indicating the carnage. "Look!
Nothing but women and children! This was a wedding re-

ception! Where are the terrorists?" He grabbed a camera-man by the arm, showed him the corpses stretched out on the grass, and said, "The real terrorists are the bastards who fired the missile at us."

My hands bandaged, my shirt torn, and my pants stained with blood, I left the orchards on foot and walked home like a man stumbling through fog.

# 7

* • *

I was an emotional person; I found other people's sorrows
devastating. Whenever I passed a misfortune, I bore it away
with me. As a child, I often wept in my room after locking
the door, for fear that my twin sister—a *girl*—would catch
me shedding tears. People said she was stronger than I was,
and less of a crybaby. I didn't hold any of it against her. I
was made that way, and that was all there was to it. A delicate porcelain creature. My mother tried to put me on my
guard. "You have to be tougher," she'd say. "You must learn
to give up other people's troubles—they're not good for
them, and they're not good for you. You're too badly off to
worry about someone else's fate." Her warnings were in
vain—we aren't born wise; we learn wisdom. Me, I was
born in misery, and misery raised me to share. All suffering
confided in mine and became my own. For the rest, there
was an arbiter in heaven; it was up to Him to tweak the
world as He saw fit, just as he could freely choose not to lift
His little finger.

At school, my classmates considered me a weakling.

They could provoke me all they wanted; I never returned their blows. Even when I refused to turn the other cheek, I kept my fists in my pockets. Eventually, the other kids got discouraged by my stoicism and left me in peace. In fact, I wasn't a weakling; I simply hated violence. Whenever I watched a schoolyard brawl, I hunched my shoulders around my ears and got ready for the sky to fall in on me. Maybe that's what happened at the Haitems' place: The sky fell in on me. I told myself I'd never be free of the curse that had destroyed the wedding party and turned joyous ululations into appalling cries of agony. I told myself our fates are sealed: We're united in pain until the worst of pains separates us. A voice knocking at my temples kept repeating that the death stinking up the orchards was contaminating my soul, and that I was dead, too.

In the Haitems' orchards—that is, in the land of the blessed, the filthy rich who disregarded the rest of us—I saw with my own eyes how incongruous our existence is, how flimsy our certainties, how precarious our knowledge. Chance had led me there.

You can't walk on hot coals without burning your feet.

I didn't remember ever having borne a grudge against anybody, anybody at all, and yet there I was, ready to bite something, including the hand that tried to soothe me—except that I held myself back. I was outraged, sick, tormented by a thousand thorns, like Christ at the height of His suffering, but my way of the cross wound in a circle I didn't understand. What had happened at the Haitems' wedding party wasn't anything I could figure out. You don't pass from jubilation to grief in the blink of an eye. Life, even though it often hangs by a mere thread, isn't a conjuring trick. People don't die in bulk between dance steps; no, what had happened at the Haitems' made no sense.

On the evening news, there was talk of an American drone alleged to have detected some suspicious signals coming from in or around the reception hall. The nature of these suspicious signals was not revealed. Instead, there was a suggestion that terrorist movements had previously been reported in this sector. When the local residents rejected this assertion altogether, the undaunted American hierarchy tried for a while to justify the missile strike by offering other security-related arguments; in the end, however, tired of looking ridiculous, the Americans deplored the mistake and apologized to the victims' families.

And that was the end of that—one more news item destined to travel around the world before falling onto the scrap heap, replaced by other enormities.

But in Kafr Karam, anger had unburied the war hatchet: Six young men asked the faithful to pray for them. They promised to avenge the dead and vowed not to return to the village until the last "American boy" had been sent back home in a body bag. After the customary embraces, the young men went out into the night and soon merged with the darkness.

A few weeks later, the district police superintendent was shot to death in his official car. That same day, a military vehicle was blown up by a homemade bomb.

Kafr Karam went into mourning for its first *shaheeds*, its first martyrs—six all at once, surprised and cut down by a patrol as they prepared a fresh attack.

The tension in the village was reaching deranged proportions. Every day, young men vanished from Kafr Karam. I never stepped into the street anymore. I could bear neither the reproachful looks from the elders, startled to see me still around when all the brave lads of my age had joined the resistance, nor the sardonic smiles of the youngsters, which reminded me of the way my classmates used to smile when they called me a weakling. I shut myself up in my room and took refuge in books or in the audiocassettes Kadem sent me. As a matter of fact, I was indeed angry, I held a bitter grudge against the coalition forces, but I couldn't see myself indiscriminately attacking everyone and everything in sight. War wasn't my line. I wasn't born to commit violence—I considered myself a thousand times likelier to suffer it than to practice it one day.

And then one night, the sky fell in on me again. At first, when the door of my room flew open with a crash, I imagined another missile. Then came shouted insults and cones of blinding light. I didn't have time to reach for the lamp switch. A squad of American soldiers barged into my privacy. "Lie back down! If you move, I'll blow you up!" "Stand up!" "Lie down!" "Stand up! Hands on your head! Don't move!" Flashlights nailed me to the bed; weapons were aimed at me. "Don't move or I'll blow your brains out!" Those shouts! Atrocious, demented, devastating. Capable of unraveling you thread by thread and making you a stranger to yourself. Hands seized me, pulled me from my bed, and flung me across the room. Other hands caught me and crushed me against the wall. "Hands behind your back!" "What have I done? What is it?" The GIs smashed my wardrobe, overturned my dresser drawers, and kicked my things in all directions. A booted foot stamped my old radio into fragments. "What's going on?" "Where are the fucking weapons, shithead?" "I have no weapons. There aren't any weapons here." "We'll see about that, mother-fucker. Put this asshole with the others." A soldier grabbed me by the neck; another kneed me in the groin. I was swept up into a tornado and tossed from one tumult to another, caught in a waking nightmare like a sleepwalker assailed by poltergeists. I had the vague sensation of being dragged across the roof terrace and rushed downstairs; I couldn't tell whether I was tumbling or gliding. A similar upheaval was taking place on the top floor. My nephews' weeping cut through the surrounding racket. I heard Bahia grumble before falling silent all at once, struck by a fist or a rifle butt. Pallid and half-dressed, my sisters were penned up at the other end of the hall with the children. The eldest, Aisha, pressed a couple of her kids against her skirts. She was trembling like a leaf, unaware that her naked breasts were hanging out of her blouse. On her right stood my second sister, Afaf, the seamstress, swaying and clutching her cloth-ing. She'd been snatched from her sleep so abruptly that she'd forgotten her wig on her night table; her bald head, as pitiful as a stump, shone under the ceiling lights. Mortified, she ducked and hunched her shoulders as if she wanted to take refuge in her own body. Bahia was standing firm. A nephew in her arms, her hair disheveled, and her face drained of blood, she silently defied the weapon pointed at her; a bright red thread dripped down the nape of her neck.

I felt faint. My hand searched in vain for something to hold on to.

Hellish insults erupted from the end of the hall. My mother, ejected from her room, immediately collected her-self and went to help her invalid husband. "Leave him alone.

He's sick." Soldiers brought out the old man. I'd never seen him in such a state. With his threadbare undershirt hanging loosely from his thin shoulders and his stretched-out drawers fallen nearly to his knees, he was the very image of boundless distress, walking misery, an affront personified in all its absolute boorishness. "Let me get dressed," he moaned. "My children are here. It's not right; what you're doing isn't right." His quavering voice filled the corridor with inconceivable sorrow. My mother tried to walk in front of him, to spare us the sight of his nakedness. Her terrified eyes implored us, begging us to turn away. I couldn't turn away. I was hypnotized by the spectacle the two of them presented to my eyes. I didn't even see the brutes who surrounded them. I saw only a distraught mother and a painfully thin father in shapeless underwear, his eyes wounded, his arms dangling at his sides, stumbling as the soldiers shoved him along. With a final effort, he pivoted on his heels and tried to go back to the bedroom to fetch his robe—and the blow was struck. Rifle butt or fist, what difference does it make? The blow was struck, and the die was cast. My father fell over backward; his miserable undershirt flapped up over his face, revealing his belly, which was concave, wrinkled, and gray as the belly of a dead fish. . . . And I saw, while my family's honor lay stricken on the floor, I saw what it was forbidden to see, what a worthy, respectable son, an authentic Bedouin, must never see: that flaccid, hideous, degrading thing, that forbidden, unspoken-of, sacrilegious object, my father's penis, rolling to one side as his testicles flopped up over his ass. That sight was the edge of the abyss, and beyond it, there was nothing but the infinite void, an interminable fall, nothingness. Suddenly, all our tribal myths, all the world's legends, all the stars in the sky lost their gleam. The sun could keep on rising, but I'd never be able to distinguish day from night anymore. A Westerner can't understand, can't suspect the dimensions of the disaster. For me, to see my father's sex was to reduce my entire existence, my values and my scruples, my pride and my singularity, to a coarse, pornographic flash. The gates of hell would have seemed less catastrophic! I was finished. Everything was finished—irrecoverably, irreversibly. I had been saddled, once and for all, with infamy; I'd plunged into a parallel world from which I'd never escape. I found myself hating my arms, which seemed grotesque, translucent, ugly, the symbols of my impotence; hating my eyes, which refused to turn away and pleaded for blindness; hating my mother's screams, which discredited me. I looked at my father, and my father looked back at me. He must have read in my eyes the contempt I felt toward everything that had counted for us and my sudden pity for the person I revered above everything, despite everything. I looked at him as though from atop a blasted cliff on a stormy night; he looked at me from the bottom of disgrace. At that very instant, we already knew that we were looking at each other for the last time. And *at that very instant*, when I dared not turn a hair, I understood that nothing would ever again be as it had been; I knew I'd no longer consider things in the same way; I heard the foul beast roar deep inside me, and it was clear that sooner or later, whatever happened, I was *condemned to wash away this insult in blood*, until the rivers and the oceans turned as red as the cut on Bahia's neck, as my mother's eyes, as the fire in my guts, which was already preparing me for the hell I knew was waiting. . . .

❖  •  ❖

I don't remember what happened after that. I didn't care. Like a piece of wreckage, I let myself drift wherever the waves took me. There was nothing left to salvage. The soldiers' bellowing didn't reach me anymore. Their weapons, their gung-ho zeal hardly made an impression. They could move heaven and earth, erupt like volcanoes, crack like thunder; I could no longer be touched by that sort of thing. I watched them thrashing about as though I were looking through a picture window in a microcosm of shadows and silence.

They scoured the house. Nary a weapon; not so much as a puny penknife.

Rough hands propelled me into the street, where some young men were crouched with their hands on their heads.

Kadem was one of them. His arm was bleeding.

In the neighboring houses, orders were shouted, sending the residents into hysterics.

Some Iraqi soldiers examined us. They carried lists and pages printed with photographs. Someone lifted my chin, shined his light in my face, checked his papers, and went on to the next man. Off to one side, guarded by overexcited GIs, suspects waited to be taken away. They lay facedown in the dust, their hands bound behind them and their heads in bags.

Two helicopters flew over the village, sweeping us with searchlights. There was something apocalyptic about the rumbling of their rotors.

The sun rose. Soldiers escorted us to an area behind the mosque, where a large tent had just been pitched. We were interrogated separately, one by one. Some Iraqi officers showed me photographs; several of them had been taken in the morgue or at the scene of the carnage and showed some of the faces of the dead. I recognized Malik, the "blasphemer" from the other day at the Safir. His eyes were staring and his mouth was wide open; blood ran out of his nose and formed tiny rivulets on his chin. I also recognized a distant cousin, curled up at the foot of a streetlight, his jaw shattered.

The officer asked me to name all the members of my family. His secretary noted down all my declarations in a register, and then I was set free.

Kadem was waiting for me on the street corner. He had a nasty gash on his arm, running from the top of his shoulder to his wrist. His shirt was stained with sweat and blood. He told me that the GIs had smashed his grandfather's lute—a fabulous lute of inestimable value, a tribal and even national heirloom. I only half-listened. Kadem was crushed. Tears veiled his eyes. His monotonous voice disgusted me.

We sat for long minutes leaning against a wall, empty, panting, holding our heads in our hands. Light slowly grew in the sky, and on the horizon, as though rising from an open fracture, the sun prepared to immolate itself in its own flames. The first noisy kids could be heard; soon they would overrun the square and the open lots. The roar of the trucks signaled the withdrawal of the troops. Some old men left their patios and hurried to the mosque, eager to learn who had been arrested and who had been spared. Women wailed in their doorways, calling out the names of husbands or sons whom the soldiers had carried off. Little by little, as despair spread from one hovel to the next and the sound of sobbing rose above the rooftops, Kafr Karam filled me with a flood of venom. "I have to get away from here," I said.

Kadem stared at me in alarm. "Where do you want to go?" he asked.

"Baghdad."

"To do what?"

"There's more to life than music."

He nodded and pondered my words.

All I had were the clothes I was wearing—namely, an undershirt that had seen better days and a pair of old pajama pants. No shoes. I asked, "Can you do me a favor, Kadem?"

"That depends."

"I need to get some stuff from home."

"So what's the problem?"

"The problem is, I can't go back to my house."

He frowned. "Why not?"

"Because I can't, that's all. Will you get my things for me? Bahia will know what to put in my bag. Tell her I'm going to Baghdad to stay with our sister Farah."

"I don't understand. What happened? Why can't you go back home?"

"Kadem, please. Just do what I'm asking you to do."

Kadem guessed that something very serious had taken place. I'm sure he was thinking in terms of rape.

"Do you really want to know what happened, cousin?" I cried. "Do you really insist on hearing about it?"

"That's all right, I get it," he grumbled.

"You don't get a thing. Nothing at all."

His cheekbones quivered as he pointed a finger at me.

"Watch it," he said. "I'm older than you. I won't permit you to talk to me like that."

"I'm afraid I no longer need anyone's permission for anything, cousin." I looked him straight in the eye. "And what's more, I don't care a rotten fig about what happens to me from this moment on. From this second. Are you going to pick up my fucking stuff for me, or do I have to leave like this? I swear, I'll jump on the first bus I see in just this undershirt and these pajama pants. Nothing matters anymore, not ridicule, not even lies. . . ."

"Come on, get a hold of yourself."

Kadem tried to grab my wrists. I pushed him away. "Listen," he said, breathing slowly so he could keep calm. "Here's what we're going to do. We'll go to my house—"

"I want to leave from here."

"Please. Listen to me, just listen. I know you're completely—"

"Completely what, Kadem? You don't know a damn thing. It's something you can't even imagine."

"All right, but let's go to my house first. You can take some time and think about this calmly, and then, if you're still sure you want to leave, I'll personally accompany you to the nearest town."

"Please, cousin," I said in a toneless voice. "Go get me my bag and my walking stick. I've got to say a few words to the good Lord."

Kadem saw that I was in no condition to listen to anyone at all. "Okay," he said. "I'll go and get your things."

"I'll wait for you behind the cemetery."

"Why not here?"

"Kadem, you ask too many questions, and I've got a headache."

He gestured with both hands, beseeching me to take it easy, and then he went away without looking back.

＊　●　＊

I wandered around the cemetery for a bit. Everywhere I looked, I saw the *abominable thing* I'd glimpsed in the hall the previous night. Twice I had to crouch down and puke. My body swayed unsteadily on my heels as the spasms overwhelmed me. I opened my mouth, but all that came out was something that sounded like a wild beast's death rattle. After a while, I sat down on a little mound and started digging rocks out of the ground around me and throwing them at a scrawny tree whose dusty branches were hung with plastic packets. Every time I snapped my arm, I let out a grunt of rage. I was chasing away the cloud of ill omen that was gathering over my thoughts; I was plunging my hand into my memory of the previous evening in order to tear out its heart.

The whole place stank in the morning heat. A decomposing corpse, no doubt. That didn't bother me. I kept on excavating rocks and hurling them at the little tree, so many rocks that my fingers were bleeding.

Behind me, the village was getting out of the wrong side of the bed. The voices of the fed up could be heard here and there—a father speaking roughly to his kid, a younger brother rising up against an older one. I didn't recognize myself in that anger. I wanted something greater than my misery, vaster than my shame.

I'd just finished stoning the little tree when Kadem came back, slipping among the graves. From a distance, he showed me my bag. Bahia was following him, her head wrapped in a muslin scarf. She was wearing the black dress of farewells. "We thought the soldiers had taken you away," she said, her face waxen.

Apparently, she hadn't come to dissuade me from leaving. That wasn't her style. She understood my motives and obviously approved them all, without reservations and without regrets. Bahia was a daughter of her tribe. In the ancestral tradition, honor was supposed to be the domain of men, but even so, she knew how to recognize it and require it.

I snatched the bag out of Kadem's hand and started digging around inside it. Although my sister clearly noticed the violence of my movements, she didn't reproach me in any way. She merely said, "I've put in two undershirts, two shirts, two pairs of trousers, some socks, your toilet bag—"

"How about my money?"

She reached into her bosom, drew out a little packet, carefully folded and tied with string, and handed it to Kadem, who immediately turned it over to me. "I don't want any money but mine," I said to my sister. "Not a penny more."

She said, "There's nothing in there but your savings, I promise you. I packed a cap for you, too," she added, repressing a sob. "Because of the sun."

"Very good. Now turn around so I can change."

I put on a pair of pinstriped trousers, my checked shirt,

and the shoes my cousin had given me. "You forgot my belt," I said.

"It's in the outside pocket of the bag," Bahia said. "Along with your pocket light."

"Very good."

I finished getting dressed, and then, without a glance at my sister or my cousin, I grabbed my bag and started down the steep path in the direction of the main trail. Don't turn around, an interior voice admonished me. You're already gone. There's nothing for you here. Don't turn around. I turned around—and saw my sister, standing on the mound, looking ghostly in her windblown dress, and my cousin, with his hands on his hips and his chin against his chest. I retraced my steps. My sister pressed herself against me. Her tears wet my cheeks. I felt her frail body shudder in my embrace. "Please," she said. "Take care of yourself."

Kadem opened his arms to me. We flung ourselves against each other. We hugged for what seemed like a very long time.

"Are you sure you don't want me to go with you to the next town?" he asked in a strangled voice.

"It's not worth the trouble, cousin," I said. "I know the way."

I waved at them and hurried off toward the trail without turning around.

BAGHDAD

# 8

＊　●　＊

I walked to the crossroads about ten kilometers from the village. From time to time, I looked back in hopes of seeing a vehicle coming my way, but no cloud of dust rose from the trail. I was in the middle of the desert, alone and infinitesimally small. The sun rolled up its sleeves. The day would be a scorcher.

The junction featured a makeshift bus shelter. Formerly, the bus that served Kafr Karam used to stop at that shelter. Now the place seemed to have been abandoned. Pieces of torn metal dangled down over the bench from a hole in the corrugated-tin roof. I sat in the shade and waited two hours. There was no sign of movement anywhere on the horizon.

I continued on my way, heading for an access road normally used by the refrigerated trucks that furnished the isolated communities of the region with fruits and vegetables. Since the embargo, such vehicles made far fewer trips, but it sometimes happened that an itinerant grocer went down that road. It was a hell of a hike, and I was crushed by the ever-increasing heat.

I noticed two black spots on a small hill overlooking the access road. They turned out to be two young men in their early twenties. They were squatting in the sun, immobile and impenetrable. The younger-looking of the two gave me a sharp look; the other drew circles in the dust with a stick. They were both wearing grimy white sweatpants and wrinkled, dirty shirts. A large bag lay at their feet like some fresh-killed prey.

I sat on a little sand mound and pretended to busy myself with my shoelaces. Every time I raised my eyes to look at the two strangers, a peculiar feeling came over me. The younger of the two had a disagreeable way of bending over his companion to whisper into his ear. The other nodded and kept working his stick. Just once, he shot me a glance that made me uncomfortable. After about twenty minutes, the younger one got to his feet abruptly and started walking in my direction. His bloodshot eyes grazed me, and I felt his hot breath lash my face. He moved past me and went to urinate on a withered bush.

I made a show of consulting my watch and continued on my way at a quicker pace. A desire to turn around tormented me, but I resisted. After I got far enough away, I checked to see whether they were following me. They were back on their hillside, crouched over their sack like two carrion birds watching over a carcass.

A few kilometers farther on, a van caught up with me. I stood on the side of the trail and waved my arms. The van nearly knocked me down as it passed in a din of scrap metal and overworked valves. Glancing into the cabin, I recognized the two individuals of a little while ago. They were looking straight ahead.

By midday, I was exhausted. Sweat steamed off my clothes. I veered toward a tree—the only one for miles around—standing atop a rise in the ground. Its bare, thorny branches cast a skeletal shadow, which I quickly occupied.

Hunger and thirst accentuated my fatigue. I took off my shoes and lay down under the tree in such a way that I could keep the dirt road in sight. Hours passed before I made out a vehicle in the distance. It was still nothing but a grayish dot sliding through the glare, but I was able to identify it from the irregular flashes of reflected light it gave off. I immediately put my shoes back on and ran toward the trail. To my great disappointment, the dot changed direction and gradually slid out of sight.

According to my watch, it was four o'clock. The nearest village was about forty kilometers to the south. To reach it, I would have had to leave the dirt road, and I didn't much like the idea of just wandering. I went back to the tree and waited.

The sun was going down when a new glinting dot appeared on the horizon. I considered it a good idea to be certain the dot was coming my way before leaving the shelter of my tree. And along came a rattling old truck whose fenders had been torn off. The truck came toward me. I hurried to intercept it, praying to my patron saints not to let me fall. The truck slowed down. I heard its brake shoes grind and scream.

The driver was a small, dehydrated fellow, with a face that looked like papier-mâché and two arms as thin as baguettes. He was transporting empty crates and used mattresses.

"I'm going to Baghdad," I said, climbing up on the running board.

"That's not exactly next door, my boy," he said, looking me over. "Where do you come from?"

"Kafr Karam."

"Ah, the asshole of the desert. I'm going to Basseel. Not the most direct route, but you can find a taxi there to take you to the city."

"Suits me fine."

The driver considered me suspiciously. "You mind if I take a look inside your bag?"

I handed it to him through the window. He set the bag on the dashboard and went through its contents carefully. "Okay," he said. "Get in on the other side."

I thanked him and walked around the front of the truck. He leaned over and opened the passenger door, whose exterior handle was missing. I settled into the seat, or, to be more precise, what was left of it.

The driver took off in a racket of shivering metal.

I said, "Would you have any water?"

"There's a goatskin bag right behind you. If you're hungry, look in the glove compartment. There's some of my snack left."

He let me eat and drink in peace. Then a troubled look came over his emaciated face, and he said, "Don't be annoyed at me for going through your things. I'm just trying to avoid problems. There are so many armed men on the roads. . . ."

I said nothing. We traveled several kilometers in silence.

"You're not very talkative, are you?" the driver said. He'd probably been hoping for a little company.

"No."

He shrugged and forgot about me.

After we reached a paved road, we passed some trucks going full speed in the opposite direction and a series of banged-up Toyota taxicabs loaded with passengers. Lost in thought, my driver drummed on the steering wheel with his fingertips. The wind rushing in through the open windows tangled the thick lock of white hair on his forehead.

At a checkpoint, soldiers ordered us off the road and onto a freshly bulldozed track. The new trail was fairly well laid out, but bumpy, and it included some turns so tight that it wasn't possible to go faster than ten kilometers an hour. The truck bounded in and out of deep fissures, nearly snapping its suspension. Soon, however, we caught up with other vehicles that had been diverted by the soldiers at the checkpoint. A large, groaning van was parked on the edge of the trail with its hood up; its passengers—some women swathed in black and several children—had left the van to watch the driver grapple with the motor. No one stopped to lend them a hand.

"You think the highway's too messed up to drive on?" I asked.

"We wouldn't have a pleasant trip," the truck driver replied. "First, they'd go over us and the truck with a fine-tooth comb, and then they'd let us bake in the sun and maybe even spend the night in the open. Obviously, there's a military convoy on the way. To foil suicide bombers in cars and trucks, the soldiers divert every vehicle onto the desert trails, ambulances included."

"So we're going to make a big detour?"

"Not so big. We'll get to Basseel before nightfall."

"I'm hoping to find a taxi to take me to Baghdad."

"A cab, at night? There's a curfew, strictly enforced. As soon as the sun goes down, all Iraq must go to ground. I hope you've got your ID papers at least."

"I do."

He passed his arm over his mouth and said, "You'd better."

We turned onto an old trail, wider and flatter than the one we'd been on, and accelerated, making up for lost time. Raising clouds of dust, the other vehicles were soon far ahead of us.

The driver gestured with his chin toward a military installation on a nearby hilltop. "I supplied this outfit with provisions," he said. "Before."

The barracks were open to the four winds, the ramparts collapsed. Looters had carried off the doors and windows from every building, including the huts. The main compound, which must have housed the unit's headquarters and administration building, looked as though it had gone through a seismic episode. A jumble of blackened beams was all that was left of the roofs. The shattered facades bore the marks of missile strikes. An avalanche of papers had escaped from the offices and was piled up against the wire fence behind the sheds. The carcasses of various bombed-out military vehicles were sprawled in the parking area, and a water tower mounted on metal scaffolding, apparently blown off its base, lay on top of the charred watchtower it had crushed. On the front wall of one of the modern barracks, automatic-weapons fire had blasted away fragments of a portrait of Saddam Hussein, chubby-cheeked and smiling a carnivore's smile.

"It seems our guys didn't fire so much as a shot," the driver said. "They ran like rabbits before the American troops arrived. The shame!"

I gazed at the desolation on the hilltop. Sand was insidiously invading everything. A scrawny brown dog came out of the sentry box in front of the main entrance to the barracks. The dog stretched, sniffing the ground on the way to a pile of rocks, and disappeared behind them.

❉   ●   ❉

Basseel was a small town wedged between two enormous rocks, polished by time and sandstorms. The town lay curled up in a basin, which in the summer heat recalled a Turkish bath. Its hovels of clay and straw clung desperately to several hillsides, the hills separated from one another by a labyrinth of winding alleyways barely wide enough for a cart. The main thoroughfare, an avenue cut into a riverbed—the river having disappeared long ago—traversed the town like the wind. The black flags on the roofs indicated that this was a Shiite community; the residents wished to distance themselves from the doings of the Sunnis and to line up on the side of those who were burning incense to the new regime.

Ever since the checkpoints started to proliferate on the national highway, slowing traffic and transforming quick trips into interminable expeditions, Basseel had become an obligatory overnight stopping place for frequent travelers. Bars and cheap eating places, their locations marked by strings of paper lanterns visible for kilometers at night, had grown up like mushrooms on the outskirts, while the town itself lay plunged in darkness below. Not a single streetlight illuminated the alleys.

About fifty vehicles, most of them tanker trucks, were lined up shoulder-to-shoulder on a makeshift parking lot at the entrance to the town. One family was bivouacked a little apart, near their truck. Kids wrapped up in sheets were sleeping here and there. Off to one side, some truck drivers had built a fire and were sitting around a teapot, chatting; their swaying shadows merged in a kind of reptilian dance.

My benefactor managed to slip in among the haphazardly parked vehicles and stopped his truck near a little inn that looked like a bandits' hideout. In front of it, there was a small courtyard with tables and chairs, all of them already occupied by a pack of dull-eyed travelers. Above the hubbub, a cassette player was spitting out an old song about the Nile.

The driver invited me to accompany him to a small restaurant located nearby but practically hidden by an arrangement of tarpaulins and worm-eaten palms. The room was filled with hairy, dusty people crowded around bare tables. Some were even sitting on the floor, apparently too hungry to wait for an available chair. This entire fraternity of shipwreck survivors sat hunched over their plates, their fingers dripping with sauce and their jawbones working away: peasants and truck drivers, worn out from a grueling day of checkpoints and dirt roads, trying to regain their strength in order to face whatever trials the morrow might bring. They all reminded me of my father, because they all carried on their faces the unmistakable mark of the defeated.

My benefactor left me standing in the doorway of the restaurant, stepped over a few diners, and approached the counter, where a fat fellow in a djellaba took orders, made change, and berated his workers, all at the same time. I looked over the room, hoping to see some acquaintance. I didn't recognize anyone.

My driver came back, looking crestfallen. "Well," he said, "I'm going to have to leave you now. My customer won't be here until tomorrow evening. You're going to have to manage without me."

✤  •  ✤

I was asleep under a tree when the roar of engines woke me up. The sky wasn't yet light, but already the truckers were nervously maneuvering their vehicles, eager to leave the parking area. The first convoy headed for the steep road that skirted the town. I ran from one vehicle to another, searching for a charitable driver. No one would take me.

As the parking area gradually emptied, a feeling of frustration and rage overcame me. When only three vehicles remained, my despair verged on panic. One of them was a family truck whose engine refused to start, and the other two were old crates with nobody in them. Their occupants were probably having breakfast in one of the neighboring joints. I awaited their return with a hollow stomach.

A man standing in the doorway of a little café called to me. "Hey! What're you doing over there? Get away from my wheels right now, or I'll tear your balls off."

He gestured as though trying to shoo me away. He took

me for a thief. I walked over to him with my bag slung across my back. As I drew nearer, he put his fists on his hips and gazed at me with disgust. He said, "Can't a man drink his coffee in peace?"

A beanpole with a copper-colored face, he was wearing clean cotton trousers and a checked jacket over a sweater of bottle-green wool. A large watch was mounted on the gold bracelet that encircled his wrist. He had a face like a cop's, with a brutish grin and a way of looking at you from on high.

"I'm going to Baghdad," I told him.

"I couldn't care less. Just stay away from my wheels, okay?"

He turned his back on me and sat at a table near the door.

I went back to the stony road that skirted the town and sat down under a tree.

The first car that passed me was so loaded down that I didn't have the nerve to follow it with my eyes as it bounced off in a northerly direction.

The truck that wouldn't start a little while ago almost brushed me as it went down the trail, clattering metallically. The sun came up, heavy and menacing, from behind a hill. Down below, closer to town, people were emerging from their burrows.

A car appeared, some way off. I got up and stretched out my arm, prominently displaying my thumb. The car passed me and kept going for a few hundred meters; then, just as I was preparing to sit back down, it rolled to a stop. I couldn't figure out whether the driver was stopping for me or having a mechanical problem. He honked his horn and then stuck his hand out the window, motioning to me. I picked up my bag and started running.

The driver was the man from the café, the one who had taken me for a thief.

As I approached the car, he said without prologue, "For fifty dinars, I'll take you to Al Hillah."

"It's a deal," I said, glad to get out of Basseel.

"I'd like to know what you've got in your bag."

"Just clothes, sir," I said, emptying the bag onto his hood.

The man watched me, his face masked in a stiff grin. I lifted my shirt to show him I wasn't hiding anything under my belt. He nodded and invited me to get in with a movement of his chin. "Where are you coming from?" he asked.

"From Kafr Karam."

"Never heard of it. Pass me my cigarettes, will you? They're in the glove compartment."

He flicked his lighter and exhaled the smoke through his nostrils. After looking me over again, he pulled away.

We drove along for half an hour, during which he was lost in thought. Then he remembered me. "Why are you so quiet?" he asked.

"It's in my nature."

He lit another cigarette and tried again. "These days, the ones who talk the least are the ones who do the most. Are you going to Baghdad to join the resistance?"

"I'm going to visit my sister. Why do you ask me that?"

He pivoted the rearview mirror in my direction. "Take a look at yourself, my boy. You look like a bomb that's about to go off."

I looked in the mirror and saw two burning eyes in a tormented face. "I'm going to see my sister," I said.

He mechanically returned the rearview mirror to the proper angle and shrugged his shoulders. Then he proceeded to ignore me.

After an hour of dust and potholes, we reached the national highway. My vertebrae had taken quite a pounding, and I was relieved to be on a paved road. Buses and semitrailers were chasing one another at top speed. Three police cars passed us; their occupants seemed relaxed. We went through an overpopulated village whose sidewalks were jammed with shops, stalls, and people. A uniformed policeman was maintaining order, his helmet pushed back on his head, his shirt soaked with sweat in the back and under the arms. When we got to the center of the village, our progress was slowed by a large gathering, a crowd besieging a traveling souk. Housewives dressed in black scavenged among the stalls; bold though they were, their baskets were often empty. The odor of rotten vegetables, together with the blazing heat and the swarms of flies buzzing around the piles of produce, made me dizzy. We witnessed a serious crush around a bus halted at a bus stop on the far side of the square; although the conductor was frantically dealing out blows with a belt, he was unable to hold back the surge of would-be passengers.

"Just look at those animals," my driver said, sighing. I didn't share his attitude, but I made no comment.

About fifty kilometers farther on, the highway widened from two lanes to three, and after that, the traffic rapidly grew thicker. For long stretches, we crept along bumper-to-bumper because of the checkpoints. By noon, we weren't yet halfway to our destination. From time to time, we came upon the charred remains of a trailer, pushed to the shoulder of the highway to keep it clear, or passed immense black stains, all marking places where a vehicle had been surprised by an explosion or a barrage of small-arms fire. Shards of broken glass, burst tires, and metal fragments lined the highway on both sides. Around a curve, we passed what was left of an American Humvee, lying on its side in a ditch, probably blown there by a rocket. The spot was made for ambushes.

The driver suggested that we stop and get something to eat. He chose a service station. After filling his tank, he invited me to join him at a sort of kiosk that had been turned into a refreshment stand. An attendant served us two passably cold sodas and some skewers of dubious meat in a gut-wrenching sandwich dripping with thick tomato sauce. When I tried to pay my share, the driver refused with a wave of his hand. We relaxed for about twenty minutes before getting back on the road.

The driver had put on sunglasses, and he was steering his car as though he were alone in the world. I had settled into my seat and soon let myself drift away, lulled by the rumble of the engine. . . .

When I woke up, traffic was at a standstill. There seemed to be a terrible mess up ahead, and the sun was white-hot. People had left their vehicles and were standing on the roadway, grumbling loudly.

"What's going on?"

"What's going on is, we're screwed."

A low-flying helicopter passed overhead and then suddenly veered away, making a terrifying racket. It flew to a distant hill, turned, and hovered. All at once, it fired a pair of rockets; they whistled shrilly as they sped through the air. We saw two masses of flames and dust rise over a ridge. A sudden shiver ran along the highway, and people hurried back to their vehicles. Some nervous drivers made U-turns and sped away, thus provoking a chain reaction that reduced the traffic jam by half in less than ten minutes.

His eyes glinting with amusement at the panic that seized our fellow travelers, my driver took advantage of their defection and rolled forward several hundred meters. "Not to worry," he reassured me. "That copter's just flushing out game. The pilot's putting on a show. If it was serious, there'd be at least two Cobras up there covering each other. After eight months as a 'sand nigger' for the Americans, I know all their tricks."

All of a sudden, the driver seemed engaged. "I was an interpreter with the American troops," he went on. "'Sand niggers'—that's the name they give their Iraqi collaborators. . . . In any case, there's no way I'm turning around. Al Hillah's only a hundred kilometers away, and I don't feel like spending another night out in the open. If you're afraid, you can get out."

"I'm not afraid."

Traffic returned to normal about an hour later. When we reached the checkpoint, we started to understand a little about what had produced the terrible mess. Two bullet-riddled bodies lay on an embankment, each of them clothed in bloodstained white sweatpants and a filthy shirt. They were the two men I'd seen near Kafr Karam the previous day, crouching on a mound with a big bag at their feet.

"Another little blunder," my driver grumbled. "The

American *boys*"—he said the word *boys* in English—"they shoot first and verify later. That was one of the reasons why I quit them."

My eyes were riveted on the rearview mirror; I couldn't stop looking at the two corpses.

"Eight months, man," the driver continued. "Eight months putting up with their arrogance and their idiotic sarcasm. Real American GIs have nothing to do with the Hollywood marketing version. That's just loud dema-goguery. The truth is, they don't have any more scruples than a pack of hyenas let loose in a sheep barn. I've seen them fire on children and old people as though they were cardboard training targets."

"I've seen that, too."

"I don't think so, kid. If you haven't lost your mind yet, that's because you haven't seen very much. Me, I've gone off the deep end. I have nightmares every night. I was an inter-preter with a regular army battalion—angels compared to the Marines—but it was still pretty hard to take. Plus, they got their kicks making fun of me and treating me like shit. As far as they were concerned, I was just a traitor to my country. It took me eight months to realize that. Then, one evening, I went to the captain and told him I was going home. He asked me if something was wrong. 'Everything,' I said. In fact, the main thing was that I didn't want to have anything more to do with those bleating, dim-witted cow-boys. Even if I'm on the losing side, I'm worth more than that."

Some policemen and soldiers made vigorous gestures in our direction, urging us to get a move on. They weren't checking anyone; they were too busy trying to free up the congestion on the highway. My driver stepped on the gas. "They think all Arabs are retarded," he muttered. "Imagine: Arabs, the most fabulous creatures on earth. We taught the world table manners; we taught the world hygiene and cooking and mathematics and medicine. And what do these degenerates of modernity remember of all that? A camel caravan crossing the dunes at sunset? Some fat guy in a white robe and a keffiyeh flashing his millions in a gambling casino on the Côte d'Azur? Clichés, caricatures . . ."

Upset by his own words, he lit a cigarette and ignored me until we reached Al Hillah. He was plainly eager to get rid of me; he drove directly to the bus station, stopped the car, and held out his hand. "Good luck, kid," he said.

I took my packet of money—still tied with string—out of my back pocket so I could pay him. "What are you doing?" he asked.

"I owe you fifty dinars," I said.

He rejected my money with the same backhand gesture he'd made at the service station a few hours ago. "Keep your little nest egg intact, my boy," he said. "And forget what I told you. Ever since I went off the deep end, I talk nonsense. You never saw me, all right?"

"All right."

"Good. Now fuck off."

He helped me get my bag, made a U-turn, and left the bus station without so much as a wave.

# 9

§ • §

The bus, a backfiring old relic stinking of burned oil and overheated rubber, seemed to be on its last legs. It didn't roll so much as crawl along, like a wounded animal on the point of giving up the ghost. Every time it slowed down, I felt a tightness in my chest. The sun was blazing hot, our progress had been interrupted three times (two blowouts and one breakdown), and the spare tires, as smooth and worn as the two flats, didn't look very encouraging.

When the driver, who was clearly exhausted, stowed his jack the second time, he reeled a little. One of his hands was bandaged—the result of a recalcitrant tire—and he seemed generally to be in a bad way. I didn't take my eyes off him; I was afraid he might pass out on the steering wheel. From time to time, he put a bottle of water to his lips and drank at length, without paying any attention to the road; then he went back to wiping his face on a towel he kept hanging from a hook on the back of his seat. Although probably around fifty, he looked ten years older, with sunken eyes and an egg-shaped skull, hairy at the temples and bald on the crown. He insulted his fellow motorists continually.

Silence reigned inside the bus. The air-conditioning didn't work, and the heat inside was deadly, even though all the windows were open. Sunk in their seats, the passengers were mostly dozing, except for a few who gazed absently at the fleeting landscape. Three rows behind me, a young man with a furrowed brow insisted on fiddling with his pocket radio, spinning the dial from one station to another and filling the air with static. Whenever he found a song, he'd listen to it for a minute and then start looking for another station. He was seriously getting on my nerves, and I couldn't wait to get out of that coffin on wheels.

We'd been rolling along for three hours without interruption. Fixing the two blowouts and patching the burst radiator hose had put the driver well behind schedule, and we'd had to cancel the planned stop for a snack at a roadside inn.

The previous day, after my benefactor dropped me off at the station, I'd missed the Baghdad bus by a few minutes and had to wait for the next one, which was supposed to leave four hours later. It arrived on time, but there were only about twenty passengers. The driver explained that his bus wouldn't leave without at least forty passengers on board; otherwise, he couldn't cover his expenses for the trip. So we all waited, praying for other passengers to show up. The driver circled the bus, shouting "Baghdad! Baghdad!" Sometimes, he approached people loaded down with baggage and asked them if they were going to Baghdad. When they shook their heads, he moved on to the next group of travelers. Very late in the afternoon, the driver came back to the bus and asked us to get off and retrieve our luggage from the baggage hatch. There were a few protests, and then everyone gathered on the sidewalk and watched the bus return to the depot. Those who were local residents went home; the rest of us spent the night in the bus station. And what a night! Some thieves tried to rob a sleeping man, but their victim turned out to be armed with a cudgel, and they couldn't get near him. They retreated for a while but then returned with reinforcements, and since the police were nowhere to be seen, the rest of us witnessed a disgraceful thrashing. We remained apart from the scene, barricaded behind our suitcases and our bags, none of us daring to go to the victim's aid. The poor fellow defended himself valiantly. For a while, he gave as good as he got, blow for blow. In the end, however, the thieves knocked him to the ground and assailed him with a vengeance. Then they relieved him of his belongings and left, taking him with them. By then it was about three o'clock in the morning, and nobody slept a wink after that.

Another military roadblock. A long line of vehicles advanced slowly, gradually squeezing closer to the right side of the road. There were road signs in the middle of the highway, along with large rocks marking the boundaries of the two lanes. The soldiers were Iraqis. They were checking everyone who went through, inspecting automobile trunks and bus hatches and baggage; men whose looks the soldiers didn't like were gone over with a fine-tooth comb. They came into our bus, asked for our papers, and compared certain faces to the photographs of the people they were looking for.

"You two, off the bus," a corporal ordered. Two young

men stood up and walked down the aisle with an air of resignation. Outside, a soldier searched them and then told them to get their things and follow him to a tent pitched on the sand about twenty meters away.

"All right," the corporal said to our driver. "You can shove off."

The bus coughed and sputtered. We watched our two fellow passengers, who were standing before the tent. They didn't look worried. The corporal hustled them inside, and they disappeared from our sight.

Finally, the buildings on the outskirts of Baghdad appeared, wrapped in an ocher veil. A sandstorm had blown through, and the air was laden with dust. It's better this way, I thought. I wasn't eager to see what the city had become—disfigured, filthy, at the mercy of its demons. In the past, I'd really loved Baghdad. The past? It seemed like a former life. Baghdad was a beautiful city then, with its great thoroughfares and its posh boulevards, bright with gleaming shop windows and sunny terraces. For a peasant like me, it was truly the Elysian fields, at least the way I imagined them from deep in the boondocks of Kafr Karam. I was fascinated by the neon signs and the store decorations, and I passed a good part of my nights ambling along the avenues in the refreshing evening breeze. Watching so many people strolling down the street, so many gorgeous girls swaying their hips as they walked on the esplanades, I had the feeling that all the journeys my condition prevented me from taking were there within my reach. I had no money, but I had eyes to gaze until I got dizzy and a nose to inhale the heady scents of the most fabulous city in the Middle East, set astride the beneficent Tigris, which carried along in its meanders the enchantment of Baghdad's legends and love songs. It's true that the shadow of the Rais dimmed the lights of the city, but that shadow didn't reach me. I was a young, dazzled student with marvelous prospects in my head. Every beauty that Baghdad suggested to me became mine; how could I surrender to the charms of the city of houris and not identify with it a little? And even then, Kadem told me, I should have seen it before the embargo. . . .

Baghdad might have survived the United Nations embargo just to flout the West and its influence peddling, but the city assuredly wouldn't survive the affronts its own misbegotten children were inflicting on it.

And there I was, come to Baghdad in my turn to spread my venom there. I didn't know how to go about it, but I was certain I'd strike some nasty blow. It was the way things had always been with us. For Bedouin, no matter how impoverished they may be, honor is no joking matter. An offense must be washed away in blood, which is the sole authorized detergent when it's a question of keeping one's self-respect. I was the only boy in my family. Since my father was an invalid, the supreme task of avenging the outrage he'd suffered fell to me, even at the cost of my life. Dignity can't be negotiated. Should we lose it, all the shrouds in the world won't suffice to veil our faces, and no tomb will receive our carcasses without cracking.

Prodded on by some evil spell, I, too, was going to rage: I was going to defile the walls I'd caressed, spit on the shop windows I'd groomed myself in, and unload my quota of corpses into the sacred Tigris, the anthropophagous river, once greedy for the splendid virgins who were sacrificed to the gods, and today full of undesirables whose decomposing remains polluted its virtuous waters. . . .

The bus crossed a bridge and traveled alongside the river. I didn't want to look at the public squares, which I imagined devastated, or at the sidewalks, teeming with people I already no longer loved. How could I love anything after what I'd seen in Kafr Karam? How could I appreciate perfect strangers after I'd fallen in my own self-esteem? Was I still myself? If so, who was I? I wasn't really interested in knowing that. It had no sort of importance for me anymore. Some moorings had broken, some taboos had fallen, and a world of spells and anathemas was springing up from their ruins. What was terrifying about this whole affair was the ease with which I passed from one universe to another without feeling out of place. Such a smooth transition! I had gone to bed a docile, courteous boy, and I'd awakened with an inextinguishable rage lodged in my very flesh. I carried my hatred like a second nature; it was my armor and my shirt of Nessus, my pedestal and my stake; it was all that remained to me in this false, unjust, arid, and cruel life.

I wasn't returning to Baghdad to relive happy memories, but to banish them forever. The blooming innocence of first love was over; the city and I no longer had anything to say to each other. And yet we were very much alike; we'd lost our souls, and we were ready to destroy others.

The bus stopped at the station square, which had been occupied by a horde of ragged urchins with crafty faces and wandering hands: feral, garbage-eating street kids whom the bankrupt orphanages and reform schools had dumped onto the city. They were a recent phenomenon, one whose existence I hadn't even suspected. The first passengers had hardly stepped out of the bus when someone cried out, "Stop, thief!" A group of kids had gathered around the hatches and helped themselves amid the crowd. Before anyone realized what had happened, the band was already across the street and moving fast, their booty on their shoulders.

I pinned my bag tightly under my arm and got away from there in a hurry.

The Thawba clinic was several blocks from the bus station. I decided to walk there, as I was stiff from sitting so long. There were a few cars scattered across the clinic's parking lot, a little square surrounded by bashed-up palm trees. Times had changed, and so had the clinic; it was merely the shadow of its former self, with scary-looking windows and a tarnished facade.

I walked up the outside staircase and came to a security officer, who was cleaning his teeth with a match. "I'm here to see Dr. Farah," I said.

"Let me see your appointment slip."

"I'm her brother."

He asked me to wait on the landing, entered a small, windowed office, and spoke to the clerk, who shot a suspicious look in my direction before picking up the telephone. After two minutes or so, I saw him nod his head and make a sign to the officer, who came back and escorted me to a waiting room furnished with exhausted sofas.

Farah came in about ten minutes later, radiant in her long white apron, her stethoscope dangling on her chest. She was carefully made up, but she'd put on a little too much lipstick. She welcomed me without enthusiasm, as if we saw each other every day. Her work, which allowed her no rest, had probably worn her out, and she'd obviously lost weight. Her kisses were fleeting and accompanied by a lifeless embrace.

"When did you get here?" she asked.

"Here in Baghdad? Just a few minutes ago."

"Bahia phoned me to announce your visit the day before yesterday."

"We lost a lot of time on the road. With all those military roadblocks and the obligatory detours—"

"Did you have to come?" she asked, a hint of reproach in her voice.

I didn't understand right away, but her unwavering stare helped me to see the light. She wasn't acting like that because she was exhausted or because of her work; my sister was simply not overjoyed to see me.

"Have you had lunch?"

"No."

"I've got three patients to attend to. I'm going to take you to a room. Then, first thing, you're going to have a nice shower, because you smell really strong. After that, a nurse will bring you something to eat. If I'm not back by the time you're finished, just lie down on the bed and rest until I come."

I picked up my bag and followed her along a corridor and then upstairs to the next floor. She let me into a room furnished with a bed and a night table. There was a little television set on a wall bracket and, behind a plastic curtain, a shower.

"Soap, shampoo, and towels are in the closet," Farah said. "The water's rationed—don't use more than you need." She looked at her watch. "I have to hurry."

And she left the room.

I stood where I was for a good while, staring at the spot where my sister had vanished and wondering if, somehow, I had made a bad choice. Of course, Farah had always been distant. She was a rebel and a fighter, the only girl from Kafr Karam who'd ever dared to violate the rules of the tribe and do exactly what she wanted to do. Her audacity and insolence obviously conditioned her temperament, making her more aggressive and less conciliatory, but the welcome I'd received disturbed me. Our last meeting had been more than a year ago, when she visited the family in Kafr Karam. Even though she didn't stay as long as she'd said she would, there wasn't a moment when she seemed disdainful of us. True, she rarely laughed, but nothing had suggested she'd receive her own brother with such indifference.

I took off my clothes, stood under the shower, and soaped myself from head to foot. When I stepped out, I felt as though I had a new skin. I put on some clean clothes and stretched out on the sponge mattress, which was covered with an oilcloth spread. A nurse brought me a tray of food. I devoured it like an animal and fell asleep immediately afterward.

When Farah returned, the sun was going down. She seemed more relaxed. She half-sat on the edge of the bed and put her white hands around one of her knees. "I came by earlier," she said, "but you were sleeping so soundly, I didn't want to wake you up."

"I hadn't slept a wink for two days and two nights."

Farah released her knee and scratched her temple. A look of annoyance crossed her face. "You've picked a bad time to turn up here," she said. "Right now, Baghdad's the most dangerous place on earth."

Her gaze, so steady a while ago, started eluding mine.

I asked her, "Does it bother you that I'm here?"

She stood up and went to switch on the ceiling light. This was a ridiculous thing to do, as the room was brightly illuminated already. Suddenly, she turned around and said, "Why have you come to Baghdad?"

Once again, there was that hint of reproach.

We'd never been very close. Farah was much older than I was, and she'd left home early, so our relations had remained rather vague. Even when I was attending the university, we saw each other only occasionally. Now that she was standing in front of me, I realized that she was a stranger, and—worse—that I didn't love her.

"There's nothing but trouble in Baghdad," she said. She passed her tongue over her lips and continued. "We're overwhelmed here at the clinic. Every day, we get a new flood of sick people, wounded people, mutilated people. Half of my colleagues have thrown up their arms in despair. Since we've stopped being paid, there are only about twenty of us left, trying to salvage what we can."

She took an envelope from her pocket and held it out to me.

"What's that?"

"A little money. Get a hotel room for a few days. I need some time to figure out where to put you up."

I couldn't believe it.

I pushed the envelope away. "Are you telling me you don't have your apartment anymore?"

"I've still got it, but you can't stay there."

"Why not?"

"I can't have you."

"How do you mean? I'm not following you. At home, if someone needs a place to stay, we work something—"

"I'm not in Kafr Karam," she said. "I'm in Baghdad."

"I'm your brother. You don't shut your door in your brother's face."

"I'm sorry."

I looked her up and down. She wouldn't meet my eyes. I didn't recognize her anymore. She was nothing like the image of her I had in my head. Her features meant nothing to me; she was someone else.

"You're ashamed of me—that's it, isn't it? You've renounced your origins. You're a city girl now, all modern and all, and me, I'm still the hick who spoils the decor, right? Madame is a physician. She lives by herself in a chic apartment where she no longer receives her relatives, for fear of becoming the laughingstock of her neighbors on the other side of the landing—"

"I can't let you stay with me because I live with someone," she said, interrupting me curtly.

An avalanche of ice landed on me.

"You live with someone? How can that be? You got married without letting the family know?"

"I'm not married."

I bounded to my feet. "You live with a man? You live in sin?"

She gave me a dry look. "What's sin, little brother?"

"You don't have the right. It's . . . it's forbidden by,

by . . . Look, have you gone mad? You have a family. Do you ever think about your family? About its honor? About yours? You are—you can't live in sin, not you. . . ."

"I don't live in sin; I live my life."

"You don't believe in God anymore?"

"I believe in what I do, and that's enough for me."

# 1 O

✳   •   ✳

I wandered around the city until I could no longer put one
foot in front of the other. I didn't want to think about anything or see anything or understand anything. People
swirled around me; I ignored them. I don't know how many
times I stepped off a sidewalk, only to be blown back by a
blaring horn. I'd emerge from my personal darkness for a
second and then plunge into it again as though nothing had
happened. I felt at ease in my black thoughts, safe from my
torments, out of reach of troublesome questions, alone inside my rage, which was digging channels in my veins and
merging with the fibers of my being. Farah was ancient history. As soon as I left her, I'd banished her from my
thoughts. She was nothing but a succubus, a whore, and she
had no more place in my life. In our ancestral tradition,
when a relative went astray, that person was systematically
banished from the community. When the sinner was a
woman, she was rejected all the more swiftly.

Night caught up with me on a bench in a hapless square
next to a car wash. Suspicious characters of every stripe

were loitering about, spurned by angels and devils alike, beached on that square like whales cast out of the ocean. There was a bunch of dead-drunk bums shrouded in rags, urchins stoned on shoemaker's glue, destitute women sitting under trees and begging with their infants on their laps. This part of town hadn't been like this when I was in Baghdad before the invasion. The neighborhood wasn't fashionable then, but it was tranquil and tidy, with well-lit shops and innocuous pedestrians. Now, it was infested with famished orphans, tatterdemalion young werewolves covered with sores, who would stop at nothing.

With my bag pressed against my chest, I observed a pack of cubs prowling around my bench.

A snot-nosed brat sat down beside me. "What do you want?" I asked him. He was a kid of about ten, with a slashed face and streaming nostrils. His tangled hair hung down over his brow like the nest of snakes on Medusa's head. He had disturbing eyes and a treacherous smile playing about his mouth. His long shirt reached his calves, his trousers were torn, and he was barefoot. His damaged toes, black with dirt, smelled like a dead animal.

"I've got a right to sit here, don't I?" he yapped, meeting my eye. "It's a public bench; it's not your property."

A knife handle protruded from his pocket.

A few meters away, three little rascals were feigning interest in a patch of grass. In reality, they were observing us on the sly, waiting for a sign from their comrade.

I got up and walked away. The kid on the bench hissed an obscenity in my direction and lifted his shirt to show me his crotch. His three pals sneered and stared at me. The eldest of them wasn't yet thirteen, but they stank of death like carrion.

I walked faster.

A few blocks farther on, shadows rose up out of the darkness and charged at me. Taken by surprise, I flattened myself against a wall. Hands clutched my bag and tried to tear it away from me. I kicked out, struck someone's leg, and retreated into a doorway. The would-be muggers came at me with increased ferocity. I felt the straps of my bag giving way and started dealing blows blindly. At the end of a desperate struggle, my assailants released their grip and ran away. When they passed under a streetlight, I recognized the four wolf cubs of a little while ago.

I crouched down on the sidewalk, clutching my head, and took several deep breaths to get my wind back. "What country is this?" I heard myself pant.

When I stood up, I had the impression that my bag was lighter. And in fact, one side of it had been cut open, and half of my things were gone. I put my hand on my back pocket and was relieved to find that my money was still there. That was when I started running toward the city center, jumping aside every time a shadow passed me.

⁕   •   ⁕

I ate at a place that served grilled meats. I sat at a table in the corner, far from the door and the windows, with one eye on my brochettes and the other on the steady stream of customers entering and leaving. I recognized no one, and I grew irritated every time somebody's eyes settled on me. I was uncomfortable in the midst of all those hairy creatures, who filled me with suspicion and dread. They didn't have very much in common with the people of my village, except perhaps for their human form, which did nothing to temper their brutish aspect. Everything about them filled me with cold animosity. I had the feeling I'd ventured into enemy territory—or, worse, into a minefield, and I expected to be blown to pieces at any moment.

"Relax," the waiter said, putting a plate of fries in front of me. "I've been holding out this plate to you for a good minute, and you just stare right through me. What's wrong? Have you escaped a raid? Or maybe survived an attack?"

He winked at me and went to take care of another customer.

After eating my brochettes and my fries, I ordered more, and then more after that. I'd never been so hungry, and the more I ate, the more my hunger increased. I consumed two baskets of bread and a good twenty brochettes, to say nothing of the fries, and washed everything down with a one-liter bottle of soda and a pitcher of water. My sudden appetite scared me.

To put an end to this gorging, I asked for the check. While the cashier was giving me my change, I asked, "Is there a hotel near here?"

He raised an eyebrow and looked at me askance. "There's a mosque at the other end of the street, behind the square. It'll be on your left as you step out. They provide accommodations for transients at night. At least you'll be able to rest easy there."

"I want to go to a hotel."

"You're obviously not from here. All the hotels are under surveillance. And the police give the managers so much shit that most of them have closed their places down. Go to the mosque. The police don't show up there very often, and besides, it's free."

"If I were you, that's what I'd do," the waiter said as he slipped past.

I picked up my bag and went out into the street.

⁜   •   ⁜

Actually, the mosque was on the ground floor of a two-story warehouse wedged between a large disused store and another building. A large room in the warehouse had been transformed into a prayer hall. The neighborhood had a cutthroat look I disliked right away. The meager light from a streetlamp picked out the boarded-up fronts of two grocer's shops, one across from the other. It was eleven o'clock at night, and except for the cats rummaging around in the piles of garbage on the sidewalks, there wasn't a living soul in sight.

The prayer hall had been evacuated and the homeless people lodged in another room large enough to accommodate about fifty persons. The floor was covered with old blankets. A chandelier cast its beams upon various shapeless masses curled up here and there. There were about twenty wretches on the floor, all of them sleeping in their clothes, some with their mouths open, others in a fetal position; the place smelled like rags and feet.

I decided to lie down in a corner alongside an old man.

Using my bag as a pillow, I fixed my eyes on the ceiling and waited.

The chandelier went out. Snores came from all sides, intensified, and then became intermittent. I listened to the blood beating in my temples and heard my breathing accelerate; waves of nausea rose from my stomach, ending in stifled belches. Once only, the image of my father falling over backward flashed through my head; I immediately drove it out of my mind. I was too badly off to burden myself with disturbing memories.

I dreamed that a pack of dogs were chasing me through a dark wood where the branches had claws and the air was loud with screams. I was naked, my arms and legs were bloody, and my hair was streaming with bird droppings. Suddenly, the undergrowth parted, revealing a precipice. I was about to step into the void, when the muezzin's call woke me up.

Most of last night's sleepers, including the old man beside me, had left the room. Only four miserable wretches remained in tattered heaps on the floor. As for my bag, it wasn't there anymore. I put my hand on my back pocket; my money had disappeared.

＊　　●　　＊

Sitting on the sidewalk with my chin in my hands, I watched uniformed policemen checking cars. They asked for the passengers' papers as well as the drivers' and inspected all of them carefully; sometimes they made everyone get out of the car and then began a systematic search, sifting through the contents of the trunk and looking under the hood and the chassis. The previous evening, in this same spot, the interception of an ambulance had turned dramatic. The physician on board the ambulance had tried to explain that the case was an emergency, but the policemen didn't want to hear about that. Eventually, the doctor became upset, and a police corporal punched him in the face. Things degenerated from there. Threats were answered by insults, blows were struck by both sides, and finally the corporal pulled out his pistol and shot the doctor in the leg.

This part of town had a bad reputation. Two days before the ambulance incident, someone had been murdered in the exact spot where the police roadblock now stood. The victim, a man in his fifties, had come out of the shop across the way with a shopping bag in his arms. As he was getting ready to climb into his car, a motorbike pulled up beside him. Three shots, and the fellow collapsed on the pavement, his head resting on his purchases.

A few days before that, in the same place, a young deputy in the Iraqi parliament had likewise been cut down. He'd been driving his car when a motorbike caught up with him. There was a volley of shots, and the windshield suddenly seemed to be covered with spiderwebs. The vehicle skidded onto the sidewalk and flattened a female pedestrian before crashing into a lamppost. The hooded killer hurried over to the car, opened the door, pulled out the young deputy, laid him on the ground, and riddled him with bullets at point-blank range. Then, without haste, the gunman got back on his motorbike and roared away.

The police had no doubt taken over the neighborhood with the intention of stopping the killing. But the city was a sieve; it leaked everywhere. Murderous attacks were the order of the day. When the authorities plugged one hole, they freed up others that were more dangerous. Baghdad was no longer an urban center; the lovely city I remembered had become a battlefield, a firing range, a gigantic butcher's shop. Several weeks before the Allied bombardments began, people had still believed a miracle was possible. All over the world, in Rome and in Tokyo, in Madrid and in Paris, in Cairo and in Berlin, there were mass demonstrations and marches—millions of strangers converging on their city centers to say no to war. Who listened to them?

For two weeks, I wandered around in rubble, without a penny and without a goal. I slept anywhere and ate anything and flinched at every explosion. It was like being at the front, with the endless rolls of barbed wire marking off high-security areas, the makeshift barricades, the antitank obstacles against which suicide bombers occasionally detonated their cars, the watchtowers rising above the facades of buildings, the caltrop barriers lying across roadways, and the sleepwalking people who had no idea where to turn but nevertheless, whenever an attack was carried out, rushed to the scene of the tragedy like flies to a drop of blood.

Baghdad was decomposing. After spending a long, tortured time docked in repression, the city had broken from its moorings and gone adrift, fascinated by its own suicidal rage and the intoxications of impunity. Once the tyrant had fallen, Baghdad found much that was still intact: its forced silences, its vengeful cowardice, its large-scale misery. Now that all proscriptions were removed, the city drained the cup of resentment, the source of its wounds, to the dregs. Exhilarated by its suffering and the revulsion it aroused,

Baghdad was trying to become the incarnation of all that it couldn't bear and rejecting its former public image. And from the grossest despair, it drew the ingredients of its own agony.

Baghdad was a city that preferred exploding belts and banners cut from shrouds.

I was exhausted, demoralized, appalled, and nauseated, all at once. Every day, my contempt and my rage rose another notch. One morning, I looked in a shop window and didn't recognize myself. My hair was bushy, my face wrinkled, my eyes white-hot and hideous, my lips chapped; my clothes left a lot to be desired; I had become a bum.

Now I was sitting on the sidewalk across from the checkpoint. I don't know how many hours I'd spent in that position when a voice barked, "You can't stay there."

The speaker was a cop. It was a few moments before I realized he was addressing me. With a scornful wave, he signaled to me to clear off. "Let's go, let's go, move on." I got to my feet, a little dazed by my nagging hunger. When I reached out a hand for support, I found only empty air. I drew myself up and staggered away.

※ • ※

I walked and walked. It was as though I were marching through a parallel world. The boulevards opened up before me like giant maws. I went reeling along amid the crowd with blurry eyes and shooting pains in my calves. Now and then, an exasperated arm pushed me away. I straightened up and continued on aimlessly.

A crowd gathered around a vehicle burning on a bridge. I passed through the throng easily.

The river lapped at its banks, deaf to the clamor of the damned. A gust of sand-laden wind stung my face. I didn't know what to do or where to go.

"Hey!"

I didn't turn around. I didn't have the strength to turn around; one false move, and I'd collapse. It seemed to me that the only way to stay on my feet was to walk, to look straight ahead, and, especially, to avoid all distractions.

A horn sounded—once, twice, three times. After an interval, running footsteps came up behind me, and then a hand grabbed my shoulder.

"Are you deaf, or what?"

A pudgy form straddled my path. My clouded vision prevented me from recognizing the interloper right away. He spread out his arms, inadvertently displaying his oversized belly. "It's me," he said.

It was as if an oasis had emerged out of my delirium. I don't think I've ever known such a sensation of relief or felt so happy. The smiling man before me brought me back to life, revived me, became at once my only recourse and my last chance. It was Omar the Corporal.

"You're amazed, aren't you?" he exclaimed with delight, turning in a circle in front of me. "Check this outfit. A real knockout, right?"

He smoothed the lapels of his sport jacket and fingered the crease in his trousers. "Not a drop of grease, not a wrinkle. Your cousin is impeccable. Like a brand-new penny. You remember, in Kafr Karam? I always had oil or grease stains on my clothes. Well, since I've been in Baghdad, that doesn't happen anymore."

All of a sudden, his enthusiasm subsided. He'd just realized that I wasn't well, that I was having trouble staying upright, that I was on the point of fainting.

"My God! Where have you been?"

I stared at him and said, "I'm hungry."

## I I

•

Omar took me to a cheap eating place. All the while I ate, he said not a single word. He saw that I wasn't in a position to understand anything at all. I bent over my plate, looking only at the wilted fries, which I devoured by the fistful, and the bread, which I tore apart ferociously. It seemed to me that I wasn't even taking the trouble to chew the food. The giant mouthfuls flayed my throat, my fingers were sticky, and my chin was covered with sauce. Other customers seated nearby gawked at me in horror. Omar had to frown to make them turn their eyes away.

When I'd finished stuffing myself, he took me to a shop to buy me some clothes. Then he dropped me off at the public baths. I took a shower and felt a little better.

Afterward, with a hint of embarrassment, Omar said, "I assume you have nowhere to go."

"No, I don't."

He scratched his chin.

Overly sensitive, I said, "You're under no obligation."

"It's not that, cousin. You're in good hands—it's just that they're not completely free. I share a little studio flat with an associate."

"That's all right. I'll manage."

"I'm not trying to get rid of you. I just need to think. There's no chance I'm going to abandon you. Baghdad wastes no pity on strays."

"I don't want to bother you. You've done enough for me already."

With an upraised hand, he asked me to let him give the matter some thought. We were in the street; I was standing on the sidewalk, and he was leaning against his van, his arms crossed and his chin resting on an index finger, his great belly like a barrier between us.

"That's the way it'll have to be," he said abruptly. "I'll tell my roommate to beat it until we find you something. He's a nice guy. He's got family in Baghdad."

"You're sure I'm not causing you trouble?"

He straightened up with a thrust of his hips and opened the passenger door for me. "Get in, cousin," he said. "Things are going to be tight."

As I hesitated, he grabbed me by the shoulder and shoved me into the van.

Omar lived in Salman Pak, an outlying neighborhood in the southeastern part of the city. His flat was on the second floor of a flaking apartment building that stood on a side street overrun by packs of children. The outside steps were falling into ruin, and the doors were halfway off their hinges. In the stairwell, miasmal odors lingered, and the mailboxes hung askew; there were empty spaces where some of them had been wrenched away completely. The cracked stairs mounted into an unhealthy, pitch-black darkness.

"There's no light," Omar explained. "Because of thieves. You replace a bulb, and the next minute they rip it off."

Two little girls, quite young, were playing on the landing. Their faces were revoltingly dirty.

"Their mother's a head case," Omar whispered. "She leaves them there all day long and doesn't care what they do. Sometimes, pedestrians have to bring them in from the street. And the mother doesn't like it at all when someone advises her to keep an eye on her kids. . . . The world's full of lunatics."

He opened the door and stepped aside to let me enter. The room was small and meagerly furnished. There was a double mattress on the floor, a wooden crate with a little television set on it, and a stool against the wall. A padlocked closet faced the window, which overlooked the courtyard. That was it. A jail would offer its prisoners more amenities than Omar's studio apartment offered his guests.

"Behold my realm," the Corporal exclaimed, gesturing theatrically. "In the closet, you'll find blankets, some cans of food, and some crackers. I don't have a kitchen, and when I want to shit, I have to suck in my gut to get to the toilet." He jerked a thumb in the direction of the tiny bathroom. "The water's rationed. It comes once a week, and not much at that. If you're not here or you forget, you have to wait for the next distribution. Grumbling does no good. In the first place, it's boring, and in the second, it only increases your thirst. I have two jerricans in the bathroom. For washing your face, because the water isn't drinkable."

He opened the padlock, took off the little chain, and

showed me the contents of the closet. "Make yourself at home," he said. "I've got to run if I don't want to get fired. I'll be back in three hours, four at most. I'll bring some food and we'll talk about the good old days. Maybe we can conjure them up again."

Before he left, he advised me to double-lock the door and to sleep with one eye open.

*    •    *

When Omar returned, the sun was going down. He sat on the stool and looked at me as I lay on the mattress, stretching. "You've been asleep for twenty-four hours," he announced.

"You're kidding!"

"It's true, I assure you. I tried to wake you up this morning, but you didn't budge. When I came back around noon, you were still in a deep sleep. You even slept through our local explosion."

"There was an attack?"

"We're in Baghdad, cousin. When it's not a bomb going off, it's a gas cylinder blowing up. This time, it was an accident. Some people got killed, but I didn't look at the figures. I'll bring myself up-to-date next time."

I wasn't feeling great, but I was happy to know I had a roof over my head and Omar at my side. My intensive two-week Introduction to Vagrancy course had done me in. I wouldn't have been able to hold out much longer.

"Will you tell me why you've come to Baghdad?" Omar asked, scrutinizing his fingernails.

"To avenge an offense," I said without hesitation.

He raised his eyes and gave me a sad look. "These days, people come to Baghdad to avenge an offense they've suffered elsewhere, which means they tend to mistake their targets—by a lot. What happened in Kafr Karam?"

"The Americans."

"What did they do to you?"

"I can't talk about it."

He nodded. "I understand," he said, getting off his stool. "Let's go for a little walk. Afterward, we'll have a bite in a restaurant. It's better to chat on a full stomach."

※　●　※

We walked the length and breadth of the neighborhood, talking about trifles, leaving the main subject until later. Omar was concerned. A nasty wrinkle creased his forehead. He shuffled along with his chin on his clavicle and his hands behind his back, as though a burden were wearing him down. And he wouldn't stop kicking whatever tin cans he found along the way. Night fell softly on the city and its delirium. From time to time, police cars passed us, their sirens wailing, and then the ordinary racket of a densely populated quarter returned, a din so banal as to be almost imperceptible.

We ate in a little restaurant on the square. Omar knew the owner. He had only two other customers; one of them, with his wire-rimmed glasses and his sober suit, looked like a young leading man, and the other, a dust-covered driver, never took his eye off his truck, which was parked in front of the restaurant, within reach of a pack of kids.

"How long have you been in Baghdad?" Omar asked.

"About two and a half weeks, more or less."

"Where did you sleep?"

"In squares, on the banks of the Tigris, in mosques. It depended. Generally, I lay down wherever I was when my legs gave way."

"For pity's sake! How did you wind up in such a fix? You should have seen your mug yesterday. I recognized you from a distance, but when I got closer, I had my doubts. You looked as though some fat whore had pissed on you while you were eating her out."

There he was in all his glory, the Corporal of Kafr Karam. Oddly enough, his obscenity didn't repulse me as much as usual. I said, "I came with the idea of staying with my sister, at least for a while, but it wasn't possible. I had a little money with me, enough to make it for a month at most. By then, I thought, I'll have found some kind of place. But the first night, I slept in a mosque, and in the morning, my money and my belongings were gone. After that, I'll let you guess." Then, trying to change the subject, I asked, "How did your roommate take the news?"

"He's a good guy. He knows what's what."

"I promise not to take advantage of your hospitality."

"Don't talk shit, cousin. You're not causing me any hardship. If I were in your situation, you'd do the same thing for me. We're Bedouin. We don't have anything to do with these people here. . . ."

He put his joined hands over his mouth and stared at

me with great intensity. "Now will you explain to me why you want revenge? And what exactly do you intend to do?"

"I have no idea."

He swelled his cheeks and let out an irrepressible sigh. His right hand moved over the table, picked up a spoon, and started stirring the cold soup still left in his bowl. Omar guessed what I had in mind. There were legions of peasants streaming in from the hinterlands to swell the ranks of the fedayeen. Every morning, buses discharged contingents of them at the Baghdad stations. Various motivations activated these men, but they all shared a single, blindingly obvious objective.

"I'm in no position to oppose your choice, cousin. No one owns the truth. Personally, I don't know whether I'm right or wrong, and so I can't lecture you about anything. You've suffered an offense; only you can decide what's to be done about it."

His voice was full of false notes.

"It's a question of honor, Omar," I reminded him.

"I don't want to quibble over that. But you have to know exactly what you're getting into. You see what the resistance does every day. It's killed thousands of Iraqis. In exchange for how many Americans? If the answer to that question doesn't matter to you, then that's your problem. But as for me, I disagree."

He ordered two coffees to gain time and gather his arguments; then he went on. "To tell you the truth, I came to Baghdad to do some damage. I've never been able to get over the way Yaseen insulted me in the café. He disrespected me, and ever since, when I think about it—which is to say several times a day—I start gasping for air. You'd think Yaseen made me asthmatic."

Evoking the shaming incident in Kafr Karam made Omar ill at ease. He pulled a handkerchief from his pocket and mopped his face. "One thing I'm sure of: My ass is going to have that offense stuck to it until the insult is washed away in blood," he declared. "There's no doubt about it—sooner or later, Yaseen will pay for it with his life."

The waiter placed two cups of coffee next to our plates. Omar waited to watch him withdraw before reapplying the handkerchief to his face and neck. His plump shoulders vibrated. He said, "I'm ashamed of what happened in the Safir. Staying drunk did no good, none at all. I decided I had to get lost. I was all psyched up. I wanted to turn the country into an inferno from one end to the other. Everything I put in my mouth tasted like blood; every breath I took stank of cremation. My hands were itching for a gun—I swear, I could feel the trigger move when I curled my finger. While the bus was taking me to Baghdad, I imagined myself digging trenches in the desert, making shelters and command posts. I was thinking like a military engineer—you see what I mean? And I happened to arrive in Baghdad the day a false alert caused an enormous crush on a bridge—you remember—and a thousand demonstrators got killed. When I saw that, cousin, when I saw all those bodies on the ground, when I saw those mountains of shoes at the site where the panic took place, those kids with blue faces and their eyes half-closed—when I saw that whole mess, caused to Iraqis by Iraqis, I said to myself, right away, This is not my war. It was a clean break, cousin."

He brought the coffee cup to his lips, drank a mouthful, and invited me to do the same. His face was quivering, and his nostrils made me think of a fish suffocating in the open air. "I came here to join the fedayeen," he said. "It was all I thought about. Even the Yaseen thing was deferred until later. I'd settle his account when the time came. But first, I had to come to terms with the deserter in me. I had to find the weapons I'd left on the battlefield when the enemy approached; I had to deserve the country I couldn't defend when I was supposed to be ready to die for it. . . . But, hell, you don't make war on your own people just to piss off the world."

He awaited my reaction—which did not come—and then rummaged in his hair with a discouraged look. My silence embarrassed him. He understood that I didn't share his emotions, and that I was solidly camped on my own. That's the way we are, we Bedouin. When we keep quiet, that means that everything's been said and there's nothing more to add. He saw the mess on the bridge again; I saw nothing, not even my father falling over backward. I was in the postshock, postoffense period; it was my duty to wash away the insult, my sacred duty and my absolute right. I didn't know myself what that represented or how it was constructed in my mind; I knew only that an obligation I couldn't ignore was mobilizing me. I was neither anxious nor galvanized; I was in another dimension, where the only reference point I had was the certainty that I would carry out to the fullest extent the oath my ancestors had sealed in blood and sorrow when they placed honor above their own lives.

"You listening to me, cousin?"

"Yes."

"The actions of the fedayeen are lowering us in the eyes of the world. We're Iraqis, cousin. We have eleven thousand years of history behind us. We're the ones who taught men to dream."

He drained his cup in a single swallow and wiped his lips with the back of his hand. "I'm not trying to influence you."

"You know very well that's impossible."

⁂   •   ⁂

Night had fallen. A hot wind hugged the walls. The sky was covered with dust. On an esplanade, some kids, not at all bothered by the darkness, were playing soccer. Omar trudged alongside me, his heavy feet scraping the ground. When we reached a streetlight, he stopped to look me over.

"Do you think I'm putting my nose in something that's none of my business, cousin?"

"No."

"I wasn't trying to put anything over on you. I'm not on anybody's side."

"That didn't even occur to me."

I looked him over in turn. "Life has rules, Omar, and without some of them, humanity would return to the Stone Age. Sure, they don't all suit us, and they aren't infallible or even always reasonable, but they help us hold a certain course. You know what I'd like to be doing right now? I'd like to be home in my room on the roof, listening to my tinny radio and dreaming about a piece of bread and some cool water. But I don't have a radio anymore, and I couldn't go back home without dying of shame before I crossed the threshold."

※　　●　　※

Omar worked as a deliveryman for a furniture dealer, a former warrant officer he'd known in the army. They'd met by
chance in a woodworker's shop. Omar had recently landed
in Baghdad, and he was looking for some comrades from
his unit, but the addresses he had were no longer current;
many of the men had moved away or disappeared. Omar
was about to offer his services to the woodworker, when the
warrant officer came in to order some tables and cup-
boards. The two of them, Omar and the warrant officer,
had flung themselves into each other's arms. After the embraces and the customary questions, Omar revealed his situation to his former superior. The warrant officer wasn't
exactly flush with money and didn't really have enough
business to afford new hires, but team spirit won out over
bottom-line considerations, and the deserting Corporal was
engaged on the spot. His employer provided Omar with the
blue van he drove and devotedly maintained and also found
him the studio flat in Salman Pak. The salary Omar received was modest and sometimes several weeks late, but

the warrant officer didn't cheat. Omar knew from the beginning that he was going to work hard for peanuts, but he had a roof, and he wasn't starving. When he compared his situation with what he saw around him, he could only praise his saints and marvel at his luck.

Omar took me to see his employer, with the idea of angling for a job. He warned me beforehand that this was going to be a complete waste of effort. Business was in general decline, and even the people with the deepest pockets were having trouble feeding their families. Everyone had too many other priorities, too many pressing concerns, to think about buying a new sideboard or changing armchairs. The warrant officer, a long-limbed personage who resembled a wading bird, received me with great respect. Omar introduced me as his cousin and spoke highly of merits that were not necessarily mine. The warrant officer nodded and raised admiring eyebrows, his smile suspended on his face. When Omar came to the reasons for my presence in the warehouse, the warrant officer's smile went away. Without saying a word, he disappeared through a concealed door and returned with a register, which he displayed under our noses. The lines of writing, in blue ink, went on and on, but not the lines of figures, which were underlined in red. The payments received were almost nonexistent, and as for the section in green ink with the heading "Orders," it was as succinct as an official bulletin.

"I'm very sorry," he said. "We're high and dry."

Omar didn't insist.

He called a few friends on his mobile phone and dragged me from one end of the city to the other; no potential employer we spoke to would so much as promise to let us know if an opening should occur. Our failures depressed Omar; as for me, I had the feeling that I was overburdening him. After the fifth day of not being able to get a foot in any door, I decided not to bother him further and said so.

Omar's response was to call me an idiot. "You're staying with me until you can stand on your own two feet. What would our family think if they learned I'd dropped you just like that? They already find my foul language and my reputation as a drunkard impossible to bear; I'm not going to let them say I'm two-faced, as well. I have a lot of faults, I surely do—no way I'm getting into paradise—but I have my pride, cousin, and I'm holding on to it."

One afternoon, while Omar and I were twiddling our thumbs in a corner of the apartment, a young man, practically a boy, knocked on the door. He was thin-shouldered and frightened, with a girlish face and eyes of crystalline limpidity. He must have been my age, about twenty or so. He was wearing a tropical shirt—open at the neck, revealing his pink chest—tight jeans, and shoes that were new but scuffed on the sides. Chagrined at finding me there, he fixed the Corporal with an insistent stare that dismissed me out of hand.

Omar hastened to introduce us. He, too, had been caught unprepared; his voice trembled oddly as he said, "Cousin, this is Hany, my associate and roommate."

Hany held out a fragile hand that almost dissolved in mine, and then, without showing much interest in me, signaled to Omar to follow him out onto the landing. They closed the door behind them. A few minutes later, Omar came back to say that he and his associate had some problems to deal with in the apartment; he wondered if I would mind waiting for him in the café on the corner.

"Just in time. I was starting to go numb in here," I said.

Trying to make sure that I wasn't taking it badly, Omar accompanied me to the bottom of the stairs. "Order whatever you want; it's on me."

His eyes were glinting with a strange jubilation.

"Sounds like good news," I said.

He said, "Ah," and trailed off in confusion. "Who knows? Heaven doesn't always send bad luck."

I brought my hand to my temple in a salute and went to the café. An hour later, Omar joined me. The discussion with his associate seemed to have been satisfactory.

Hany paid us several more visits. Each time, Omar asked me to go to the café and wait for him. Eventually, his roommate, who still couldn't bring himself to share any sort of friendly exchange with me, came over one evening and declared that he'd been very patient and that now it was time for him to return to his normal daily life; in short, he wanted to reclaim his share of the apartment. Omar tried to reason with him. Hany persisted. He declared that he wasn't comfortable with the people who'd taken him in; he was fed up with being subjected to their hypocrisy when he didn't have to be. Hany had made up his mind. His set face and fixed stare allowed no possibility of negotiations.

"He's right," I said to Omar. "This is his place, after all. He's been very patient."

Hany's eyes were still fixed on his associate. He didn't even see the hand I put out to bid him farewell.

Omar's irritation was audible as he stepped between me and his roommate and said to him, "Fine. You want to come back? The door is open. But this guy is my cousin, and I'm not about to kick him out. If I don't find him a place this evening, I'll sleep with him on a bench, tonight and every night until he's got a roof over his head."

I tried to protest. Omar pushed me onto the landing and slammed the door behind us.

First, we went to an acquaintance of Omar to see if there was any chance she might accommodate me for two or three days, but the two of them were unable to reach an agreement; then he fell back on his employer, who suggested I could sleep in his warehouse. Omar accepted the offer as a possible last resort and continued knocking on other doors. When they all rang hollow, we went back to the warehouse and acted like night watchmen.

By the end of the week, Omar had grown less and less talkative. He retreated inside himself and stopped paying attention to what I said to him. He was unhappy. The precariousness of our situation hollowed his cheeks and left its traces deep in his eyes. I felt responsible for his listlessness.

One morning, he asked me, "What do you think of Sayed, the Falcon's son?"

"Nothing much, one way or the other. Why?"

"I've never been able to figure out that boy. I don't know what he's up to, but he's got a household-appliances shop in the city center. Would you be willing to go and see if he's in a position to give you a hand?"

"Of course. Why do you seem bothered?"

"I don't want you to think I'm trying to get rid of you."

"If I had such a thought, I wouldn't forgive myself." I patted him on the wrist to reassure him. "Let's go see him, Omar. Right away."

We took the van and headed for the center of Baghdad. An attack on a district police station caused us to turn back and drive around a large part of the city in order to reach a wide and very lively avenue. Sayed's store stood on a corner next to a pharmacy, in the extension of a small, still-intact public garden. Omar parked about a hundred meters away. He was uneasy.

"Well, we're lucky," he said. "Sayed's at the cash register. We won't have to hang around the premises. You go and see him. Pretend you happened to be walking by and you thought you recognized him through the window. He's sure to ask what brings you to Baghdad. Just tell him the truth: You've been living in the street for weeks, you don't have anywhere to go, and your money's all gone. Then, he'll either come up with something for you or make up a bunch of crap to fend you off. If you get situated, don't even think about visiting me at the warehouse. Not anytime soon, in any case. Let a week or two pass. I don't want Sayed to know where I stay or what I do. I'd appreciate it if you never said my name in his presence. Me, I'm going back to the warehouse. If you don't come back this evening, I'll know you've been taken on."

Rather eagerly, he pushed me out of the van, showed me his thumb, and quickly rejoined the vehicles slaloming around pedestrians.

Sayed was making entries in a register. He'd rolled up his shirtsleeves, and beside him, a little fan whirled its noisy blades. When he noticed my indecisive silhouette in the doorway, he pushed his glasses up on his forehead and squinted. We'd never been very close, and it took him a little while to situate me in his memory. My heart started racing. Then his face lit up in a broad smile.

"I don't believe it," the Falcon's son cried, spreading his arms in welcome.

He folded me in a long embrace. Then he asked, "What brings you to Baghdad?"

I told my story almost exactly the way Omar had suggested. Sayed listened to me with interest, but otherwise his face was expressionless. It was hard for me to tell whether my distress touched him or not. When he raised his hand to interrupt me, I thought he was about to kick me out. To my great relief, he put it on my shoulder and declared to me that my cares were his from that moment on; should I care to, he said, I could work in his store and live in a little storeroom on the upper floor.

"I sell television sets here, parabolic antennas, microwave ovens, et cetera. Naturally, everything that comes in and everything that goes out must be recorded. Your job would be to keep those records up-to-date. If memory serves, you attended the university, right?"

"I was a first-year humanities student."

"Excellent! Bookkeeping's nothing more than a question of honesty, and you're an honest boy. For the rest, you'll learn it as you go along. As you'll see, it's not all that difficult. I'm really very happy to welcome you here."

He led me upstairs to show me my room. It was occupied by a young night watchman, who was relieved to be assigned to other duties, which meant he'd be able to go home after the store closed for the day. I liked the accommodations: There was a camp bed, a TV set, a table, and a wardrobe where I'd be able to keep my things. Sayed advanced me some money so I could go have a bath and buy myself a toilet kit and some clothes. He also invited me to a meal in a real restaurant.

That night, I slept like a stone.

At 8:30 the next morning, I raised the store's rolling shutter. The first employees—there were three of them—were already waiting on the sidewalk outside. A few minutes later, Sayed joined us and performed the introductions. His workers shook my hand without displaying much enthusiasm. These were young city dwellers, mistrustful and little inclined to conversation. The tallest of them, Rashid, worked in the rear of the store, an area to which he had sole access. His job was to supervise deliveries of incoming merchandise and store it properly. The eldest of the three, Amr, was the deliveryman, and the third, Ismail, an electronics engineer, was in charge of after-sale service and repair.

Sayed's office served as the reception area. He sat as though enthroned, facing the large shop window, and ceded the rest of the store to product display. Metal shelving ran the length of the walls. Small- or large-screen television sets with Asian brand names, accompanied by satellite dishes and every kind of sophisticated accessory, took up most of the available surface area. There were also electric coffee machines, food processors, grills, and other cooking appliances. Unlike the furniture dealer's enterprise, Sayed's store, located on an important commercial avenue, was constantly filled with shoppers, who jostled one another on the display floor all day long. Of course, the majority of them were there just for the sake of gawking; nonetheless, a steady stream of customers carrying purchases exited the store.

I was fine until the afternoon, when I returned to the store after a cheap lunch and Sayed informed me that some "very dear friends" were waiting for me in my room on the upper floor. Sayed led the way. When he opened the door, I saw Yaseen and the twins, Hassan and Hussein, sitting on my camp bed. A shiver went through me. The twins were overjoyed to see me again. They jumped on me and pounded me affectionately, laughing all the while. As for Yaseen, he didn't get up. He remained seated on the bed, unmoving, his spine erect, like a cobra. He cleared his throat, a signal to the two brothers to cut out the hilarity, and fixed me with the gaze that no one in Kafr Karam dared to withstand.

"It took you a while to wake up," he said to me.

I failed to grasp what he meant by that.

The twins leaned against the wall and left me in the center of the little room, facing Yaseen. "So how are things?" he asked.

"I can't complain."

"I can," he said. "I pity you."

He fidgeted, successfully liberating the tail of his jacket from under his behind. He'd changed, Yaseen had. I'd have thought he was ten years older than was actually the case. A few months had been enough to harden his features. His stare was still intimidating, but the corners of his mouth were furrowed, as if they'd cracked under the pressure of his fixed grin.

I decided not to let him upset me. "Are you going to tell me why you pity me?" I asked.

He shook his head. "You think you're not pitiful?"

"I'm listening."

"He's listening. Finally, he can hear, our dear well-digger's son. Now, how shall we aggravate him?" He looked me up and down before going on. "I wonder what goes on in your head, my friend. You have to be autistic not to see what's happening. The country's at war, and millions of fools act as if everything's cool. When something explodes in the street, they go back inside and close their shutters and wash their hands of the whole affair. The trouble is, things don't work that way. Sooner or later, the war will knock their houses down and surprise them in their beds. How many times did I tell you and everybody else in Kafr Karam? I told you all: If we don't go to the fire, the fire will come to us. Who listened to me? Hey, Hassan. Who listened to me?"

"Nobody," Hassan said.

"Did *you* sit around waiting for the fire to come?"

"No, Yaseen," Hassan said.

"Did you wait until some sons of bitches came and yanked you out of your bed in the middle of the night before you opened your eyes?"

"No," Hassan said.

"How about you, Hussein? Did some sons of bitches have to drag you through the mud to wake you up?"

"No," Hussein said.

Yaseen looked me over again. "As for me, I didn't wait, either. I became an insurgent before someone spat on my self-respect. Was there anything I lacked in Kafr Karam? Did I have anything to complain about? I could have closed my shutters and stopped up my ears. But I knew that if I didn't go to the fire, the fire was going to come to my house. I took up arms because I didn't want to wind up like Sulayman. A question of survival? No, just a question of logic. This is my country. Scoundrels are trying to extort it from me. So what do I do? According to you, what do I do? You think I wait until they come and rape my mother before my eyes, and under my roof?"

Hassan and Hussein bowed their heads.

Yaseen breathed slowly, moderating the intensity of his gaze, and then spoke again. "I know what happened at your house."

I frowned.

"Oh, yes," he continued. "What men consider a grave is a vegetable garden as far as their better halves are concerned. Women don't know the meaning of the word *secret*."

I bowed my head.

Yaseen leaned back against the wall, folded his arms over his chest, and gazed at me in silence. His eyes made me uncomfortable. He crossed his legs and put his palms on his knees. "I know what it is to see your revered father on the floor, balls in the air, thrown down by a brute," he said.

My throat clamped shut. I couldn't believe he was going to reveal my family's shame! I wouldn't stand for it.

Yaseen read on my face what I was shouting deep inside. It meant nothing to him. Jerking his chin toward the twins and Sayed, he went on. "All of us here—me, the others in this room, and the beggars in the street—we all know *perfectly well* what the outrage committed against your family signifies. But the GI has no clue. He can't measure the extent of the sacrilege. He doesn't even know what a sacrilege is. In his world, a man sticks his parents in an old folks' home and forgets them. They're the least of his worries. He calls his mother 'an old bag' and his father 'an asshole.' What can you expect from such a person?"

Anger was smothering me. Clearly recognizing my condition, Yaseen raised the bidding. "What can you expect from a snot-nosed degenerate who would put his mother into a home for the moribund, his *mother*, the woman who conceived him fiber by fiber, carried him in her womb, labored to bring him into the world, raised him step by step, and watched beside him night after night like a star? Can you expect such a person to respect *our* mothers? Can you expect him to kiss the foreheads of *our* old men?"

The silence of Sayed and the twins increased my anger. I had the feeling they'd pulled me into a trap, and I resented them for it. If Yaseen was meddling in a matter that was none of his business, well, that was pretty consistent with his character and his reputation; but for the others to act as his accomplices without really getting completely involved—that enraged me.

Sayed saw that I was on the point of imploding. He said, "Those people have no more consideration for their elders than they do for their offspring. That's what Yaseen's trying to explain to you. He's not chewing you out. He's telling you facts. What happened in Kafr Karam has shaken all of us, I assure you. I knew nothing about it until this morning. And when I heard the story, I was furious. Yaseen's right. The Americans have gone too far."

"Seriously, what did you expect?" Yaseen growled, annoyed by Sayed's intervention. "You thought they'd modestly avert their eyes from the nakedness of a handicapped, terrorized sexagenarian?" He made a little circle with his hand. "Why?"

I had lost the power of speech.

Sayed took advantage of my tongue-tied state to land a

few blows of his own. "Why should they turn away? These are people who can catch their wives in bed with their best friends and act as though nothing's wrong. Modesty's a virtue they've long since lost sight of. Honor? They've distorted its codes. They're just infuriated retards, smashing valuable things, like buffalo let loose in a porcelain shop. They arrive here from an unjust, cruel universe with no humanity and no morals, where the powerful feed on the flesh of the downtrodden. Violence and hatred sum up their history; Machiavellianism shapes and justifies their initiatives and their ambitions. What can they comprehend of *our* world, which has produced the most fabulous pages in the history of human civilization? *Our* fundamental values are still intact; *our* oaths are unbroken; *our* traditional points of reference remain the same. What can they understand about us?"

"Not very much," Yaseen said, getting up and approaching me until we were nose-to-nose. "Not very much, my brother."

Sayed went on. "They know nothing of our customs, our dreams, or our prayers. They're particularly ignorant of our heritage and our long memories. What do those cowboys know about Mesopotamia? Do you think they have a clue about this fantastic Iraq they're trampling down? About the Tower of Babel, the Hanging Gardens, Harun al-Rashid, the *Thousand and One Nights*? They know nothing of these things! They never look at this side of history. All they see in our country is an immense pool of petroleum, which they intend to lap dry, even if it costs the last drop of our blood, too. They're bonanza seekers, looters, despoilers, mercenaries. They've reduced all values to the single dreadful question of cash, and the only virtue they recognize is profit. Predators, that's what they are, formidable predators. They're ready to march over the body of Christ if they think it'll help fill their pockets. And if you aren't willing to go along with them, they haul out the heavy artillery."

Yaseen pushed me toward the window, crying out, "Look at them! Go ahead, take a look at them, and you'll see what they really are: machines."

"And those machines will hit a wall in Baghdad," Sayed said. "Our streets are going to witness the greatest duel of all time, the clash of the titans: Babylon against Disneyland, the Tower of Babel against the Empire State Building, the Hanging Gardens against the Golden Gate Bridge, Scheherazade against Bonnie Parker, Sindbad against the Terminator. . . ."

I was completely bamboozled. I felt as though I were in the thick of a farce, in the midst of a play rehearsal, surrounded by mediocre actors who'd learned their roles but didn't have the talent the text deserved, and yet—and yet—and yet, it seemed to me that this was exactly what I wanted to hear, that their words were the very words I was missing, the ones I'd sought in vain while the effort filled my head with migraines and insomnia. It made no difference whether Sayed was sincere, or whether Yaseen was speaking his real thoughts to me, speaking from his guts; the only certitudes I had were that the farce suited me, that it fit me like a glove, that the secret I'd chewed on for weeks was shared, that my anger wasn't unique, and that it was giving me back my determination. I found it difficult to define this particular alchemy, which under different conditions would have made me laugh out loud, but now it gave me great relief. That bastard Yaseen had pulled a nasty thorn out of my side. He'd known how to touch me in exactly the right spot, how to stir up all the crap that had filled my head ever since the night when the sky fell in on me. I had come to Baghdad to avenge an offense. I didn't know how to go about it, but from now on, my ignorance was no longer a concern.

And so, when Yaseen finally opened his arms to me, he seemed to be opening up the path that would lead me to retrieve what I wanted more than anything else in the world: my family's honor.

# 13

⁕ • ⁕

Yaseen and his two guardian angels, Hassan and Hussein, didn't return to the store. Sayed invited all four of us to dinner at his house to celebrate our reunion and seal our oath; then, after the meal was over, the three companions bade us farewell and disappeared. It would be a while before I saw them again.

I resumed my work as night watchman, which meant I opened the store for the other employees in the morning and closed it behind them in the evening. Weeks passed. My colleagues hardly warmed to me. They said "Good morning" when they arrived and "Good evening" when they left, but nothing in between. Their indifference exasperated me. I tried for a while to gain their confidence; eventually, however, I started ignoring them, too. I still had enough pride to stop myself from foolishly smiling at people who offered no smile in return.

I took my meals nearby, in a restaurant with questionable hygiene. Sayed had made an arrangement with the manager, who ran a tab for me and sent the bill to the store at the end of the month. He was a small, swarthy fellow, sprightly and jovial. We got on well together. Later, I found out that Sayed owned the restaurant, along with one newspaper kiosk, two grocery stores, a shoe store on the avenue, a photographer's studio, and a telephone store.

At the end of each week, Sayed paid me a good salary. I bought myself various necessities and miscellaneous items with it and socked away the rest of my pay in a leather pouch meant for Bahia; I intended to send her everything I managed to save.

Things fell into place without difficulty. I carved out a little routine, custom-made for myself. After the store closed, I went for a walk in the city center. I loved walking, and there were new spectacles every day in Baghdad. Attacks were answered with barrages of gunfire, raids were carried out in retaliation for ambushes, and the coalition's response to protest marches was often racist violence. People made the best of the situation. The area where an explosion or summary execution had taken place was barely cleared before the crowd poured back into it. The population was fatalistic, stoic. Several times, I came upon some still-smoking scene of carnage and stopped to ogle the horror until help and the army arrived. I watched ambulance drivers picking pieces of flesh from sidewalks, firemen evacuating blasted buildings, cops interrogating the neighborhood residents. I stuck my hands in my pockets and whiled away hours in this pursuit, inuring myself to the exercise of rage. While the victims' relatives raised their hands to heaven, howling out their grief, I asked myself if I was capable of inflicting the same suffering on others and registered the fact that the question didn't shock me. I strolled calmly back to the store and my room. The nightmares of the street never caught up with my dreams.

Around two A.M. one night, I was awakened by muffled sounds. Switching on the lights, I went downstairs to see whether a burglar had slipped in while I was sleeping. There was nobody in the store, and none of the merchandise appeared to be missing. The noises were coming from the area in the back of the store reserved for repairs and off-limits to all nonauthorized personnel. The door was locked from the inside, and I didn't have permission go in there anyway, so I stayed in the showroom until the intruders departed. The next day, I reported the incident to Sayed. He explained that the technician, the engineer, sometimes came to work at odd hours to satisfy demanding customers, and he reminded me that my duties didn't extend to the repair shop. I detected a peremptory warning in his tone.

One Friday afternoon, as I was rambling among the palms on the banks of the Tigris, Omar the Corporal approached me. I hadn't seen him for weeks. He was wearing the same jacket and trousers, which now looked faded, and new, grotesque sunglasses. The front of his shirt, stretched tight over his belly, was splattered with grease.

He started talking right away. "Are you sulking, or what? Every day, I ask for you at the warehouse and the warrant officer tells me he hasn't seen you. You're pissed off at me, right?"

"For what? You've been more than a brother to me."

"So why are you avoiding me?"

"I'm not avoiding you. I've been very busy, that's all."

He was uneasy, trying to read my eyes to see whether I

was hiding something from him. "I've been worried about you," he confessed. "You can't imagine how much I regret thrusting you into Sayed's arms. Every time I think about it, I tear my hair."

"You're wrong. I'm doing fine with him."

"I'd never forgive myself if he got you involved in some shady business . . . in some . . . in some bloodshed."

He had to swallow several times before he could bring up that last bit. His sunglasses hid his eyes from me, but the expression on his face gave him away. Omar was in dire straits, tormented by pangs of conscience. He was letting his beard grow as a sign of contrition.

"I didn't come to Baghdad to get a job and settle down, Omar. We've already discussed that. No use going over it again."

Omar was far from reassured by my words, which, in fact, offended him. More apprehensive than ever, he clutched at his hair.

"Come on," I said. "Let's go have a bite to eat. On me."

"I'm not hungry. To tell you the truth, I haven't been eating much, not since I had that harebrained idea of entrusting you to Sayed."

"Please . . ."

"I have to run. I don't want to be seen with you. Your friends and I aren't tuned to the same frequency."

"I'm free to see anybody I want."

"Not me."

Nervously squeezing his fingers, he cast suspicious looks all around us before he spoke again. "I talked to an army buddy of mine about you. He's prepared to take you in for a while. He's a former lieutenant, a really nice guy. He's about to start up a business, and he needs someone he can trust."

"I'm exactly where I want to be."

"Are you sure?"

"Positive."

He nodded, but his heart was heavy. "Well," he said, extending his hand. "If you know what you want, all I can do is let the matter drop. But should you happen to change your mind, you know where to find me. I'm someone you can count on."

"Thanks, Omar."

He pressed his chin against his throat and walked away.

After about a dozen steps, he changed his mind and came back. His cheek muscles were twitching spasmodically.

"One more thing, cousin," he whispered. "If you insist on fighting, do it properly. Fight *for* your country, not *against* the whole world. Keep things in perspective; don't mistake wrong for right. Don't kill just for killing's sake. Don't fire blindly—we're losing more innocent people than bastards who deserve to die. You promise?"

I said nothing.

"You see? You're already on the wrong track. The world isn't our enemy. Remember all the people who protested the invasion all over the world, millions of them marching in Madrid, Rome, Paris, Tokyo, South America, Asia. All of them were on our side, and they still are. We got more support from them than we got from the other Arab countries. Don't forget that. All nations are victims of the avarice of a handful of multinational companies. It would be terrible to lump them all together. Kidnapping journalists, executing

NGO workers who are here only to help us—those kinds of things are alien to our customs. If you want to avenge an offense, don't commit one. If you think your honor must be saved, don't dishonor your people. Don't give way to madness. If I see pictures of you mistaking arbitrary execution for a feat of arms, I'll hang myself."

He wiped his nose on his wrist, nodded once again with his shoulders around his ears, and concluded: "I'd hang myself for sure, cousin. From now on, remind yourself that everything you do concerns me directly."

And he hurried away to melt into the confused crowds wandering along the riverbank.

❖　●　❖

Two months after my conversation with Omar, my schedule hadn't changed a bit. I got up at six o'clock in the morning, lifted the rolling shutter in front of the store entrance two hours later, posted the previous day's incoming and outgoing merchandise, and closed the store in the late afternoon. After the departure of the other employees, we locked the door, Sayed and I, and busied ourselves with drawing up a sales balance sheet and making an inventory of new acquisitions. Once we'd assessed the take and made provisions for the following day, Sayed handed me the big key ring and took away a bag stuffed with banknotes. The routine was starting to weigh on me, and my universe was shrinking down to nothing. I stopped going to cafés—stopped going out altogether, in fact. My daily itinerary ran between two points a hundred meters apart: the store and the restaurant. I ate dinner late, bought some lemonade and cookies in the grocery store on the corner, and shut myself up in my room. I spent my time staring at the TV set, zapping mindlessly from channel to channel, unable to concentrate on a program or a movie. This situation accentuated my disgust and warped my character. I became increasingly touchy and decreasingly patient, and an aggressiveness I didn't recognize in myself began to characterize my words and my gestures. I no longer put up with the way my colleagues ignored me, and I missed no opportunity to make that clear to them. If someone failed to respond to my smile, I muttered "Dickhead" loud enough for him to hear me, and if he had the gall to frown, I confronted and taunted him. But things never went beyond that, and so I was left unsatisfied.

One evening, unable to take it anymore, I asked Sayed what he was waiting for to send me into action. He replied in a hurtful tone of voice: "Everything in its time!" I felt like small fry, like someone who counted for nothing. Just you wait, I thought. I'll show you what I can do one of these days. For the moment, the initiative didn't depend on me; I contented myself with chewing over my frustrations and elaborating fantastic revenge schemes, all of which served to enliven my insomnia.

And then a chain of events was set in motion. . . .

After seeing off the store's last customer, I was pulling down the rolling shutter when two men came up and waved me aside so they could enter. Two other employees, Amr and Rashid, who had been putting up their things and preparing to leave for the day, stopped what they were doing. Sayed put his glasses on; when he recognized the two intruders, he stood up from his desk, opened a drawer, took out an envelope, and propelled it across the table with a flick of his finger. His visitors exchanged looks and folded their hands. The taller of the two was a man in his fifties with a sinister-looking mug resting on his fat neck like a gargoyle on a church. A hideous burn scar extended high enough on his right jaw to cause a slight pucker in his eyelid. The fellow was a downright brute, complete with treacherous eyes and a sardonic grin. He was wearing a leather jacket worn at the elbows and a bottle-green knit shirt sprinkled with dandruff. His companion, thirty-something, displayed his young wolf's fangs in an affected smile. His casual demeanor betrayed the go-getter eager to go very far very fast, assured by the cop's badge that he wore. His new jeans were turned up at the ankles, revealing a pair of worn moccasins. He stared at Rashid, who was perched on a stool.

"Greetings, my good prince," the older man said.

"Hello, Captain," Sayed replied, tapping his finger on the envelope. "It's been waiting for you."

"I've been on special assignment these past few days." The captain slowly approached the table, picked up the envelope, felt its weight, and grumbled, "Thinner than usual."

"The amount's correct."

The officer flashed a skeptical grimace. "You know my family problems, Sayed. I have a whole tribe to maintain, and we haven't been paid our salaries for six months." He jerked a thumb toward his colleague. "My buddy here's in the shit, too. He wants to get married, but he can't find so much as a fucking bedroom he can afford."

Sayed pressed his lips together before plunging his hand back into the desk drawer. He pulled out a few supplementary bills, which the captain, as swiftly as a conjurer, caused to disappear.

"You're a good prince, Sayed. God will repay you."

"We're going through a rough patch, Captain. We have to help one another out."

The captain scratched his damaged cheek, pretended to be embarrassed, and looked to his teammate for the strength to get to the heart of the matter. "To tell you the truth," he said, "I didn't come here for the envelope. My buddy and I are about to start up a business, and it occurred to me that you might perhaps be interested in it and maybe you could give us a hand."

Sayed sat down and clasped his mouth between his thumb and his index finger.

The captain settled into the chair facing the desk and crossed his legs. He said, "I'm starting a little travel agency."

"In Baghdad? You think Iraq's a tourist destination?"

"I have some relatives in Amman who think it would be a good idea for me to invest in Jordan. I've been knocking around here long enough, you know, and frankly, I don't see any light at the end of the Iraq tunnel. We've got a second Vietnam on our hands. I'd like to get out while I'm more or less intact. I'm already carrying around three slugs in my body, and a Molotov cocktail nearly took my face off. So I've decided to turn in my badge and make my fortune in Jordan. This is quite a juicy business I'm talking about. One hundred percent profit. And legal. If you want, I'll let you come in as a partner."

"I've got enough hassles with my own business."

"Stop it. You do just fine."

"Not really."

The captain thrust a cigarette between his lips, lit it with a disposable lighter, and blew the smoke in Sayed's face. Sayed limited himself to slightly turning his head.

"Too bad," the policeman said. "You're letting a real opportunity get away, my friend. Tell me the truth—doesn't it tempt you a little?"

"No."

"Well, that's all right. Now, shall we move on to the reason for my visit?"

"I'm listening."

"Do you trust me?"

"How do you mean?"

"In all the time I've been keeping an eye on your businesses, have I ever tried to double-cross you?"

"No."

"Have I been greedy?"

"No."

"And if I ask you to advance me a little money so I can get started, will you think I'm not going to pay you back?"

Sayed had been expecting the conversation to reach this point. He smiled and spread out his arms. "You're an honorable man, Captain. I'd advance you millions without so much as a second thought, but I have debts up to here, and my sales are tanking."

"Don't give me that crap!" the captain said, crushing out his barely smoked cigarette on the glass desktop. "You're rolling in dough. What do you think I do all day long? I sit at a table in the café across the street and watch your delivery vans coming and going. And I make notes. Your deliveries can't keep up with your sales. Why, just today," he went on, pulling out a little notebook from the inside pocket of his jacket, "you unloaded two big refrigerators, four washing machines, and four television sets, plus a bunch of customers left the store with various boxes. And it's only Monday. The way you're turning your stuff over, you ought to found your own bank."

"So you're spying on me, Captain?"

"I'm your lucky star, Sayed. I watch over all your little scams. Have you had any tax problems? Have any other cops come in here to hit you up for money? Because of me, everything's cushy for you. I know your bills are as phony as your word of honor, and I make sure no one calls you to account. And what do you do? You slip me some crumbs and you think I should be grateful. I'm not a beggar, Sayed."

He stood up abruptly and headed straight for the storeroom. Sayed didn't have enough time to stop him. The captain plunged into the rear of the shop and made a sweeping gesture toward the innumerable boxes stacked in tiers and filling three-quarters of the room. He said, "I'll bet none of this merchandise has ever passed through a customs post."

"Come on. Everybody in Baghdad works off the books."

Sayed was perspiring and very angry, but he tried to contain himself. The two cops had the air of calm assurance that people get when they're running the show with an iron hand. They knew what they wanted and how to obtain it. Getting your palm greased was the primary vocation of each and every functionary in the service of the state, particularly those in the security forces. This ingrained practice was an inheritance from the former regime and continued to flourish under the occupation, facilitated by the confusion and the galloping impoverishment that reigned in the country, where villainous kidnappings, bribes, embezzlements, and extortions were the order of the day.

The captain called over to his colleague, "How much you think all this is worth?"

"Enough to buy an island in the Pacific Ocean."

"Do you think we're being piggish, Detective?"

"We eat like birds, Chief."

Sayed mopped his brow with a handkerchief. Amr and Rashid were standing in the doorway behind the two policemen, on the alert for a sign from their boss. "Let's go back to the office," Sayed mumbled to the captain. "We'll see what I can do to help you with your business venture."

"Now you're being sensible," the captain said, spreading out his arms. "But look, if you're talking about another skinny envelope like the one you just gave me, you can forget it."

"No, no," said Sayed, eager to exit the storeroom. "We'll work something out. Come on back to the office."

The captain frowned. "It almost seems as though you have something to hide, Sayed. Why are you shoving us out? What do you keep in this stockroom, besides what we can see?"

"Nothing, I assure you. It's just that it's after closing time, and I have an appointment with someone who lives on the other side of the city."

"Are you sure?"

"What would I be hiding in here? This stuff is all my merchandise. It hasn't even been unpacked yet."

The captain squinted his right eye. Did he suspect something? Was he about to give Sayed a very hard time? He stepped over to the walls of boxes, rummaged about here and there, and then suddenly whipped around to see whether Sayed was holding his breath or not. Amr and Rashid's rigid posture gave him a moment's pause. He crouched down to peer under the stacked cartons, the piles of television sets and various small appliances. When he spotted a concealed door in a corner, he started walking toward it. "What's that back there?"

"It's the repair shop. It's locked. Our technician left an hour ago."

"Can I have a look around?"

"It's locked from inside. The technician gets in through another door."

Suddenly, just as the captain was preparing to let the matter drop, there was a loud crash inside the repair shop. Sayed and his employees froze. The captain raised an eyebrow, delighted to catch Sayed out.

Sayed said, "I swear I thought he'd left, Captain."

The captain knocked on the door. "Open up, pal, or I'll kick my way in."

"Just a moment. I'm soldering something. Almost finished."

You could hear creaking sounds, followed by some metallic screeching; a key turned in the lock, and the door opened. The engineer, wearing an undershirt and tracksuit bottoms, peered out. The captain saw a table cluttered with wires, tiny screws, screwdrivers, little pots of paint and glue and soldering material, and, in the midst of the clutter, a dismantled television set. Its back cover, which had been replaced too hastily, hung askew, revealing a skein of multi-colored wires inside the shell. The captain squinted his right eye again. The moment he detected the bomb, which lay half-concealed in the place where the picture tube should have been, his throat tightened, and then his face suddenly turned somber when the engineer poked the mouth of a pistol into the back of his neck.

The detective, who had remained in the background, didn't immediately comprehend what was going on, but the heavy silence that had just fallen on the room caused him instinctively to bring his hand to his belt. He never reached his weapon. Amr jumped him from behind, put one hand over his mouth, and with the other thrust a dagger deep into his back, just under the shoulder blade. His eyes wide in disbelief, the detective shivered from head to foot and slowly collapsed onto the floor.

The captain was trembling in every limb. He could neither lift his arms in surrender nor lean forward. He said, "I won't say anything, Sayed."

"Only the dead know how to keep their mouths shut, Captain. I'm awfully sorry for you, Captain."

"I beg you. I've got six kids—"

"You should have thought of them before."

"Please, Sayed, please spare me. I swear I won't say anything. If you want, take me into your cell. I'll be your eyes and ears. I've never cheered for the Americans. I hate them. I'm a cop, but—you can check—I've never laid a hand on anyone in the resistance. I'm on your side, all the way. . . . Sayed, what I said was true: I'm hoping to get out of here.

Don't kill me, for the love of heaven, don't. I've got six kids, and the oldest isn't even fifteen yet."

"Were you spying on me?"

"No, I swear I wasn't. I just got a little greedy, that's all."

"In that case, why didn't you come alone?"

"He was my partner."

"I'm not talking about the jackass who came in with you. I mean the boys waiting for you outside in the street."

"No one's waiting for me outside, I swear to you. . . ."

There was a silence. The captain raised his eyes; when he saw Sayed's satisfied smile, he realized the seriousness of his mistake. He should have been a little craftier and pretended he wasn't alone. The unfortunate man had no luck at all.

Sayed ordered me to go to the front of the store and lower the rolling shutter completely. I did as he said. When I returned to the storeroom, the captain was on his knees, with his hands tied behind his back. He'd shit his pants and was crying like a child.

Sayed asked me, "Did you look around outside?"

"I didn't notice anything unusual."

"Very good."

Sayed slipped a plastic packing bag over the captain's head and then, with Rashid's help, forced him to the floor. The officer struggled wildly. Mist filled the plastic bag. Sayed held its mouth closed very tightly around the captain's throat. He ran out of air quickly and started wriggling and writhing. His body was racked by violent convulsions; it took a long time for them to become less frequent and then subside; after a final jerk, they stopped altogether. Sayed and Rashid kept bearing down on the captain with all their weight; they didn't let up until the corpse was completely still.

"Get rid of these two stiffs," Sayed ordered Amr and Rashid. Then, turning to me, he said, "And you, clean up this blood before it dries."

# 14

· 

After Sayed charged Amr and Rashid with making the two corpses disappear, the engineer proposed demanding a ransom from their families. The idea was to throw people off by making them think the men had been kidnapped. Sayed's response was, "It's your problem," and then he told me to follow him. We got in his black Mercedes and went across the city to the other bank of the Tigris. Sayed slipped a CD of Eastern music into the slot, turned up the sound, and drove calmly. His natural composure made me relax, too.

I'd always dreaded the moment when I would step over the line; now that it was behind me, I didn't feel anything in particular. I'd witnessed the killings of the two officers with the same detachment I observed when I contemplated the victims of terrorist attacks. I was no longer the delicate boy from Kafr Karam. Another individual had taken his place. I was stunned by how easy it was to pass from one world to another and practically regretted having spent so much time being fearful of what I'd find. The weakling who had vomited at the sight of blood and lost his head when shots rang out was far, far away, and so was the wimp who'd passed out during the screwup that cost Sulayman his life. I was born again as someone else, someone hard, cold, implacable. My hands didn't tremble. My heart beat normally. In the side-view mirror on my right, my face betrayed no trace of an expression; it was a waxen mask, impenetrable and inaccessible.

Sayed took me to a posh little building in a residential neighborhood. As soon as the security guards recognized his Mercedes, they lifted the barrier. Sayed seemed to receive a great deal of deference from the guards. He parked his car in a garage and led me to a luxury apartment. It wasn't the same one where he'd convened Yaseen, the twins, and me. The place had a caretaker, a secretive old man who served as a general factotum. Sayed suggested that I take a bath and join him later in the living room, whose windows were festooned with taffeta curtains.

The bathtub had a chrome faucet the size of a teakettle. I took off my clothes and stepped in. The scalding water quickly warmed me to my bones.

The old man served us a late supper in a small dining room filled with glittering silver objects. Sayed was wrapped in a dark red dressing gown, which made him look rather like a nabob. We ate in silence. The only audible sound was the clicking of the silverware, occasionally interrupted by the ringing of Sayed's cell phone. Each time, he looked at the dial and decided whether or not to answer the call. Once, it was the engineer, calling about the two corpses. Intermittently grunting, Sayed listened to him and then clicked his phone shut. When Sayed looked up at me, I understood that Rashid and Amr had carried out their assignment successfully.

The old man brought us a basket of fruit. Sayed, as before, scrutinized me in silence. Perhaps, I thought, he expects me to make conversation. I couldn't imagine any topic of mutual interest. Sayed was by nature taciturn, not to mention haughty. I didn't like the way he ordered his employees around. He had to be obeyed to the letter, and once he'd reached a decision, there was no appeal. Paradoxically, I found his authority reassuring. Working for a guy of his stature meant I had no reason to ask questions; he saw to everything and seemed prepared to face any eventuality.

The old man showed me to my room. Pointing to a bell on the night table, he informed me that should I require his services, I had only to ring. Having ostentatiously verified that everything was in order, he withdrew on tiptoe.

I got into bed and turned off the lamp.

Sayed came to inquire as to whether I needed anything. Without turning on the light, he hovered in the doorway, with one hand on the doorknob. "Everything all right?" he asked.

"Everything's fine."

He nodded, closed the door halfway, and then opened it wide again. "I very much appreciated your composure in the storeroom," he said.

●

The next day, I went back to the store and my upstairs room. The business resumed at its normally accelerated pace. Nobody came to inquire whether we'd seen two police officers in the area. A few days later, photographs of the captain and his detective adorned the front page of a newspaper that announced their kidnapping and the amount of the ransom demanded by the kidnappers in exchange for the officers' liberation.

Rashid and Amr no longer shunted me off to one side and no longer slammed the door in my face; from this time forward, I was one of them. The engineer continued installing his bombs in place of television picture tubes. To be sure, he modified only one set out of ten, and so only a minority of his customers was engaged in the transport of death. I noticed that the people who took delivery of the TV bombs were always the same, three large young men squeezed into mechanics' overalls; they arrived in small vans stamped on the sides with a huge logo, accompanied by writing in Arabic and English: HOME DELIVERY. They parked behind the storeroom, signed some release papers, loaded their merchandise, and drove away again.

Sayed disappeared for a week. When he returned, I informed him that I wanted to join Yaseen and his group. I was dying of boredom, and Baghdad's diabolical odor was polluting my thought processes. Sayed asked me to be patient. To help me occupy my nights, he brought me a selection of DVDs. On each of them, someone had written a place name with a felt-tipped pen—Baghdad, Basra, Mosul, Safwan, and so forth, followed by a date and a number. The DVDs contained videos recorded from televised newscasts or made by amateurs on the spot, showing various atrocities committed by the coalition forces: the siege of Fallujah; the racist assaults carried out by British troops on some Iraqi kids seized during a popular demonstration; a GI's summary execution of a wounded civilian inside a mosque; an American helicopter's night attack on some peasants whose truck had broken down in a field—the visual chronicle, in short, of our humiliation, and of the awful blunders that had become so commonplace. I watched every DVD without blinking. It was as if I were downloading into my brain all the possible and imaginable reasons I'd need to blow up the fucking world. The result was, no doubt, just what Sayed had hoped: I got an eyeful, and my subconscious stored away a maximum load of anger, which (when the time came) would give me enthusiasm for whatever violence I might commit and even lend it a certain legitimacy. I wasn't fooled; I figured I'd already had an overdose of hatred and it wasn't really necessary to add any more. I was a Bedouin, and no Bedouin can come to terms with an offense unless blood is spilled. Sayed must have lost sight of that constant, inflexible rule, which has survived through ages and generations; his city life and his mysterious peregrinations had surely taken him far from the tribal soul of Kafr Karam.

I saw Omar again. He'd spent the day bouncing around from dive to dive. He suggested we go and get something to eat, his treat, and I accepted on condition that he not start in on me again. He understood, he said, and during the meal everything was fine until, all at once, his eyes filled with tears. For the sake of propriety, I refrained from asking him what was bothering him. Nevertheless, with no prompting from me, he spilled the beans. He told me about the little problems his roommate, Hany, was causing him.

Hany was planning to leave the country and go to live in Lebanon, and Omar didn't like the idea. When I asked him why Hany's decision troubled him so much, he declared that Hany was very dear to him and that he wouldn't be able to survive if Hany should leave. We said good night on the banks of the Tigris; Omar was dead drunk, and I was disgusted at the thought of returning to my room and my melancholy cogitations.

The store routine started to seem like a sentence to the gallows. The weeks passed over me like a herd of buffalo. I was suffocating. Boredom was slicing me to pieces. I had long since stopped going to the sites of terrorist attacks, and the sirens of Baghdad no longer reached me. Since I almost never ate, I grew visibly thinner, and every night I lay in bed with my head on fire, waiting to fall asleep. Sometimes, when I was hanging around in the store, I caught my reflection in the shop window, soliloquizing and gesticulating. I felt as though I'd lost the thread of my own story; all I could see was exasperation. At the end of my rope, I decided to talk to Sayed again and tell him that I was *ready,* that this farce was unnecessary, that I didn't need to be drawn in any further.

He was in his little office, filling out some forms. After contemplating his pen at some length, he laid it down on a stack of papers, pushed his glasses up on top of his head, and pivoted his chair to face me.

"I'm not trying to string you along, cousin. I'm awaiting instructions in your behalf. I think we have something for you, something extraordinary, but it's still in the conceptual stage."

"I can't wait any longer."

"You're wrong. We're not trying to get into a stadium; we're at war. If you lose patience now, you won't be able to keep cool when you have to. Go back to your work and learn how to overcome your anxieties."

"I'm not anxious."

"Yes, you are."

And with that, he dismissed me.

One Wednesday morning, a truck detonated at the end of the boulevard; the explosion leveled two buildings, left a crater two meters deep, and destroyed most of the storefronts in the area. I'd never seen Sayed in such a state. He stood on the sidewalk, holding his head with both hands and teetering as he contemplated the devastation. As the neighborhood had been spared ever since the beginning of hostilities, I assumed that things hadn't gone according to plan.

Amr and Rashid lowered the metal shutter in front of the store, and Sayed and I immediately drove to the other side of the Tigris. Along the way, he spoke to several "associates" on the telephone, telling them to meet him at once at "number two." He used a coded language that sounded like a banal conversation between businessmen. We came to a suburban area bristling with decrepit buildings and inhabited by a population abandoned to its own devices; then we turned into a courtyard and parked next to two vehicles that had arrived just ahead of us. Their occupants, two men wearing suits, accompanied us into the house. Yaseen joined us there a few minutes later. Sayed had been waiting for him to begin the proceedings. The meeting lasted barely a quarter of an hour and essentially concerned the attack that had taken place on the boulevard. The three men looked at one another with inquiring eyes, unable to propose an explanation. They didn't know who had been behind the explosion. It looked to me as though Yaseen and the two strangers were the leaders of the groups that operated in the neighborhoods traversed by the boulevard; the attack had clearly taken all three of them by surprise. Sayed therefore concluded that a new, unknown, and obviously breakaway group was trying to horn in on their territory. It was absolutely imperative, he said, for the other three to identify this group and stop it from interfering with their plans of action and, as a consequence, disrupting the operational schedule currently in force. The meeting was adjourned. The two men who'd arrived before us left first; then Sayed also drove away, but not before consigning me to Yaseen "until further orders."

Yaseen was not exactly delighted to take me under his wing, especially now that some unknown rivals had encroached on his turf. He contented himself with driving me to a hideout on the north side of Baghdad, a rat hole a little larger than a polling booth, furnished with a bunk bed and a miniature armoire. The place was occupied by a spindly young man with a face like a knife blade, its prominent feature a large hooked nose, whose effect was softened by a thin blond mustache. He was sleeping when we arrived. Yaseen explained to him that he would have to share the place with me for two or three days. The young man nodded. After Yaseen left, my new roommate invited me to have a seat on the lower bunk.

"Are the cops after you?" he asked.

"No."

"Have you just arrived in Baghdad?"

"No."

Seeing that I was in no mood for conversation, he gave up. We remained seated, side by side, until noon. I was furious at Yaseen, and also at what was happening to me. I had the impression that I was being tossed about like some worthless bundle.

"Well," the young man said. "I'm going to buy some sandwiches. Chicken or lamb brochettes?"

"Bring me whatever you feel like."

He slipped on a jacket and went out onto the landing. I heard his footsteps going down the stairs, and then nothing. I listened closely. Not a sound. It was as though the building had been abandoned. I stepped to the window and watched the young man hurrying toward the square. A veiled sun shed its light on the neighborhood. I felt like opening the window and puking.

The young man brought me a chicken sandwich wrapped in newspaper. After two bites, my stomach tightened. I put the sandwich on top of the little armoire.

"My name's Obid," the young man said.

"What the hell am I doing here?"

"Dunno. I've been here only a week myself. Before that, I lived downtown. That was where I operated. Then the police raided the place, but I got away. Now I'm waiting to be assigned to another sector, if not to another city. How about you?"

I pretended I hadn't heard the question.

That evening, I was relieved to see one of the twins, Hussein, turn up. He informed Obid that a car would come to pick him up the next day. Obid leapt for joy.

"And me?"

Hussein favored me with a broad smile. "You? You're coming with me pronto."

Hussein piloted a beat-up little car. He kept running into curbs and drove so badly in general that people got out of his way instinctively. He laughed, amused by the panic he was causing and by the things he was knocking down. I thought he was drunk or drugged, but neither was the case; he simply didn't know how to drive, and his license was as fake as the car's registration papers.

I asked him, "Aren't you afraid of getting busted?"

"For what?" he replied. "I haven't run over anybody yet."

I relaxed a little once we'd made it out of the heavily populated areas. Hussein was giggling and making jokes. I'd never known him to be like that. In Kafr Karam, he'd certainly always seemed like a nice guy, but a bit slow on the uptake.

Hussein stopped his jalopy at the entrance to a suburb that had been severely damaged by missile fire. The hovels looked deserted. Only after we crossed a kind of line of demarcation did I realize that the townspeople were holed up indoors. Later, I would learn that this was the sign of the fedayeen's presence. To avoid attracting the attention of soldiers or the police, the local people were ordered to keep a very low profile.

We walked up an alleyway until we reached a grotesque three-story house. The other twin, Hassan, and a stranger opened the door for us. Hussein performed the introductions. The other man was the home owner, Tariq, a pallid individual who looked like an escapee from an operating room. We went to table at once. The meal was sumptuous, but I failed to do it justice. Shortly after nightfall, we heard the belch of a distant bomb. Hassan looked at his watch and said, "Good-bye, Marwan! We'll meet again in heaven." Marwan must have been a suicide bomber.

Then Hassan turned to me. "You can't imagine how delighted I am to see you again, cousin."

"There's only you three in Yaseen's group?"

"Don't you think that's enough?"

"What happened to the others?"

Hussein burst out laughing. His brother tapped him on the shoulder to calm him down. He said, "Who do you mean by 'the others'?"

"The rest of your band in Kafr Karam. Adel, Salah, Bilal."

Hassan consented to answer me. "Salah's with Yaseen at the moment. It seems that some splinter group's trying to take over from us. As for Adel, he's dead. He was supposed to blow himself up in a police recruiting center. I was against sending him on such a mission from the start. Adel wasn't all there, you know? But Yaseen said he could do it, so they put an explosive belt on him and off he went. By the time Adel got to the recruiting center, he'd forgotten how to detonate the thing, even though it was quite simple—all he had to do was press a button. Nevertheless, Adel got confused, and then he got pissed off. He removed his jacket and started pounding on the explosive belt with his fists. When the other guys in the recruitment line saw what Adel was wearing around his waist, they got the hell out of there, and so the only potential recruit left in front of the center was Adel, still trying to remember how to make his bomb explode. Of course, the cops shot him to pieces. Our Adel disintegrated without hurting a soul."

Hussein guffawed, writhing in his chair. "Only Adel could go out like that!"

"How about Bilal?" I asked.

"Nobody knows where he is. There was this important guy, a leader of the resistance, and Bilal was supposed to drive him to Kirkuk. The bigwig waited for him at the pre-arranged meeting place, but Bilal never showed up. We still don't know what happened to him. We've looked in the morgues, the hospitals, everywhere, even in the police stations and army barracks where we've got people, but . . . nothing. No trace of the car he was driving, either."

I stayed at Tariq's place for a week, enduring Hussein's outbursts of incongruous laughter. He was a bit cracked, Hussein was. There was something broken in his mind. His brother entrusted him with domestic errands only. Hussein whiled away his unoccupied hours settled in an armchair, watching TV and loitering until the next time he was sent out to buy supplies or pick somebody up.

One single time, Yaseen authorized me to go on a mission with Hassan and Tariq. We were to transfer a hostage from Baghdad to a cooperative farm. We left in broad daylight. Tariq knew all the shortcuts and back roads and circumvented every checkpoint. The hostage was a European woman, a member of an NGO, kidnapped from the clinic where she worked as a physician. She'd been shut up in the cellar of a villa not far from a police station. We took her out of there with no problem, right under the cops' noses, and delivered her to another group headquartered on a farm about twenty kilometers south of the city.

After this accomplishment, I thought I'd earned a higher level of trust, and I expected to be sent on a second mission shortly. I expected in vain. Three weeks dragged by, and still no sign from Yaseen. He visited us from time to time and talked at length with Hassan and Tariq, and sometimes he shared a meal with us; but then, Salah, the blacksmith's son-in-law, came by to pick him up, and I was left unsatisfied.

# 15

*   •   *

I slept badly. I think I dreamed about Kafr Karam, but I'm not sure. I lost the thread the second I opened my eyes. My head was stuffed with indistinct images, fixed on a screen that smelled of burning, and I woke up with the odor of my village in my nose.

From my deep, echoless sleep, I kept only the stabbing pain that racked my joints. I wasn't overjoyed to recognize the room where I'd been wasting away for weeks, waiting for I knew not what. I felt like the smallest in a set of Russian nesting dolls; the room was the next-size doll, the house the next after that, and so on, with the foul-smelling neighborhood as the lid. I was inside my body like a rat in a trap. My mind raced in every direction but found no way out. Was this, I wondered, claustrophobia? I needed to come unglued, to explode like a bomb, to be useful somehow.

I staggered to the bathroom. The terry-cloth towel, filthy beyond expression, hung from a nail. The windowpane had last been touched by a cleaning rag several decades ago. The place smelled like stale urine and mildew; it made me nauseous.

On the dirty sink, a battered piece of soap lay next to an intact tube of toothpaste. The mirror showed me the haggard face of a young man at the end of his rope. I looked at myself the way you look at a stranger.

There was no water. I went downstairs. Hussein was sunk in his armchair, watching an animated film on TV and chuckling as he nibbled roasted almonds from a plate beside him. On the screen, a band of alley cats, fresh from their garbage cans, were mistreating a terrified kitten. Hussein relished the fear the little animal embodied, lost in the suburban jungle.

"Where are the others?" I asked him.

He didn't hear me. I went to the kitchen, made myself some coffee, and returned to the living room. Hussein had switched channels and was now absorbed in a wrestling match.

"Where are Hassan and Tariq?"

"I'm not supposed to know," he grumbled. "They said they'd be back before nightfall, and they're still not here."

"Has anyone called?"

"No one."

"You think something's gone wrong?"

"If my brother had run into problems, I would have felt it."

"Maybe we should call Yaseen and find out what's up."

"Forbidden. He's always the one who does the calling."

I glanced out the window. The streets were bathed in the bright morning light. Soon people would emerge from their miserable houses and kids would invade the neighborhood like crickets.

Hussein manipulated the television's remote control, making a sequence of different broadcasts flash by on the screen. None of the programs interested him. He fidgeted in his chair, but he didn't turn off the TV. Then, abruptly, he said, "May I ask you a question, cousin?"

"Of course."

"You mean it? You'll answer me straight out?"

"Why not?"

He threw back his head and laughed that absurd, cringe-inducing laugh of his, which I was really starting to loathe; as usual, it seemed to have no cause and come from nowhere. It was all I heard, day and night, because Hussein never slept. He was in his armchair round the clock, clutching the remote control like a magic wand, changing worlds and languages every five minutes.

"So you'll be frank?"

"I'll do my best."

His eyes gleamed in a funny way; I felt sorry for him. He said, "Do you think I'm . . . nuts?"

His throat tightened on the last word. He looked so wretched, I was embarrassed.

"Why are you asking me that?"

"That's not an answer, cousin."

I started to avert my eyes, but his dissuaded me. "I don't think you're . . . nuts," I said.

"Liar! In hell, you're going to hang from your tongue over a barbecue. You're just like the others, cousin. You say one thing and think the opposite. But don't kid yourself—I'm not crazy. I've got a full tank and all the accessories. I know how to count on my fingers, and I know how to read people's eyes to see what they're hiding from me. It's true that I can't stop myself from laughing, but that doesn't mean I've flipped out. I laugh because . . . because . . . well, I don't know exactly why. Some things can't be explained. I caught the laughing bug watching that simpleton Adel get all frazzled because he couldn't find the button to blow himself up. I wasn't far away, and I was observing him as he mingled with the other candidates in front of the police recruiting center. At that moment, I was in a panic. And when the cops fired on him and he exploded, it was as if I disintegrated along with him. He was someone I really liked. He grew up on our patio. I sincerely mourned him, but then the mourning was over, and now, whenever I picture him stabbing at his explosive belt and cursing, I burst out laughing. It was so insane . . . but that doesn't make me a nutcase. I can count on my fingers, and I can tell what's right and wrong."

"I never said you were a nutcase, Hussein."

"Neither have the others. But they think it. You imagine I don't see that? Before, they used to send me on real missions. Ambushes, kidnappings, executions—I was at the top of the list. Now they let me buy provisions or pick up someone in my old car. When I volunteer for a serious job, they tell me not to bother, they've got all the guys they need, and they don't want to expose our flank. What does that mean, 'expose our flank'?"

"They haven't given me anything to do yet, either."

"You're lucky, cousin. Because I'm going to tell you what I think. Our cause is just, but we're defending it very badly. If I laugh from time to time, maybe that's the reason why."

"You're talking rubbish, Hussein."

"Where's it getting us, this war? Can you see the end of it?"

"Shut up, Hussein."

"But I'm speaking the truth. What's going on makes no sense. Killing, killing, and more killing. Day and night. On the squares, in the mosques. Nobody knows who's who anymore, and everyone has it in for everyone else."

"You're raving. . . ."

"You know how Adnan, the baker's son, died? The story is, he flung himself heroically against a checkpoint, but that's a crock. He was sick of all the slaughter. He'd been in action full-time, sniping one day, blowing things up the next. Targeting markets and civilians. And then one morning, he blew up a school bus, killed a lot of kids, and one of the bodies wound up in a tree. When the emergency units arrived on the scene, they picked up the dead and wounded, put them in ambulances, and took them to the hospital. It was only two days later that people on the ground began to smell the dead kid decomposing up in the tree. Adnan happened to be in the area that day—just by chance—and he saw the volunteers pulling the kid out of the branches. I'm telling you, Adnan did a U-turn on the spot. He completely flipped. He stopped being the dedicated warrior we all knew. And one night, he put on a belt stuffed with loaves of bread—baguettes, all around his waist, so they looked like sticks of dynamite—and he went to a checkpoint and started taunting the soldiers. After a bit of that, he suddenly opened his coat and revealed the harness he was wearing, and the soldiers turned him into a sieve. As long as the belt didn't explode, they kept firing. They used up all

their clips and their comrades' clips, too. Adnan was reduced to a pulp. Afterward, you couldn't tell the chunks of
flesh from the chunks of bread. And that's the truth,
cousin. Adnan didn't die in combat; he went to his death of
his own free will, without a weapon and without a battle
cry. He simply committed suicide."

There was no chance that I was going to stay in Hussein's
company one minute longer. I placed my cup on the low
table and made for the door.

Hussein stayed in his armchair. He said, "You haven't
killed anyone yet, cousin. So get the hell out. Set your sails
for another horizon and don't look back. I'd do the same
thing if I didn't have a battalion of ghosts holding on to my
coattails."

I looked him up and down, trying to make him dissolve
with my eyes. I said, "I think Yaseen's right, Hussein. Running errands is all you're good for."

And I hastened to slam the door behind me.

◈　　●　　◈

I went to look at the Tigris. Turning my back on the city, I
fixed my gaze on the water and tried to forget the buildings
on the other bank. Kafr Karam occupied my mind. I imagined the sandy stadium where youngsters chased soccer
balls; I saw the two recovering palm trees, the mosque, the
barber clipping away at the skulls of his clientele, the two
cafés majestically ignoring each other, the clouds of dust
swirling along the silver-gray desert trails, and then I saw

the gap where Kadem and I listened to Fairuz, and the horizons, as dead as the seasons. . . . I tried to retrace my steps,
to return to the village; my memories refused to follow me.
The images blurred, stopped, and disappeared under a
great brown stain, and Baghdad caught up with me again,
with its streets bled white, its ghost-populated esplanades,
its ragged trees, and its tumult. The sun beat down like a
brute, so close that you could have reached it with a fire-
man's hose. I think I'd walked across a good part of the city,
but I remembered nothing of what I might have encoun-
tered, seen, or heard. I'd been wandering around ever since
I left Hussein.

As the river didn't suffice to drown my thoughts, I
started walking again, without any notion of where to go.
I was lost in Baghdad, my obsession drowned out by the
roar of the void, surrounded on all sides by whirling shadows—a grain of sand in a storm.

I didn't love this city. For me, it represented nothing.
Meant nothing. I traversed it like a land accursed. We were
two incompatible misfortunes, two parallel worlds that ran
side by side and never met.

On my left, under a metal footbridge, a broken-down
van attracted a group of children. Farther off, near the stadium—now fallen silent—some American trucks were leaving a military installation. In the roar of the convoy, Kafr
Karam reappeared. Our house was in shadow, and I could
see only the indefinable tree, under which no one was sitting
anymore. There was nobody on the patio, either. The house
was empty, soulless and ghost-free. I looked for my sisters,
my mother . . . and found no one. Except for the cut on

Bahia's neck, I saw no face or furtive shape. It was as though my loved ones, once so dear to me, had been banished from my memory. Something in me had broken and collapsed, burying all trace of my family. . . .

A bellowing truck made me jump back up on the curb. "Wake up, asshole!" the driver shouted. "You think you're in your mama's backyard?"

Some pedestrians stopped, ready to gather other rubberneckers around them. It was crazy, but in Baghdad the smallest incident attracted a huge crowd of spectators. I waited for the truck driver to continue on his way before I crossed the street.

My feet were burning. I'd been pounding the pavement for hours.

I sat down at a table on a café terrace and ordered a soda. I hadn't eaten all day, but I wasn't hungry. I was just worn-out.

"I don't believe it," someone behind me said.

What joy I felt, what relief, when I recognized Omar the Corporal. His new overalls were stretched tightly across his belly.

"What are you doing in these parts?"

"I'm drinking a soda."

"You can get a soda anywhere. Why here?"

"You ask too many questions, Omar. I can't think straight."

He spread his arms to embrace me and pressed his lips insistently against my cheeks. He was genuinely happy to see me again. Dropping into a chair, he mopped his face with his handkerchief. "I'm sweating like a Camembert," he said breathlessly. "But I'm truly happy to find you here, cousin. Really."

"Likewise."

He hailed the waiter and ordered a lemonade. "So," he said. "What's new?"

"How's Hany?"

"Oh, him. He's a lunatic. You never know what you're getting with him."

"Is he still planning to become an expatriate?"

"He'd get lost in the countryside. That one is a certified city dweller. If he loses sight of his building, he cries for help. He was playing games with me, know what I mean? He wanted to make sure I cared about him. . . . What's up with you?"

"Are you still with your old warrant officer?"

"Where else could I go? With him, at least, when things get tight, I know he'll advance me some cash. He's a nice guy. And you still haven't told me what you're up to around here."

"Nothing. All I do is go in circles."

"I see. Look, I don't have to tell you, you can always count on me. If you want, I could talk to my boss again. We might be able to work something out."

"You wouldn't be thinking about paying a visit to Kafr Karam, would you? I've got a little money I want to send to my family."

"Not anytime soon. Why don't you just go back home— I mean, if you think there's nothing for you in Baghdad?"

Omar was trying to sound me out. He was dying to know whether he could bring up certain delicate subjects again without making me mad. What he read in my face made him recoil. He lifted up his hands and said in a conciliatory voice, "It was just a question, that's all."

According to my watch, it was a quarter past three. "I have to go back," I said.

"Is it far?"

"A fair distance."

"I could give you a ride. You want? My van's in the square, close by."

"No, I don't want to trouble you."

"You won't be troubling me, cousin. I've just dropped off a sideboard, and now I've got nothing else to do."

"Well, I'm warning you, it's 'way out of your way. You're going to have to go the long way around."

"I've got plenty of gas."

He downed his lemonade in one swallow and signaled to the cashier not to let me pay. "Put this on my tab, Saad."

The cashier refused my money and jotted down the amount of the check on a piece of paper, next to Omar's name.

      ⬧    ●    ⬧

Night was starting to fall. The last glints of the sun splashed the upper stories of buildings. The noises of the street subsided. The day had been a rough one: three attacks in the city center and a skirmish around a suburban church.

We were in Tariq's house. He, Yaseen, Salah, and Hassan had shut themselves up in a room on the second floor, no doubt refining the plans for the next operation. Hussein and I weren't invited to the meeting. Hussein pretended not to care about this slight, but I sensed that it had stung him. As for me, I was beside myself, and like Hussein, I brooded over my anger in silence.

The upstairs door creaked, and a babble of conversation signaled the end of the conference. Salah came down first. He'd changed a great deal. He was enormous, with a mug like a bouncer and hairy fists constantly clenched, as if he were strangling a snake. Everything in him seemed to be boiling, like the inside of a volcano. He seldom spoke, never gave an opinion, and maintained his distance from the others. All his attention was focused on Yaseen, from whom he was inseparable. When we saw each other for the first time since Kafr Karam, Salah hadn't even greeted me.

Yaseen, Hassan, and Tariq stopped and chatted for a while at the top of the stairs before coming down to join us. Their faces expressed neither tension nor enthusiasm. They all sat on the padded bench facing us. With great reluctance, Hussein picked up the remote control that was lying on the floor at his feet and turned off the little set.

Yaseen asked him, "You burned up the engine on that car of yours?"

"No one told me I had to put oil in it."

"You have a warning light on your dashboard."

"I saw a red light come on, but I didn't know why."

"You could have asked Hassan."

"Hassan pretends I'm not there."

"What do you mean by that?" Hassan asked angrily.

Hussein made a vague gesture with one hand and detached himself from his armchair.

"I'm talking to you," Yaseen said in an authoritative voice.

"I'm not deaf; I just gotta go piss."

Salah quivered from his head to his feet. He was none too pleased with Hussein's attitude. Had it been up to Salah, he would have fixed Hussein's ass on the spot. Salah couldn't bear it when anyone disrespected his leader. He snorted loudly, crossed his arms tight against his chest, and clenched his jaw.

Yaseen gave Hassan an interrogatory look. Hassan spread his arms to show he was powerless and then walked toward the bathroom. We heard him talking softly to his twin brother.

Tariq offered us a cup of tea.

"I don't have time," Yaseen said.

"It won't take more than a minute," our host said.

"In that case, you've got fifty-eight seconds."

Tariq made a dash for the kitchen.

Yaseen's cell phone rang. He put it to his ear and listened; his face contracted. He stood up abruptly, walked over to the window, and, with his back against the wall, cautiously lifted the curtain.

"I see them," he said into his phone. "What the fuck are they doing there? Nobody knows we're here. You're sure they're after us?" With his free hand, he ordered Salah to go upstairs and have a look at what was going on in the street. Salah took the steps four at a time. Yaseen kept talking into his mobile phone. "As far as I know, this area has been fairly calm."

Hassan, on his way back from the bathroom, immediately saw that something was wrong. He slipped to the other side of the window and gently moved the curtain aside. What he saw made him spring backward. He cursed and ran to an armoire, where a light machine gun was concealed. Along the way, he looked into the kitchen and alerted Tariq, who was still busy preparing tea.

Salah came back downstairs, unperturbed. "There are at least twenty cops around the house," he announced, pulling a huge gun out from under his belt.

Yaseen examined the roof of the building opposite and then twisted his neck in order to see the terraces of the buildings closer to us. He spoke again into his cell phone: "And you're where, exactly? Very good. You take them from behind and cut a hole in their trap big enough for us to get through. . . . By the street the garage is on, you're sure? How many are there? . . . That's how we'll do it. You keep them entertained on your side, and I'll take care of the rest."

He snapped his phone shut and said, "Looks like some bastard's ratted us out. There are cops on the roofs north, east, and south of here. Jawad and his men are going to help us get out of this. We're going to charge the garage. There'll be three or four collaborators for us to deal with."

Tariq was panic-stricken. "I swear to you, Yaseen, there's no mole in this sector."

"We'll talk about that later. Right now, you have to concentrate on getting out of here in one piece."

Tariq started to fetch a Soviet-made rocket launcher, but as he reached the middle of the living room, a windowpane burst into fragments, and he fell over backward, already dead. The bullet, probably fired from a neighboring roof terrace, had shattered his upper jaw. Blood began spurting from his face and branching out across the tiled floor. Immediately, a hail of projectiles crashed into the room, demolishing the silver, riddling the walls, and raising a tornado of dust and unspecific fragments all around us. We threw ourselves on the floor and began crawling toward anything that might pass for shelter. Salah fired blindly through the window, howling like a savage as he emptied his clip. Calmer than Salah, Yaseen had crouched down in the spot where he'd been standing. He stared at Tariq's contorted body as he pondered our next move. Hussein was hunched in the hallway with his fly open. When he saw Tariq stretched out on the floor, he burst out laughing.

Salah sprang to the rocket launcher, loaded it, and, with a movement of his head, ordered us to leave the living room. Hassan covered Yaseen, who ran for the hallway. The automatic-weapons fire abruptly stopped, and through the ensuing deathlike silence, we could hear the distant crying of women and children. Hassan took advantage of the lull to push me ahead of him.

The firing began again, as intensely as before, but this time we weren't the target. Yaseen explained that Jawad and his men were creating a diversion and that this was the signal for us to abandon the house by the rear entrance. Salah aimed his launcher at a terrace and fired. A monstrous, eardrum-jangling explosion was followed by a huge conflagration, which masked the living room in a cloud of thick caustic smoke. "Run!" Salah shouted. "I'll cover you!"

Stunned, I started running behind the others. Deafening bursts of reciprocal gunfire greeted me outside. Bullets ricocheted around me and whistled past my ears. Folded in half, my hands on my temples, I felt as though I were going through walls. I slipped past a doorway and fell onto a pile of garbage. Hussein laughed and ran straight ahead. His brother caught up with him and forced him into a side street. Gunfire broke out in front of us; a rocket exploded behind us. Someone screamed, apparently struck by the fragments. His cries pursued me as I clenched my teeth and ran, ran as I'd never run before in my life. . . .

# 16

•

Yaseen was in a red rage. In the hideout where we'd gone to ground after managing to escape the police raid, he was all we could hear. He punched the furniture and kicked the doors. Hassan stood with folded arms and kept his eyes cast down. His twin brother was in a heap at the end of the entrance hall, sitting on the floor with his head between his knees and his hands on the nape of his neck. Salah was missing, and that fact redoubled Yaseen's fury. He was used to ambushes, but leaving behind his most faithful lieutenant! "I want the head of the traitor who ratted on us," he fumed. "I want it on a tray."

He considered his cell phone. "Why doesn't Salah call?"

Yaseen's coolheadedness was gone, lost to a combination of anger and anxiety. When he wasn't spraying us with his whitish spittle, he was knocking over everything in his way. Although we hadn't occupied our new refuge very long, nothing was where it had been when we entered.

"There was no mole in this sector," Yaseen repeated. "Tariq was adamant. We were in that house for months, and we never had any sort of problem whatsoever. Somebody must have made a mistake, and I have no doubt it was either you"—he jabbed his finger at me—"or Hussein."

"I didn't make any mistake," Hussein growled. "And stop treating me like a retard."

Yaseen, irritated by our silence, had been waiting for just such an opening as this. He leapt on Hussein, grabbed him by his shirt collar, and lifted him off the floor. "Don't talk to me in that tone. Understand?"

Hussein let his arms hang down in a sign of submission but lifted his head high enough to show his leader he wasn't afraid of him. Yaseen pushed him away brutally and watched him slide down the wall to his initial position. When Yaseen turned in my direction, I felt his burning eyes go all the way through me.

"How about you?" he asked me. "Are you sure you haven't been dropping any white pebbles along your trail?"

I was still dazed. The explosions and the screams resounded in my head. I couldn't believe we'd escaped from that deluge of projectiles, running like madmen through a warren of side streets, ducking past more than one murderous cross fire, and now we were safe and sound. Although unable to feel my legs, I was still, somehow, on my feet, but wrung-out, dumbstruck, undone, and I really didn't need to be subjected to another ordeal. Yaseen's glare menaced me like a blade.

"Have you made some new friend? Or told somebody something you shouldn't have?"

"I don't know anyone."

"No one? Then how do you explain the shit that just went down? For months, Tariq's place is a cozy hideout, and then, all of a sudden . . . Either you're jinxed or you've been careless. My guys are veterans. They look twice before they take a step. You're the only one who's not completely up to speed. Who do you hang out with outside our group? Where do you go when you leave the hideout? What do you do with your time?"

His questions landed on me like blows, one after the other, without leaving me time to get a word in or catch my breath. My hands couldn't stifle them or fend them off. Yaseen was trying to push me to the limit. He was in a fury, he needed someone to take it out on, and I was the weak link in the chain. It was the age-old story: When you can't make sense of your misfortune, you invent a culprit for it. I strung together denials, trying hard to resist, to defend myself, to keep from getting upset, and then, suddenly, in a cry of outrage, and without realizing what I was doing, I let slip the name of Omar the Corporal. Maybe it was fatigue, or vexation, or just a way of removing myself from Yaseen's thoroughly vile scrutiny. By the time I recognized my blunder, it was too late. I would have given my soul to have my words back, but Yaseen's face had already turned crimson.

"What did you say? Omar the Corporal?"

"I see him every now and then, that's all."

"Does he know where you live?"

"No. Once he gave me a ride to the square, but only once. He never saw the house—he left me at the gas station."

I hoped that Yaseen would drop the subject and go back to harassing Hussein or maybe even turn on Hassan. I hoped in vain.

"Am I dreaming, or what? You led that worthless prick to our hiding place?"

"He picked me up along the way and kindly agreed to drop me off at the service station. Where's the harm in that? The station's a long way from Tariq's place. Omar couldn't possibly have guessed where I was going. And besides, we're not talking about just anybody; we're talking about Omar. He'd never give us up."

"Did he know you were with me?"

"Come on, Yaseen, it doesn't make any difference."

"Did he know or not?"

"Yes."

"You idiot! You moron! You dared to lead that yellow coward to our—"

"He had nothing to do with the raid."

"How do you know? Baghdad—no, the whole country— is full of snitches and collaborators."

"Wait, Yaseen, wait. You're wrong about—"

"Shut up! Not another word! You have nothing to say. Nothing, you understand? Where does that fat fuck live?"

I saw that I'd made a serious mistake; Yaseen wouldn't hesitate to shoot me down if I didn't try to redeem myself. He made me guide him to Omar's place that very night. Along the way, seeing that he seemed to have relaxed somewhat, I begged him not to do anything rash. I felt sick, very sick; I didn't know where to turn, and I was consumed by remorse and by the fear that I had caused a terrible misunderstanding. Yaseen promised me that if Omar had done nothing wrong, he'd leave him alone.

Hassan was at the wheel. He had a skinning knife hidden under his jacket, and the rigidity of his neck muscles gave me gooseflesh. Yaseen, in the front passenger seat, examined his fingernails, a blank look on his face. I cringed in the rear seat, my hands damp, my guts roiling, my thighs squeezed together to suppress an irresistible need to piss.

Avoiding the roadblocks and the main thoroughfares, we surreptitiously made our way to the poor neighborhood that had been my home for a brief while. The building in question reared up in the darkness like a landmark in the underworld. There was no light in any window and no sign of any living thing outside. It must have been three o'clock in the morning. We parked the car in a small, damaged courtyard and, after a quick look around, slipped into the building. I had a copy of the apartment key, which Yaseen confiscated and inserted into the lock. He slowly opened the door, groped for the light switch, and flicked it on. Omar was lying on the straw mattress on the floor, stark naked, with one leg wrapped around Hany, whose pallid flesh was likewise completely unclothed. At first, the sight threw us into confusion; Yaseen was the first to recover. He drew himself up, hands on his hips, and silently contemplated the two nude bodies at his feet.

"Get a load of this," he said. "I knew Omar the Drunkard, and here we have Omar the Sodomite, getting off with boys now. A charming sight."

There was so much contempt in his voice that I gulped.

The lovers were sound asleep, surrounded by empty wine bottles and soiled plates. They stank, the two of them. Hassan prodded Omar with the tip of his shoe. The Corporal shook himself heavily, gurgled, and resumed snoring.

"Go and wait for us in the car," Yaseen said. It was an order.

I was four or five years younger than he was, and he considered me insufficiently mature to witness such a spectacle, particularly in his presence.

"You promised me you'd leave him alone if he had nothing to do with the raid," I reminded Yaseen.

"Do what I tell you."

I obeyed.

A few minutes later, Yaseen and Hassan joined me in the car. Since I'd heard no screams and no shots, I believed the worst had been avoided. Then I saw Hassan wipe his bloodstained hands under the armpits of his shirt, and I understood.

"It was him," Yaseen announced as he got into the car. "He confessed."

"You stayed in there less than five minutes. How did you make him talk so fast?"

"Tell him, Hassan."

Hassan put the car in first gear and drove out of the courtyard. When we reached the end of the street, he turned to me and declared, "It was him all right, cousin. You've got nothing to reproach yourself for. That piece of shit didn't hesitate a second when he saw who we were. He spit at us and said, 'Go fuck yourselves.'"

"He knew why you were there?"

"He figured it out the second he woke up. He even laughed in our faces. Look, cousin, some things are clear, and this is one of them. We're talking about a disgusting son of a bitch, a pig and a traitor. His wild nights are over."

I tried to find out more; I asked exactly what Omar had said and what had happened to Hany. Yaseen pivoted in his seat and growled in my direction: "You want a notarized report, or what? This is war, not lace-making. If you think you're not ready, then get the hell out, right now. No one has to know."

I hated him. God, I hated him more than I believed myself capable of hating anyone. For his part, he was fully aware of the hatred he inspired in me. I know because I saw his vaunted stare waver a little before my eyes. At that precise moment, I realized I had just made myself a sworn enemy, and I understood that Yaseen would seize the next occasion to do me wrong.

*     •     *

Shortly after noon, when we were sitting around gnawing our fingernails in our new hideout, Yaseen's mobile phone rang. It was Salah, who had miraculously made it out of Tariq's house unscathed. The television news reports declared that the house itself was completely in ruins. It had collapsed under a barrage of artillery shells, and then fire had devastated a good part of the remains. According to the local residents, the pitched battle had lasted all evening, and the reinforcements sent to the scene of the clash had only intensified the confusion; electrical power had long since been cut, and after some of the neighbors were struck by stray bullets or grenade fragments, panic had spread throughout the area.

When Yaseen recognized his lieutenant's voice on the telephone, he nearly burst into tears. He chided the fortunate survivor, reproaching him for his "radio silence"; then he consented to listen without further interruption. He nodded, running his finger under his collar again and again as we watched him in silence. At last, he raised his chin and spoke into the handset: "You can't bring him here? Ask Jawad. He knows how to transfer a parcel."

Yaseen snapped the phone shut and, without a word, hurried into the next room and slammed the door in our faces.

⁂　●　⁂

The "parcel" arrived for us that evening, in the trunk of a car driven by a uniformed police officer, a tall, strapping fellow I'd seen two or three times in Sayed's store, ordering television sets from us. Whenever he'd come in, he'd been wearing civilian clothes. Now, it turned out, he was Jawad—his nom de guerre—and, to my great surprise, he was the deputy superintendent of this police district.

He explained to us that he'd been returning from a routine mission when he discovered that his unit's assault team had been sent into action. "When the duty officer read me the coordinates of the operation, I couldn't believe it. The superintendent's target was your hideout. He wanted to conduct the action on his own and score points on his rivals."

"You could have warned me immediately," Yaseen said reproachfully.

"I wasn't sure. You were in one of the most secure refuges in Baghdad. I didn't see how they could have gotten close to you, not with all the alarm bells I'd set up all around. Somebody would have warned me. But not wanting to take any chances, I went to the area where the raid was about to take place, and that's when things became clear."

He lifted the trunk of his car, which he'd parked in the garage. A half-smothered man was lying curled up inside, wrapped like a sausage in a roll of clear packing tape. His mouth was gagged, and his face looked lumpy and battered.

"It was him. He's the one who gave you up. He was there before the operation began, showing the superintendent your hideout."

Yaseen shook his head sadly.

Thrusting his muscular arms into the trunk, Salah violently extracted the prisoner, threw him to the ground, and kicked him away from the car.

Yaseen squatted down beside the stranger and tore off his gag. "If you yell, I'll poke out your eyes and throw your tongue to the rats."

The man must have been around forty years old, with a scrawny body, a malnourished face, and graying temples. He wriggled in his bonds like a maggot.

"I've seen that face before," Hussein said.

"He was your neighbor," the policeman said, strutting a little with his thumbs hooked in his belt. "He lived in the building on the corner next to the grocery, the one with the climbing plants on the front."

Yaseen stood up. "Why?" he asked the stranger. "Why did you give us up? We're fighting for you, dammit!"

"I never asked you to," the informer replied disdainfully. "You think I want to be saved by hoodlums like you? I'd rather die!"

Salah gave the man a brutal kick in the side, knocking

the breath out of him. He rolled about, gasping for air. But as soon as he got his wind back, the snitch took up where he'd left off. "You consider yourselves fedayeen," he panted. "But you're nothing but murderers. Vandals. Child-killers. I'm not afraid of you. Do what you want with me, you won't change my mind. I think you're a pack of mad dogs. Criminals, heathens, head cases. I loathe you!"

He spat at us, one after the other.

Yaseen was astounded. "Is this guy normal?" he asked Jawad.

"Perfectly," the police officer declared. "He teaches in a primary school."

Yaseen thought for a while, holding his chin between his thumb and index finger. "How did he spot us? None of us is on any poster anywhere. None of us even has a police record. How did he know what we were?"

"I'd pick that gorilla face out of a million gorilla faces," the snitch said contemptuously, jerking his head in Salah's direction. "You bastard, you dog, you son of a whore . . ."

Salah was ready to take him apart, but Yaseen held him back.

"I was there when you killed Mohammed Sobhi, the union leader," the informer said, his face crimson with fury. "I was in the car, waiting for him in the basement garage. And I saw you shoot him in the back when he stepped out of the elevator. In the back. Like the cowardly murderer you are. Disgusting pig! If my hands were free, I'd break you in half. That's all you're good for, shooting someone from behind and running like a rabbit. And afterward, you think you're a hero and you swagger around the square. If Iraq has to be defended by spineless cowards like you, I'd rather let it go to the fucking dogs. What a pathetic bunch of wankers. What a—"

Yaseen kicked him in the face, cutting him off. Then Yaseen said, "Did you understand any of that rant, Jawad?"

The police officer twisted his mouth to one side. "Mohammed Sobhi was his brother. This prick recognized Salah when he saw him going into the place where you were holed up. Then he went to the station and informed the superintendent."

Yaseen pursed his lips and looked circumspect. "Gag him again," he ordered, "and take him somewhere far from here. I want him to die slowly, bit by bit. I want him to start rotting before he breathes his last."

Salah and Hassan assured him they'd carry out his orders. They stuffed the "parcel" back in the trunk of Jawad's car, got in, and drove out of the garage, preceded by Jawad himself, who was behind the wheel of Salah's car. Hussein closed the garage door.

Yaseen, his neck bent forward, his shoulders sagging, was still standing in the spot where he'd interrogated the prisoner. I stood a few steps behind him, severely tempted to leap onto his back. I had to go to the deepest part of my being to recover my breath and say to him, "You see? Omar had nothing to do with it."

It was as if I'd opened Pandora's box. Yaseen shook from head to toe and then whipped around to face me, brandishing his finger like a dagger. His voice gave me a chill when he said, "One more word out of you, just one tiny word, and I'll tear your throat out with my teeth." Whereupon he shoved me aside with the back of his hand and went to his room to mistreat the furniture.

❖     ●     ❖

I stepped out into the night. In the anemic lights of the boulevards, while the curfew was regaining the upper hand, I measured the incongruity of people and things. Baghdad had turned away everything, even its prayers. And as for me, I no longer recognized myself in mine. I walked along with a heavy heart, hugging the walls like a shadow puppet. . . . *What have I done? Almighty God! How will Omar ever forgive me?*

# 17

• 

Sleep had become my purgatory. Almost as soon as I dozed off, I started running again, fleeing through labyrinthine corridors with a shadowy shape hot on my heels. It was everywhere, even in my frantic breathing. . . . I jerked into consciousness, drenched from head to foot, my arms waving in front of me. It was always there—in the bright light of dawn, in the silence of the night, hovering over my bed. I clutched my temples with both hands and made myself so small that I disappeared under the sheets. *What have I done?* The horrible question penetrated me at full tilt, like a falcon striking a bustard. Omar's ghost had become my companion animal, my walking grief, my intoxication, and my madness. All I had to do was to lower my eyelids and it would fill my mind, and when I opened my eyes, it hid the rest of the world. There was nothing left in the world except Omar's ghost and me. We *were* the world.

It was no use praying, no use beseeching him to spare me, if only for a minute; I supplicated in vain. He remained where he was, silent and disconcerted, so real that I could have touched him had I stretched out my hand.

A week passed, things grew more and more intense, and my inner turmoil, a compound of weakness and dread, steadily increased. I felt myself slipping deeper and deeper into depression. I wanted to die.

I went to see Sayed and informed him of my desire to get it over with. I volunteered for a suicide attack. It was the most conclusive of shortcuts, and the most worthwhile, as well. This idea, on my mind since well before the mistake that had led to the Corporal's execution, had by now become my fixation. I wasn't afraid. I had no attachment to anything anymore. I felt as qualified as any suicide bomber. Every morning, you could hear them exploding on the streets; every evening, some military post was attacked. The bombers went to their deaths as to a party, in the midst of amazing fireworks displays.

"You'll stand on line like everybody else," Yaseen later told me. "And you'll wait your turn."

Any rapport that had existed between Yaseen and me was gone. He couldn't stand me; I detested him. He was always after me, interrupting me when I tried to get a word in edgewise, rejecting my efforts to make myself useful. Our hostility made life miserable for the other members of our group, and things promised to get worse. Yaseen was trying to break me, trying to make me toe the line. I was no hothead; I never challenged his authority or his charisma. I simply hated him, and he took the contempt he aroused in me for insubordination.

Sayed eventually faced the obvious facts. My cohabitation with Yaseen was at risk of ending badly and endangering the entire group. Sayed authorized me to come back to his store, and I returned in haste to my little upstairs room. Omar's ghost joined me there; now he had me all to himself. Nevertheless, I preferred the worst of his pestering to the mere sight of Yaseen.

It was after closing time on a Wednesday. I had dinner at the greasy spoon nearby and walked back to the store. The sun was going down in flames behind the buildings of the city. Sayed was waiting for me in the doorway, his eyes glittering in the obscurity. He was extremely excited.

We went up to my room. Once we were inside, he grabbed me by the shoulders and said, "Today I received the best news of my life."

His face was radiant as he hugged me to him, and then his happiness burst out. "It's fantastic, cousin. Fantastic."

He asked me to sit on the bed, made an effort to control his enthusiasm, and finally said, "I spoke to you about a mission. You wanted to see some action, and I told you maybe I had something for you, but I wanted to wait and be sure about it. Well, the miracle has taken place. I received the confirmation less than an hour ago. This incredible mission is now possible. Do you feel capable of accomplishing it?"

"I'll say I do."

"We're talking about the most important mission ever undertaken in history. The *final* mission. The mission that will bring about the unconditional capitulation of the West and return us permanently to our proper role on the world's stage. Do you believe you could—"

"I'm ready, Sayed. My life's at your disposal."

"It's not only a question of your life. People die every day—my life doesn't belong to me, either. But this is a crucial mission. It will require total, unfailing commitment."

"Are you starting to have doubts about me?"

"I wouldn't be here talking to you if I were."

"So where's the problem?"

"You're free to refuse. I don't want to pressure you in any way."

"Nobody's pressuring me. I accept the mission. Unconditionally."

"I appreciate your determination, cousin. For what it's worth, you have my entire confidence. I've been observing you ever since you first came into the store. Every time I lay eyes on you, I feel a kind of levitation; I take off. . . . Yet it was a difficult choice. There's no lack of candidates. But it means a lot to me that the chosen one is a boy from my hometown. Kafr Karam, the forgotten, will take its place in history," he concluded. Then he took me in his arms and kissed me on the forehead.

He had lifted me up into the ranks of those who are revered. That night, I dreamed about Omar again. But I didn't run away from him.

❊   ●   ❊

Sayed came back to sound me out once more. He wanted to be sure I hadn't spoken too soon. The day before launching the preparations for the mission, he told me, "I'll give you three more days. Think hard. At the end of that time, we're off."

"I've already thought hard. Now I want to act."

Sayed assigned me to a small but luxurious apartment with a view of the Tigris. The first time I went to the place, a photographer was waiting there for me. After the photo session, a barber cut my hair, and then I took a shower. As I was to leave Baghdad within a week, I went out to the post office to send Bahia the money I'd managed to put aside.

On a Friday, after the Great Prayer, I left Baghdad in a livestock truck driven by an old peasant in a turban. I was supposed to be his nephew and his shepherd. My new papers were in order and looked properly worn. My name appeared on various documents connected to the livestock business. We negotiated the roadblocks without difficulty and reached Ar Ramadi before nightfall. Sayed was waiting for us at a farm about twenty kilometers west of the town. He made sure that everything had gone well, ate dinner with us, and gave us the itinerary for the next stage before taking his leave. At dawn the following day, we were back on the road, bound for a little village on the slopes of the Badiet esh Sham, the plateau of the Syrian desert. There, another driver took me aboard his van. He and I spent the night in a small town and drove away before sunrise, heading for Ar Rutbah, not far from the Jordanian border. Sayed, who was already there, welcomed us in the courtyard of a health clinic. A physician in a graying lab coat invited us to wash up and occupy one of the patients' rooms. Our departure from the clinic was canceled on each of the following three days because of a military redeployment in the region. On the fourth day, taking advantage of a sandstorm, the driver and I set out for Jordan. Visibility was zero, but my companion drove calmly along, following desert trails he seemed to know with his eyes closed. After several hours of absorbing shocks and inhaling sand, we made a stop on the slopes of a valley, a barren place where the wind howled unceasingly. We drove onto a natural courtyard and took refuge in a cave. We had a bite to eat, and then the driver, a small, dried-up, impenetrable fellow, climbed to the top of a ridge. I saw him take out his cell phone and, apparently with the help of some sort of navigation device, indicate our coordinates. When he came back, he declared, "I won't have to sleep outdoors tonight." That was the only time he ever addressed a word to me. He entered the cave, lay down, and pretended he wasn't there.

The sandstorm began to subside, its surges coming at longer and longer intervals. The wind still sang in the crevices, but as the landscape steadily emerged from the ocher fog of the desert, the gusts gradually died down and then suddenly fell silent altogether.

The sun burned more brightly as it touched the rim of the earth, throwing the bare, jagged hills on the horizon into bold relief. Out of nowhere, two men riding mules appeared, climbing up the valley to our cave. Later, I would learn that they belonged to a ring of former smugglers who had turned to gunrunning and occasionally served as guides for the volunteers arriving from other countries to swell the ranks of the Iraqi resistance. My driver complimented them on their punctuality, inquired about the current operational situation in the sector, and turned me over to them. Without any sort of farewell, he returned to his vehicle and sped away.

The two strangers were tall and thin, their heads wrapped in dusty keffiyehs. Both of them wore jogging pants, thick sweaters, and espadrilles. The taller of the two sought to reassure me. "Everything's going fine," he said. He offered me a big woolen pullover and a hat. "Nights get cold here."

They helped me climb up on a mule and we set out. Night fell, and the wind came up again, icy and vexing. My guides took turns riding the other mule. The goat paths branched out before us, opalescent under the moon. We hurtled down some steep escarpments and clambered up others, stopping only to prick up our ears and scrutinize the features of the landscape that lay in shadow. The journey took place without incident, as my guides had foretold. We made a brief stop in a hollow to eat and regain our strength. I devoured several slices of dried meat and emptied a goatskin of springwater. My companions advised me not to eat too fast and to try to rest. They attended to my every need, regularly asking me if I was holding up all right or if I wanted to get off my mule and walk a little. I said I wanted to keep going.

We crossed the border into Jordan at about four o'clock in the morning. Two border patrols had passed each other a few moments before, one in a military 4×4, the other on foot. The observation post, recognizable by its watchtower and the light shining on its antenna, stood atop a hillock. My guides observed the post through infrared binoculars. When the squad of scouts returned to their quarters, we took our mules by the reins and slipped along a dry riverbed. A few kilometers farther on, a little van carrying a cargo of plastic bowls bore down upon us. A man wearing a traditional tunic and a Bedouin scarf around his head was at the steering wheel. He congratulated my two guides and traced on the ground a secure itinerary for their return to Iraq. He informed them that drones were flying over the area, explained how to elude their sweeps, and recommended a way to get around a unit of coalition forces freshly deployed behind the line of demarcation. The guides asked a few practical questions; when they were satisfied, they wished us good luck and began their journey back.

"You can relax now," the new stranger said to me. "From this point on, it's a piece of cake. You're in the best hands in the business."

He was wizened and swarthy. His large head, too big for his shoulders, made him seem unsteady on his feet. His full lips opened on two rows of gold teeth that sparkled in the rising sun. He drove like a madman, with no regard for potholes and no reticence about slamming on the brakes, which he did abruptly and violently, often catapulting me against the windshield.

Sayed reappeared that evening, in my new guide's house. He embraced me for a long time.

"Two more stages," he said. "And then you'll be able to rest."

The following day, after a substantial breakfast, he drove me to a border village in a large, high-powered car. There, he turned me over to Shakir and Imad, two young men who looked like students, and he said to me, "On the other side, there's Syria, and then, right after that, Lebanon. I'll see you in Beirut in two days."

BEIRUT

# 18

\* • \*

My sojourn in Beirut is drawing to its close. I've been waiting for three weeks now. I count the hours on my fingers or stand at the window in my room, staring down at the deserted street. The rain drums on the windowpanes. On the windswept sidewalk, a tramp blows into his fists to warm his fingers. He's been there for a good while, on the lookout for a charitable soul, but I've yet to see anyone slip him a coin. His leggings are soaked through, his shoes are waterlogged, and his general appearance is simply grotesque. Living like a stray dog, practically in the gutter—that's obscene. This person, possessing not so much as a shadow, isolated in his wretchedness like a worm in a rotten fruit, can somehow forget that he's dead and over with. I feel no compassion for him. I tell myself that fate has brought him so low in order for him to function as a symbol; he focuses my awareness of life's unbearable inanity. What hopes does this man have for tomorrow? Surely he hopes for something, but for what? For manna to rain down upon him from heaven? For a passerby to notice his destitution? For

someone to take pity on him? What a fool! Is there life after pity?

Kadem was only partly right. It's not that the world's
grown base; it's that men wallow in baseness. I've come to
Beirut because I refuse to be like that tramp. I refuse to
be one of the living dead. Either live like a man or die as a
martyr—there's no other alternative for one who wants to
be free. I'm not comfortable in the role of the defeated. Ever
since that night when the American soldiers burst into our
house, overturning our ancestral values and the order of
things, I've been waiting! I'm waiting for the moment when
I'll recover my self-esteem, without which a man is nothing
but a stain. I think of myself as poised on the verge of
everything and nothing. What I've gone through, lived
through, been subjected to so far—none of that counts.
That night was like a freeze-frame. That was when the
earth stopped turning for me. I'm not in Lebanon; I'm not
in a hotel; I'm in a coma. And whether I emerge from it and
go on or stay in it and rot is up to me.

Sayed has personally seen to it that I want for nothing.
He's lodged me in one of the most expensive suites in the hotel and put at my disposal Imad and Shakir, two charming
young men who treat me most respectfully and stand ready
day or night, alert to the merest sign, poised to carry out my
most extravagant wishes. I will not let any of this go to my
head. I'm still the shy, retiring boy from Kafr Karam. Even
though I know the importance I've assumed, I haven't broken any of the rules that formed my character in simplicity
and propriety. My only caprice was to request that the television, the radio, and all the pictures on the walls be removed
from the suite; I wanted to be left with the strict minimum—

namely, the furniture and a few bottles of mineral water in the minibar. Had it been up to me, I would have chosen a cave in the desert, far from the laughable vanities of people who lead pampered lives. I wanted to be my own focus, my own reference point; I wanted to spend the remainder of my stay in Lebanon preparing myself mentally, so that I'd be equal to the task my people have entrusted to me.

I'm no longer afraid of being alone in the dark.

I've filled my lungs with the mustiness of the tomb.

I'm ready!

I've tamed my thoughts and brought my doubts to heel. I'm keeping my spirits under firm control. My agonies, my hesitations, my blackouts are all ancient history. I'm the master of what goes on in my head. Nothing escapes me; nothing resists me. Dr. Jalal has smoothed my path and filled in my gaps. As for my former fears, now I summon them of my own accord; I line them up and inspect them. The great brown blotch that hid a portion of my memories when I was in Baghdad has faded away. I can return to Kafr Karam whenever I feel like it, enter any door, step into any patio, invade anyone's privacy. My mother, my sisters, my friends and relatives all come back to me, one after the other, and I remain calm. My room is inhabited by ghosts, by those who are absent. Omar shares my bed; Sulayman blows through like a gust of wind; the wedding guests immolated in the Haitems' orchards parade around me. Even my father is here. He prostrates himself at my feet, balls in the air. I don't turn away or cover my face. And when a blow from a rifle butt knocks him down, I don't help him up. I remain upright; my sphinxlike inflexibility prevents me from bending, even over my father.

In a few days, it will be the world that prostrates itself at my feet.

*The most important revolutionary mission undertaken since man learned to stiffen his spine!* And I'm the one who's been chosen to accomplish it. What a way of getting even with destiny! The practice of death has never seemed so euphoric, so cosmic.

At night, when I lie on the sofa facing the window, I remember the painful events of my life, and they all reinforce my commitment. I don't know exactly what I'm going to do or what will be the nature of my mission. "Something that'll make September eleventh seem like a noisy recess in an elementary school," Sayed said. One thing's for certain: I won't shrink from it!

There's a knock at my door. It's Dr. Jalal. He's wearing the same tracksuit he had on yesterday evening, and he still hasn't bothered to tie his shoelaces.

It's the first time he's ever crossed my threshold. His alcoholic breath spreads out like smoke. "I was wasting away in my room," he says. "Would it disturb you if I came in for a couple of minutes?"

"You're not disturbing me."

"Thanks."

He totters over to the sofa, scratching his butt with a hand thrust down inside his drawers. I'll bet he hasn't bathed for a good long time. He casts admiring glances around the room. "Wow!" he says. "Are you some mogul's son?"

"My father was a well digger."

"Mine wasn't anything."

He realizes he's said something outlandish and waves it

away with one hand. Then, crossing his legs, he leans against the back of the sofa and squints at the ceiling. "I didn't sleep a wink last night," he complains. "These days, I can hardly fall asleep at all."

"You work too much."

He waggles his chin. "I have no doubt you're right. These lecture tours are wearing me out."

I'd heard talk of Dr. Jalal—none of it good—while I was still in high school. I'd also read two or three of his books, including a treatise on jihadist fundamentalism entitled *Why Are Muslims Angry?*—a work that aroused a great deal of indignation among the clergy. At the time, he was a very controversial figure in Arab intellectual circles, and many of his adversaries sought to hold him up to public contempt. His theories about the dysfunctions of contemporary Muslim thought were veritable indictments; the imams rejected his writings in toto, even going so far as to predict hellfire for anyone who dared to read them. For the ordinary devout Muslim, Dr. Jalal was nothing but a mountebank, a Western lackey in the pay of factions hostile to Islam in general and to Arabs in particular. I myself detested him; I thought his learning perverted, exhibitionistic, and conventional, and his contempt for his people seemed obvious to me. In my eyes, he offered one of the most repulsive examples of those traitors who proliferated like rats in European media and academic circles, fully prepared to exchange their souls for the privilege of seeing their photographs in a newspaper and hearing themselves talked about. I didn't disapprove of the fatwas that condemned him to death; the imams hoped to put an end to his incendiary rants, which he published at length in the Western press and delivered with offensive zeal in television studios. I was, therefore, amazed—and also, I must admit, rather relieved—when I learned that he'd made an about-face.

The first time I saw Dr. Jalal in the flesh was the second day after my arrival in Beirut. Sayed had insisted that I attend the doctor's talk. "He's magnificent!" Sayed declared.

The event took place in an auditorium not far from the university. There was a huge crowd, hundreds of people standing beside and behind the rows of chairs that had been taken by storm hours before the doctor was scheduled to appear. Students, women, girls, family men, government workers packed the immense room. Their hubbub sounded like a seething volcano. When the doctor appeared on the platform, escorted by militiamen, the shouts of welcome shook the walls and rattled the windows. After the applause died down, he delivered a magisterial lecture on imperialist hegemony and the disinformation campaigns behind the demonization of Muslims.

I adored the man that day. It's true that his looks are unprepossessing, that he drags his feet and dresses carelessly, that his exhalations are disconcerting and his alcoholic's laziness incorrigible, but when he starts to speak—my God, when he merely adjusts the microphone and looks at his audience!—he exalts everyone in the hall. Better than anyone, he knows how to express our anguish and the insults we suffer and the necessity of breaking our silence and rising up. "Today, we're the West's flunkies; tomorrow, *our children will be its slaves!*" he cried, stressing the final clause. And the audience erupted, experiencing en masse a kind of delirium. If some plausible joker had sicced the crowd on the enemy at that moment, all the Western embassies in Beirut would have been reduced to ashes. Dr. Jalal has a knack for mobilizing everyone. The accuracy of his analyses and the effectiveness of his arguments are a joy to consider. No imam can match him; no speaker is better at turning a murmur into a cry. He's hypersensitive and exceptionally intelligent, a mentor of rare charisma.

At the end of his lecture, responding to a student's remarks, Dr. Jalal said, "The Pentagon is out to catch the devil in his own trap. Those people are convinced they're several steps ahead of God. They were planning their war on Iraq for years before it started. September eleventh wasn't the trigger; it was the pretext. The idea of destroying Iraq goes back to the moment when Saddam laid the very first stone for the foundation of his nuclear site. The Pentagon's target was neither the despot himself nor his country's oil; it was Iraqi genius. Nevertheless, mixing business with pleasure is perfectly acceptable; you can bring a country to its knees and pump out its lifeblood at the same time. Americans love to kill two birds with one stone. What they were aiming at in Iraq was the perfect crime. But they went that one better: They made their motive for the crime the guarantee of their impunity. Let me explain. Why attack Iraq? Because Iraq is believed to possess weapons of mass destruction. How can you attack Iraq without running too great a risk yourself? By first making sure that Iraq has no weapons of mass destruction. Is this not the height of combinative genius? The rest came of its own accord, like saliva to the mouth. The Americans manipulated the planet by scaring everybody. Then, to be sure their troops wouldn't be at risk, they obliged the UN experts to do the dirty job for them, and at no cost to themselves. Once they were certain there were no nuclear firecrackers in Iraq, they unleashed their military might upon a population already and deliberately beaten down by embargoes and psychological harassment. And the deal was done."

I had an offense to wash away in blood; to a Bedouin, that duty was as sacred as prayer to the faithful. And with Dr. Jalal's words, the offense was grafted onto the Cause.

"Are you sick?" he asks me, gesturing toward the array of medications on my night table.

This catches me off guard. Since I've never imagined entertaining him in my suite, I don't have a cover story ready. I curse myself. Why have I left all those medicine boxes and bottles lying around in plain sight, instead of putting them in the bathroom cabinet, where they belong? Sayed's instructions were strict: "Don't leave anything to chance. Distrust everyone."

Intrigued, Dr. Jalal heaves himself to his feet and walks over to the night table. "Well, well," he says. "There's enough stuff here to medicate an entire tribe."

"I have some health problems," I say stupidly.

"Big ones, it seems. What are you suffering from that makes you have to take all this?"

"I'd rather not talk about it."

Dr. Jalal picks up a few boxes, turns them over in his hand, reads the names of the medications out loud, as though they were some unintelligible graffiti, and peruses one or two fact sheets. With furrowed brow, he ponders several bottles, shaking them and rattling the pills they contain. "Have you by any chance had a transplant?" he asks.

"Exactly," I say, saved by his guess.

"Kidney or liver?"

"Please, I'd rather not talk about it."

To my great relief, he puts the bottles back in their place and returns to the sofa. "In any case," he remarks, "you seem to be in good shape."

"That's because I follow the prescriptions rigorously. I'm going to have to take those medications for the rest of my life."

"I know."

To change the subject, I say, "May I ask you an indiscreet question?"

"Is it about my mother's . . . activities?"

"I wouldn't think of such a thing."

"I discussed her escapades at length in an autobiographical work. She was a whore, no different from whores everywhere. My father knew it and kept quiet. I felt more contempt for him than for her."

I'm embarrassed.

At last, he asks, "So what's your 'indiscreet' question?"

"It's one you've probably been asked hundreds of times."

"Yes?"

"You used to be the scourge of the jihadis. Now you're their spokesman. How did that happen?"

He bursts out laughing and relaxes. Obviously, he doesn't mind addressing this subject. He clasps his hands behind his neck and stretches grossly; then he licks his lips, his face suddenly turns serious, and he begins his tale. "Sometimes things dawn on you when you least expect them. Like a revelation. All of a sudden, you can see clearly, and the little details you hadn't figured into your calculations take on an extraordinary dimension. . . . I was in a bubble. No doubt, my hatred for my mother blinded me to such a degree that everything connecting me to her repulsed me, even my blood, my country, my family. The truth is, I was the West's 'nigger,' nothing more. They had spotted my flaws. The honors and requests they flooded me with were the instruments of my subjugation. I was asked to speak on every television panel imaginable. If a bomb went off somewhere, pretty soon I was up in front of the microphones and the footlights. My words conformed to Westerners' expectations. I was a comfort to them. I said what they wanted to hear, what they would have said themselves had I not been there to relieve them of that task and the hassles that went with it. I fit them, so to speak, like a glove. Then, one day, I arrived in Amsterdam, a few weeks after a Muslim had murdered a Dutch filmmaker because of a blasphemous documentary that showed a naked woman covered with verses from the Qur'an. You must have heard about this affair."

"Vaguely."

Dr. Jalal makes a face and goes on. "As a rule, there was standing room only, and not much of that, in the university hall where I spoke. This time, however, there were many empty seats, and the people who had made the effort to come were there to see the filthy beast up close. Their hatred was written on their faces. I was no longer Dr. Jalal, their ally, the man who defended their values and what they thought of as democracy. Forget about all that. In their eyes, I was only an Arab, the spitting image of the Arab who murdered the filmmaker. They had changed radically, those pioneers of modernity, the most tolerant and emancipated people in Europe. There they were, displaying their racism like a trophy. As far as they were concerned, from that point on, all Arabs were terrorists, and what was I? Dr. Jalal, the sworn enemy of the fundamentalists, the target of fatwas, who worked his ass off for them—what was I? In their eyes, I was a traitor to my nation, which made me doubly contemptible. And that's when I experienced a kind of illumination. I realized what a dupe I'd been, and I especially realized where my true place was. And so I packed my bags and returned to my people."

Having got all that off his chest, he withdraws into somber silence. I'm afraid my indiscretion has touched a particularly sensitive spot and opened a wound he'd like to let heal.

# 19

*   •   *

After dozing off on the sofa, Dr. Jalal finally leaves, and I hasten to remove my medications from sight. I'm furious at myself. What was I thinking? Even a dimwit would have been astounded at the giant battery of medicine bottles crowded onto my night table. Did Dr. Jalal suspect anything? Why, contrary to all expectation, did he come to my room? I didn't think he was in the habit of visiting other guests. Except for when he's getting drunk by himself in the bar, he's almost never to be seen in the corridors of the hotel. Moreover, he's generally sullen and aloof and returns neither smiles nor greetings. The hotel staff avoids him, because he's liable to fly into an awful rage over some triviality. On the other hand, I'm pretty sure he knows nothing about the purpose of my sojourn in Beirut. He's in Lebanon to give his lectures; I'm here for reasons that are top secret. Why did he join me yesterday on the terrace, when he's a man who abhors company?

I intrigue him; there's no doubt about it.

I take a lot of medication. For three solid days after my

arrival in Beirut, various physicians examined me, evaluated me, sounded my depths, and drew my blood, assiduously passing me back and forth between scan machines and cardiographs. After being pronounced sound of body and mind, I was introduced to a certain Professor Ghany, the only person authorized to decide whether or not I would be sent on the mission. He's a wiry old gentleman, dry as a cudgel, with a nimbus of thick, stringy hair surrounding his head. He subjected me to countless tests—some to determine what products I might be allergic to, others to prepare my body to resist possible rejection phenomena—and then he gave me my many prescriptions. Sayed informed me that Professor Ghany's a virologist, but he's also active in other scientific fields; a gray eminence without peer, Sayed says, almost a magician, who worked for decades in the most prestigious American research institutions before being kicked out *because he was an Arab and a Muslim.*

Until yesterday, everything was proceeding normally. Shakir picked me up and took me to a private clinic north of the city. He waited for me in the car until the consultations were over, and then he drove me back to the hotel. No questions asked.

Dr. Jalal's intrusion troubles me. Ever since he left, I can't stop going over our few encounters. Where did I make my mistake? When did I first arouse his curiosity? Did someone around me blow my cover? "I hope you're going to give it to them good and hard, those bastards." What was that supposed to mean? Who authorized him to address me in such a fashion?

Summoned, apparently, by my distress, Shakir finds me

pondering these mysteries. "Is anything wrong?" he asks as he closes the door behind him.

I'm stretched out on the sofa. The rain has stopped at last, but from outside you can hear the swishing sound of vehicles driving through water. In the sky, thick brown clouds are gathering, preparing for the next downpour.

Shakir grabs a chair and straddles it backward. He's not as young as I thought, thirty or so, handsome and jovial, with broad shoulders, a stubborn chin, and long hair pulled back in an austere ponytail. He must be nearly six feet tall. His blue eyes have a mineral luster, and their gaze is a little vague as they settle here and there, as though his head were somewhere else. I bonded with Shakir the moment I shook his hand, back on the Syrian border, when Sayed consigned me to him and Imad, who then brought me clandestinely into Lebanon. It's true that Shakir doesn't talk very much, but he knows how to be there. We can stand side by side and look at the same thing without exchanging a word.

But something's different now. Ever since his friend Imad was found dead of an overdose, Shakir has lost his proud assurance. Before, he was crackling with energy. You didn't have time to hang up the phone before he rang the doorbell. He put the same vigor and dedication into everything he did. Then the police discovered the body of his closest collaborator, and that was a sad jolt for Shakir. It was as though he'd hit a wall.

I didn't know Imad very well. Except for our journey from the Jordanian border to Lebanon, he and I weren't together much. He'd come with Shakir to pick me up at the hotel, and that was it. He was a shy kid, crouched in his partner's shadow. He didn't seem like a person who used drugs. When I learned how he'd been found, lying blue-mouthed on a bench in a public square, I immediately suspected that he'd actually been murdered. Shakir agreed with me, but he kept it to himself. Only once, I asked him what he thought about Imad's death; his blue eyes darkened. We've avoided the subject ever since.

"Any problems?" he asks.

"Not really," I reply.

"You look upset."

"What time is it?"

He consults his watch and tells me we still have twenty minutes before it's time to leave. I get up and go to the bathroom to wash my face. The cold water calms me down. I stay bent over the sink for a long time, dousing my face and the back of my neck. When I straighten up, I catch Shakir looking at me in the bathroom mirror. He's standing with his arms crossed over his chest, his head tilted to one side, and his shoulder against the wall. I run my wet fingers through my hair, and he watches me with a glassy gleam in his eye.

"If you're not feeling well, I'll postpone the meeting," he says.

"I'm fine."

He purses his lips skeptically. "It's your call. Sayed arrived this morning. He'll be very happy to see you again."

"He hasn't given a sign of life for more than two weeks," I point out.

"He had to go back to Iraq." Handing me a towel, he adds, "Things are getting really bad over there."

I dry my face and pass the towel around my neck. "Dr. Jalal came by to see me this afternoon," I blurt out.

Shakir raises an eyebrow. "Oh, did he?"

"He also came out on the terrace last night to chat with me."

"And?"

"It's on my mind."

"He said unpleasant things?"

I turn and face Shakir. "What kind of guy is he, this Dr. Jalal?"

"I have no idea. Not my department. But if you want my advice, don't get all worked up over nothing."

I go into my bedroom, put on my shoes and my jacket, and announce that I'm ready. "I'll go and get the car," he says. "Wait for me in front of the hotel."

❋ • ❋

The automatic gate slides open with a screech, and we enter the grounds of the clinic. Shakir takes off his sunglasses before steering his 4×4 into an interior courtyard. He parks between two ambulances and switches off the engine. "I'll wait for you here," he says.

"Very good," I reply, getting out of the vehicle.

He winks at me and leans over to pull the door closed.

I climb up a wide flight of granite steps and enter the lobby of the clinic. A male nurse intercepts me and shows me to Dr. Ghany's office on the second floor. Sayed's there, hunched in an armchair, his fingers clutching his knees. A smile lights up his face when he sees me come in. He stands up and spreads his arms, and we embrace forcefully. Sayed's lost a lot of weight. I can feel his bones through his gray suit.

The professor waits until we release each other before inviting us to take the two chairs facing him. He's nervous; he can't stop tapping the desk blotter with his pencil. "All your test results are excellent," he announces. "The treatment I prescribed has proved effective. You're perfect for the mission."

Sayed stares at me intensely. The professor lays his pencil aside, braces himself against the desk, lifts his chin, and looks me straight in the eyes. "It's not just any mission," he informs me.

I don't turn away.

"We're talking about an operation of a unique kind," the professor goes on, slightly unsettled by my stiffness and my silence. "The West has left us no choice. Sayed's just back from Baghdad. The situation there is alarming. Iraq's imploding, and its people are on the verge of civil war. If we don't act quickly, the region will go up in flames and never recover."

"The Shi'a and the Sunnis are tearing one another to pieces," Sayed adds. "The spirit of revenge is growing stronger every day."

"I think it's you two who are wasting time," I say. "Tell me what you expect of me and I'll do it."

The professor freezes, his hand on his pencil. The two men exchange furtive glances. The professor's the first to react, holding the pencil suspended in the air. "It's not an ordinary mission," he says. "The weapon we're entrusting to you is both effective and undetectable. No scanner will reveal it; no search will find it. It makes no difference how you carry it. You can do so naked, if that appeals to you. The enemy won't detect anything."

"I'm listening."

The pencil touches the blotter, rises slowly, comes down on a pile of paper, and doesn't move again. Sayed thrusts his hands between his thighs. A heavy silence weighs like a leaden cape on the three of us. One or two unbearable minutes pass. Far off, we can hear the hum of an air conditioner, or perhaps a printer. The professor picks up his pencil again, turning it round and round in his fingers. He knows that this is the decisive moment, and he fears it. After having cleared his throat and clenched his fists, he gathers himself and says abruptly, "The weapon in question is a virus."

I don't flinch, nor do I completely understand what he's said. I don't see the connection with the mission. The word *virus* passes through my consciousness. A strange term, I think, but it leaves me with a feeling of déjà vu. What's a virus? Where have I heard that word? It comes back to me, yet I still can't manage to situate it properly. Then the examinations, the X rays, and the medications fall into place in the puzzle, and the word *virus* slowly, bit by bit, gives up its secret. Microbe, microorganism, flu, illness, epidemic, treatment, hospitalization—all sorts of stereotyped images parade through my head, mingle, and blur. . . . However, I still don't see the connection.

Sayed sits beside me, unmoving, as tense as a bowstring. The professor continues his explanation. "A revolutionary virus. I've spent years perfecting it. Untold amounts of money have been sunk into this project. Men have given their lives to make it possible."

What's he telling me?

"A virus," the professor repeats.

"I understand. So what's the problem?"

"The only problem is you. Are you game for the mission or not?"

"I never back down."

"You'll be the person carrying the virus."

I'm having trouble following him. Something in his words escapes me. I'm not digesting them. It's as though I've become autistic. The professor continues: "All those tests and medications were designed to determine whether your body would be fit to receive it. Your physical reactions have been impeccable."

Only now do I see the light; all at once, everything becomes clear in my mind. The weapon in question is a virus. My mission consists in carrying a virus. That's it; I've been physically prepared to receive a virus. A virus. My weapon, my bomb, my kamikaze airplane . . .

Sayed tries to grab my wrist; I avoid his touch.

"You look surprised," the professor tells me.

"I am. But that's all."

"Is there a problem?" Sayed inquires.

"There's no problem," I say curtly.

The virologist tries to follow up. "We have—"

"Professor, I'm telling you there's no problem. Virus or bomb, what's the difference? You don't need to explain the why; just tell me the when and the where. I'm neither more nor less brave than the Iraqis who are dying every day in my country. When I agreed to follow Sayed, I divorced myself from life. I'm a dead man waiting for a decent burial."

"I never doubted your determination for a second," Sayed tells me, his voice shaking a little.

"In that case, why not move directly to concrete matters? When will I have the . . . the honor of serving my Cause?"

"In five days," the professor replies.

"Why not today?"

"We're adhering to a strict schedule."

"Very well. I won't leave my hotel. You can come and fetch me whenever you want—the sooner the better. I can't wait to recover my soul."

❖　•　❖

Sayed dismisses Shakir and invites me to get into his car. We drive across half the city without saying a word. I sense that he's searching for words but not finding any. Once, unable to stand the silence, he reaches for the radio and then draws his hand back. It's raining very hard again. The buildings seem to submit to the deluge with resignation. Their gloominess puts me in mind of the tramp I watched not long ago from the window of my hotel room.

We pass through a neighborhood with ravaged buildings. The marks of war take a long time to erase. Work sites devour large sections of the city, bristling with cranes, their bulldozers attacking the ruins like pit bulls. At an intersection, two drivers are screaming at each other; their cars have just collided. Shards of glass lie scattered on the asphalt. Sayed runs a red light and nearly crashes into a car that suddenly appears out of a side street. Drivers on all sides angrily blow their horns at us. Sayed doesn't hear them. He's lost in whatever's on his mind.

We take the coastal road. The sea is stormy, as though tormented by an immense anger. Some vessels lie in the roadstead; in the general grayness, they look like phantom ships.

We drive about forty kilometers before Sayed emerges from his fog. He discovers that he's missed his turn, twists his head around to get his bearings, abruptly veers onto the shoulder of the road, brings the car to a stop, and waits until he can put his thoughts into some order. Then he says, "It's a very important mission. Very, very important. I didn't tell you anything about the virus because no one must know. And I really believed, after all those visits to the clinic, that you would start figuring it out yourself. . . . Do you understand what I'm saying? It may look to you as though I kept quiet because I wanted to confront you with a fait accompli, but that's not the case. As of right now, nothing's set in stone. Please don't think there's any pressure on you; please don't imagine there's been any breach of trust. If you don't consider yourself ready, or if this mission doesn't suit you, you can back out and no one will hold it against you. I just want to assure you that the next candidate won't be treated any differently. He won't know anything until the last moment, either. For our security and for the success of the mission, we have to operate this way."

"Are you afraid I'm not up to it?"

"No!" he cried out before he could stop himself. His finger joints whitened as he clutched the steering wheel. "I'm sorry, I didn't mean to raise my voice. I'm just confused, that's all. If you felt cheated or trapped, I wouldn't forgive myself. I warned you in Baghdad that this would be a mission unlike any other. I couldn't tell you anything more than that. Do you understand?"

"Now I do."

He takes out his handkerchief and wipes the corners of his mouth and under his ears. "Are you angry at me?"

"Not even slightly, Sayed. I was surprised to learn that the mission involves a virus, but that has no effect on my commitment. A Bedouin doesn't lose his nerve. His word is like a rifle shot—it can't be taken back. I'll carry this virus. In the name of my family and in the name of my country."

"I haven't been able to sleep since I put you in the professor's hands. It's got nothing to do with you—I know you'll go all the way. But this operation's so . . . crucial. You have no idea how important it is. We're down to our last shot, the last cartridge in the chamber. Afterward, a new era will be born, and the West will never look at us the same way again. I'm not afraid of dying, but our deaths have to mean something. They have to change our situation. Otherwise, our martyrs aren't much use. For me, life's nothing but an insane gamble; it's the way you die that determines whether you win the bet. I don't want our children to suffer. If our parents had taken things in hand in their day, we wouldn't be so miserable. But, alas, they waited for the miracle instead of going out and finding it, and so we're compelled to change our fate ourselves."

He turns toward me. His face is deathly pale, and his eyes shimmer with furious tears. "If you could see Baghdad— if you could see what it's become: ruined sanctuaries, mosques at war with one another, fratricidal slaughter. We're overwhelmed. We call for calm, and no one listens. It's true that we were hostages back when Saddam was in power. But, good God! Now we're zombies. Our cemeteries are full, and our prayers get blown to pieces along with our minarets. How did we come to this? If I can't sleep, it's because we expect everything, *absolutely everything,* from you. You're our only recourse, our last-ditch stand. If you succeed, you'll put things back in their proper order, and a new day will dawn for us. The professor hasn't explained to you the nature of the virus, has he?"

"There's no need for that."

"Yes, there is. It's imperative that you know what your sacrifice will mean to your people and to all the oppressed peoples of the earth. You represent the end of the imperialist hegemony, the turning wheel of fortune, the redemption of the just—"

This time, *I'm* the one who grabs *his* wrist. "Please, Sayed, have faith in me. It would kill me if you didn't."

"I have complete faith in you."

"Then don't say anything. Let things take their course. I don't need to be accompanied. I'll know how to find my way all by myself."

"I'm just trying to tell you how much your sacrifice—"

"There's no point in telling me that. You know how people are in Kafr Karam. We never talk about a project if we really intend to accomplish it one day. If you don't keep your dearest wishes silent, they won't bear fruit. So let's just shut up. I want to go all the way, without flinching. In full confidence. Do you understand me?"

Sayed nods. "You're surely right. The man who has faith in himself doesn't need it from others."

"Exactly, Sayed. Exactly."

He puts the car in reverse and backs up to a gravel trail. We turn onto it and head back to Beirut.

※　●　※

I've spent a good part of the night on the hotel terrace, leaning on the balustrade, looking down at the avenue, and hoping that Dr. Jalal would turn up. I feel all alone. I try to get a hold of myself. I need Jalal's anger to fill my blank spots. But Jalal is nowhere to be found. I went and knocked on his door—twice. He wasn't in his room, nor was he in the bar. From my lookout post on the terrace, I peer down at the cars that stop at the curb, watching for his rickety silhouette. People enter and leave the hotel; their voices reach me in amplified fragments before dissolving into the other sounds of the night. A crescent moon, as sharp and white as a sickle, adorns the sky. Higher up, strings of stars sparkle in the background. It's cold; my sighs are visible. I pull my jacket tight around me and puff into my numbed fists until my eyes bulge. My mind feels empty. Ever since the word *virus* penetrated my consciousness, a toxin has been prowling around in there, waiting to be released at any moment. I don't want to give it the chance to poison my heart. That toxin's the devil. It's the trap lying in my path; it's my weakness and my ruin. And I have vowed before my saints and my ancestors never to yield. So I look away; I look at the late-night crowd in the street, the passing cars, the festive neon lights, and the thronged shops. The sights solicit my eyes, and I let them take over from my brain. This city excels in solicitation!

Just yesterday, it was draped in an immense shroud that muffled its lights and its echoes and reduced its former excesses to a cold anxiety, rooted in uncertainty and failure. Has Beirut so completely forgotten its torment that it has no compassion for its cousins in their distress? What a hopeless place! In spite of the specter of civil war that hovers over its banquets, it pretends there's nothing amiss. And those people on the sidewalk, charging around like the cockroaches in the gutters, where are they running to? What dream could reconcile them to their sleep? What dawn to their tomorrows? No, I'm not going to end up like them. I don't want to resemble them in any way. . . .

Two o'clock in the morning. There's no one left in the street. The shops have lowered their shutters, and the last ghosts have vanished. Jalal won't come back tonight. Do I really need him?

I return to my room, chilled but reinvigorated. The fresh air has done me good. The toxin that was prowling around in my mind gave up in the end. I slip under the covers and turn off the light. I'm at ease in the darkness. My dead and my living are near me. Virus or bomb, what's the difference, when you're grasping an offense in one hand and, in the other, the Cause? I don't need a sleeping pill. I've returned to my element. Everything's fine. *Life's nothing but an insane gamble; it's the way you die that determines whether or not you win the bet.* That's how legends are born.

# 2 O

❖ • ❖

A middle-aged man presents himself at the reception desk.
He's tall and bony, with the waxy complexion of an aes-
thete. His outfit includes an old gray overcoat, a dark
suit, and leather shoes worn at the heel. With his large
horn-rimmed glasses and his tie, which has seen happier
days, he exhibits the dignified and pathetic bearing of a
schoolteacher nearing retirement. A newspaper protrudes
from under one of his arms. He presses the button on the
counter and waits calmly for someone to come and attend
to him.

"May I help you, sir?"

"Good evening. Please tell Dr. Jalal that Mohammed
Seen is here."

The desk clerk turns toward the pigeonholes. Although
there's no key in number 36, he says, "Dr. Jalal's not in his
room, sir."

"I saw him come in not two minutes ago," the man in-
sists. "He may be resting, or perhaps he's very busy, but I'm

an old friend of his, and I know he'd be unhappy to learn that I came by to see him and he wasn't informed."

From my seat in the lobby, where I'm drinking a cup of tea, I catch the clerk's eye as he looks past the visitor. Then the clerk scratches his head and finally picks up the telephone. "I'll see if he's in the bar," he says. "And you are?"

"Mohammed Seen, novelist."

The desk clerk dials a number, loosens his bow tie, and bites his lip when someone answers on the other end. "Good evening, this is the front desk. Is Dr. Jalal in the bar? A gentleman named Mohammed Seen is waiting for him in the lobby. . . . Of course." He hangs up and asks the novelist to be so kind as to wait.

Dr. Jalal erupts from the elevator, his arms open wide and a smile splitting his face from ear to ear. "*Allah, ya baba!* What good wind blows you here, *habibi*? I'm overcome—the great Seen remembers me!" The two men embrace warmly and kiss each other's cheeks, delighted at this reunion; they spend a long moment in mutual contemplation and reciprocal backslapping. "What an excellent surprise!" the doctor exclaims. "How long have you been in Beirut?"

"A week. The Institut français invited me."

"Excellent. I hope you're staying awhile longer. I'd love to spend some time in your company."

"I have to go back to Paris on Sunday."

"That gives us two days. God, you look great. Come, let's go up to the terrace. The view from there is splendid. We can watch the sunset and admire the city lights."

They disappear into the elevator.

*    •    *

The two men sit in the glassed-in alcove on the hotel terrace. I hear them laughing and exchanging claps on the
shoulder before I slip surreptitiously behind a wooden
panel where they can't see me.

Mohammed Seen extricates himself from his overcoat
and lays it across the arm of his chair.

"Will you have a drink?" Jalal suggests.

"No, thanks."

"Damn, it's been a long time. Where do you live these
days?"

"I'm a nomad."

"I read your last book. I thought it was simply marvelous."

"Thank you."

The doctor sinks back into his chair and crosses his legs.
He smiles as he looks the novelist up and down, clearly
overjoyed to see him again.

The novelist leans forward with his elbows on his knees,
joins his hands like a Buddhist monk, and delicately rests
his chin on his fingertips. His enthusiasm has vanished.

"Don't make such a face, Mohammed. Is there some
problem?"

"Just one: you."

The doctor throws his head back in a short, sharp laugh.
He recovers immediately, as if he's suddenly absorbed what
the other has said. "You have a problem with me?"

The novelist straightens his back; his hands clasp his
knees. "I won't beat around the bush, Jalal. I attended your
lecture the day before yesterday. I still can't get over it."

"Why didn't you come and see me right afterward?"

"With all those people orbiting around you? To tell you the truth, I hardly recognized you. I was so baffled, I think I was the last person to leave the auditorium. I was stupe-fied, I really was. I felt as though a roofing tile had fallen on my head."

Jalal's smile disappears. His face takes on a pained, solemn expression, and furrows crease his brow. For a long time, he scratches his lower lip, hoping to eke out a word capable of breaking through the invisible wall that has just sprung up between him and the novelist. He frowns again and then says at last, "As bad as that, Mohammed?"

"I'm still stunned, if you want to know the truth."

"Well, I assume you've come to teach me a lesson, mas-ter. Have at it. Don't hold back."

The novelist lifts his overcoat, pats it nervously, and pulls out a pack of cigarettes. When he holds it out to the doctor, Jalal refuses with a brusque movement of his hand. The vi-olence of the gesture doesn't escape the novelist's notice.

The doctor barricades himself behind his disappoint-ment. His face is drawn, and his eyes are filled with cold animosity.

The writer looks for his lighter but can't put his hands on it; as Jalal doesn't offer his own, Seen gives up the idea of smoking.

"I'm waiting," the doctor reminds him in a guttural voice.

The writer nods. He puts the cigarette back in the pack and the pack back in the overcoat, which he returns to the arm of his chair. He looks as though he's trying to gain time so he can get his thoughts in order. He takes a deep breath and blurts out, "How can a man turn his coat so quickly, from one day to the next?"

The doctor trembles. His face muscles twitch. He doesn't seem to have expected such a frontal attack. After a long silence, during the course of which his eyes remain fixed, he replies, "I didn't turn my coat, Mohammed. I simply realized that I was wearing it inside out."

"You were wearing it right, Jalal."

"That's what I thought. I was wrong."

"Is it because they didn't give you the Three Academies Medal?"

"You think I didn't deserve it?"

"You deserved it, hands down. But not getting it isn't the end of the world."

"It was the end of my dream. The proof is that everything changed afterward."

"What changed?"

"The deal. Now we're the ones passing out the cards. Better yet, we set the rules of the game."

"What game, Jalal? The massacre game? Is that anybody's idea of a good time? You jumped off a moving train. You were better off before."

"As what? An Arab Uncle Tom?"

"You weren't an Uncle Tom. You were an enlightened man. We're the world's conscience now, you and I and the other intellectual orphans, jeered by our own people and spurned by the hidebound establishment. We're in the minority, of course, but we exist. And we're the only ones capable of changing things, you and I. The West is out of the race. It's been overtaken by events. The battle, the real battle, is taking place among the Muslim elite, that is, between us two and the radical clerics."

"Between the Aryan race and the non-Aryans."

"That's false and you know it. Today, our struggle is *internal*. Muslims are on the side of the person who can project their voice, the Muslim voice, as far as possible. They don't care whether he's a terrorist or an artist, an impostor or a righteous man, an obscure genius or an elder statesman. They need a myth, an idol. Someone capable of representing them, of expressing them in their complexity, of defending them in some way. Whether with the pen or with bombs, it makes little difference to them. And so it's up to us to choose our weapons, Jalal. *Us*: you and me."

"I've chosen mine. And there aren't any others."

"You don't really think that."

"Yes, I do."

"No, you don't. You're not a true believer. You're just a turncoat."

"I forbid you—"

"All right. I haven't come here to upset you. But I wanted to tell you this: We bear a heavy responsibility on our shoulders, Jalal. Everything depends on us, on you and me. Our victory will mean the salvation of the whole world. Our defeat will mean chaos. We have in our hands an incredible instrument: our double culture. It allows us to know what's going on, who's right and who's wrong, where some are flawed, why others are blocked. The West is mired in doubt. It's used to imposing its theories as though they were absolute truths, but now they're meeting resistance and coming apart. After so many centuries, the West is losing its bearings; it's no longer lulled by its illusions. Hence the metastasis that's brought us the current dialogue of the deaf, which pits pseudomodernity against pseudobarbarity."

"The West isn't modern; it's rich. And the 'barbarians' aren't barbarians; they're poor people who don't have the wherewithal to modernize."

"I couldn't agree more. But that's where we can intervene and put things in perspective, calm people down, readjust their focus, and get rid of the stereotypes this whole frightful mistake is founded on. We're the golden mean, the proper balance of things."

"That's arrant nonsense. I used to think that way, too. To survive the intellectual imperialism that snubbed me—me, an educated man, a scholar—I told myself exactly the same things you've just told me. But I was sweet-talking myself. The only risks I took were in TV studios, where I criticized my people, my traditions, my religion, my family, and my saints. They *used* me. Like a piece of charcoal. I'm not charcoal. I'm a two-edged blade. They've blunted me on one side, but I can still gut them with the other. And don't think this has anything to do with the Three Academies Medal. That was just one more disappointment among many. The truth lies elsewhere. The West has become senile. It's not aging well—in fact, it's just an old, paranoid pain in the ass. Its imperialistic nostalgia prevents it from admitting that the world has changed. You can't even reason with it. And therefore it has to be euthanized. . . . Look, you don't build a new building on top of an old one. You raze it to the ground, and then you start over, from the foundation up."

"With what? Plastic explosives, booby-trapped packages, spectacular crashes. Vandals don't build; they destroy. We have to take responsibility, Jalal. We have to learn to suffer low blows and injustices from those we consider our allies. We have to transcend our rage. It's a question of humanity's future. What can our disillusions weigh in comparison with the threat hanging over the world? They didn't treat you decently; I don't deny it—"

"Nor you, either. Remember?"

"Is that a valid reason for deciding the fate of nations—the obnoxious conceit of a handful of Templars?"

"In my view, those dim-witted Christian warriors are the incarnation of all the arrogance the West displays toward us."

"You forget your disciples, your colleagues, all the thousands of European students whom you taught and who disseminate what you taught them, even today. That's what counts, Jalal. To hell with recognition if it's granted by people who can't hold a candle to you. According to Jonathan Swift, 'When a true genius appears in the world, you may know him by this sign, that all the dunces are in confederacy against him.' It's always been the way of the world. But your triumph consists in the knowledge you bequeath to others and in the minds you enlighten. It's not possible that you can turn your back on so much joy and satisfaction and embrace instead the jealousy of a band of unthinking fanatics."

"Obviously, Mohammed, you'll never understand. You're too nice, and you're too hopelessly naïve. I'm not getting revenge; I'm laying claim to my genius, my integrity, my right to be tall and handsome and appreciated. You think I'm going to accept exclusion, or erase the memory of so many years of ostracism and intellectual despotism and ignorant segregation? Not a chance. Those days are gone. I'm a professor emeritus—"

"You used to be, Jalal. You aren't anymore. Now that you're on the obscurantist faculty, you're proving both to your former students and to the people who wounded you that you're not worth very much after all."

"They're not worth very much to me, either. The exchange rate they charged me is no longer current. I'm my own unit of measurement. My own stock market. My own dictionary. I made the decision to revise and redefine everything I knew. To prescribe *my own* truths. The time of bowing and scraping is over. If we want to straighten up the world, the spineless have to go. We have the means of our insurrection. We've stopped being dupes, and we're not hiding anymore. In fact, we're crying out from the rooftops that the West is nothing but a crude hoax, a sophisticated lie. All its seductiveness is false, like a cheap, fancy dress. Underneath, it's not such a turn-on. Believe me, Mohammed. The West isn't a suitable match for us. We've listened and listened to its lullabies, but now we've slept long enough. Once upon a time, the West could amuse itself by defining the world as it saw fit. It called indigenous men 'natives' and free men 'savages.' It made and unmade mythologies according to its own good pleasure and raised its charlatans to divine rank. Today, the offended peoples have recovered their power of speech. They have some words to say. And our weapons say exactly the same thing."

The writer claps his hands together. "You're out of your mind, Jalal. For God's sake, come back to earth! Your place isn't with people who kill and massacre and terrorize. And you know it! I know you know it. I listened to you closely the day before yesterday. Your lecture was pathetic, and I never caught so much as a glimpse of the sincerity you used to display back when you were fighting for the triumph of restraint over anger. Back when you wanted violence, terrorism, and the misery they bring to be banished from the earth—"

"Enough!" The doctor explodes. "If you like being a doormat for worthless cretins, that's your business. But don't come and tell me how delightful it is. You're living on a manure pile, goddamn it! I can tell shit when I smell it! It stinks, and so do you, you and your simpering recommendations! Let me tell you what's clear. The West doesn't love us. It will never love you, not even you. It will never carry you in its heart, because it doesn't have one, and it will never exalt you, because it looks down on you. Do you want to remain a miserable bootlicker, a servile Arab, a raghead with privileges? Do you want to keep hoping for what they're incapable of giving you? Okay. Suffer in silence and wait. Who knows? Maybe a scrap will fall out of one of their trash bags. But don't bore me with your shoeshine-boy theories, *ya waled*. I know perfectly well what I want and where I'm going."

Mohammed Seen raises his arms in surrender, gathers up his overcoat, and stands up. I hastily withdraw.

As I go down the stairs, I can hear the two of them coming down after me. Jalal's hollering at the writer. "'I offer them the moon on a silver tray. All they see is a flyspeck on the tray. How can you expect them to take a bite of the moon?' You wrote that."

"Leave my work out of it, Jalal."

"Why so bitter, Mr. Seen? Is that an admission of defeat? Why does a magnanimous man like you have to suffer? It's because they refuse to recognize your true value. They call your rhetoric 'bombastic' and reduce your dazzling flights to imprudent 'stylistic liberties.' That's the injustice I'm fighting against, that dismissive glance they deign to bend upon our magnificence—that's what has me up in arms. Those people must realize the wrong they do us. They must understand that if they persist in spitting on the best we have, they'll have to make do with the worst. It's as simple as that."

"The intellectual world's the same everywhere: shady and deceitful. It's a sort of underworld, but without scruples and without a code of honor. It spares neither its own nor others. If it's any consolation to you, I'm more controversial and hated among my own people than I am anywhere else. It's said that no one's a prophet in his own country. I would add, 'And no one's a master in foreign lands.' No one is honored as a prophet in his own country or as a master anywhere else. My salvation comes from that revelation: I want to be neither a master nor a prophet. I'm only a writer who tries to put some of his spirit into his novels for those who may wish to receive it."

"Which means you're satisfied with crumbs."

"I am, Jalal. Completely. I'd rather be satisfied with nothing than mess up everything. As long as my sorrow doesn't impoverish anyone, it enriches me. There's no wretch like the wretch who chooses to bring misfortune where he should bring life. I could lie awake dwelling on my bad luck or my friends' grief, but the darkness makes me dream."

They catch up with me in the corridor on the ground floor. I pretend to have just come out of the men's room. They're so absorbed by their intellectuals' squabble that they walk past without noticing me.

"You're caught between two worlds, Mohammed. It's a very uncomfortable position to be in. We're in the midst of a clash of civilizations. You're going to have to decide which camp you're in."

"I'm my own camp."

"That's so pretentious! You can't be your own camp; all you can do is isolate yourself."

"You're never alone if you're moving toward the light."

"Like Icarus, you mean, or maybe like a moth? What light?"

"The light of my conscience. No shadow can obscure it."

Jalal stops short and watches the novelist walk away. When Seen pushes open the double doors that lead to the lobby, the doctor starts after him but then changes his mind and lets his hands fall to his sides. "You're still in the anal stage of awareness, Mohammed," Jalal cries out. "A world's on the march and you're cross-examining yourself. They won't give you a thing, not a thing! Those crumbs they let you have? One day, they'll take them back! You'll get nothing, I tell you, nothing, nothing. . . ."

The swinging doors close with a squeak. The sound of the writer's footsteps fades and then disappears, absorbed by the carpet in the lobby.

Dr. Jalal grabs his head with both hands and mutters an unintelligible curse.

"Do you want me to blow his brains out?" I ask.

He glares at me savagely. "Leave him alone!" he says. "There's more to life than that."

※　●　※

Dr. Jalal hasn't emerged unscathed from his encounter with the writer. He seldom rises before noon, and at night I can hear him pacing in his room. According to Shakir, Jalal has called off the lecture he'd been scheduled to give at the University of Beirut, canceled several interviews with the press, and made no further progress on the book he was about to finish.

I don't see how a scholar of his stature could be flustered by a servile scribbler. Dr. Jalal's an eloquent man, a man with great rhetorical powers. The thought of such a genius allowing himself to be caught off guard by a vulgar hack disgusts me.

This afternoon, he's slouched like a sack in an armchair, his back to the reception desk. His cigarette's dying a slow death, leaving behind a little stick of ash. Staring at the blank television screen, his legs outspread, his arms hanging down over the arms of his chair, he looks like a battered boxer slumping on a stool.

He doesn't glance over at me. On the table beside him,

some empty beer bottles accompany a glass of whiskey. The ashtray is brimming with butts.

I leave the lobby. In the hotel restaurant, I order a grilled steak, fried potatoes, and a green salad. The doctor fails to appear. I wait for him, my eyes riveted on the door. My coffee gets cold. The waiter clears my dishes and takes down my room number. No one comes through the restaurant door.

I return to the lobby. The doctor's in the same place as before, but now he's leaning his head on the back of his chair and staring at the ceiling. I don't dare approach him. And I don't dare go up to my room. I step out into the street and lose myself in the crowd.

※        •        ※

Shakir slaps his hands together forcefully when he sees me come in. He's sitting on the sofa in my suite, as white as a candle. "I looked everywhere for you," he says.

"I went for a walk on the esplanade and lost track of the time."

"You could have called, dammit. One more hour and I was going to raise the alarm. We were supposed to meet here at five o'clock."

"I told you: I lost track of the time."

Shakir restrains himself from jumping on me. My composure exasperates him, and my lack of concern fills him with rage. He raises his hands and tries to calm himself. Then he reaches down to the floor, picks up a little cardboard folder, and hands it to me. "Your airplane tickets, your passport, and your university documents. Your flight to London leaves the day after tomorrow, at ten past six in the evening."

Without opening the folder, I place it on the night table.

"Something wrong?" he inquires.

"Why do you always ask me the same question?"

"That's why I'm here."

"Have I complained about anything?"

Shakir puts his hands on his thighs and stands up. He looks red-eyed and sleep-deprived. "We're both tired," he says, still furious. "Try to rest. I'll come by tomorrow morning at eight o'clock. We're going to the clinic. Don't eat or drink anything beforehand."

He wants to add something but then decides it's not necessary. He asks, "May I go?"

"Of course," I say.

He wags his head, gives the cardboard folder one last glance, and leaves. I don't hear any steps fading away in the corridor. He must be standing guard at the door, stroking his chin and wondering I don't know what.

I lie down on the bed, clasp my hands on the back of my neck, contemplate the chandelier above me, and wait for Shakir to go away. I've come to know him; when he can't figure something out, he's incapable of making any decision before the matter is settled. Finally, I hear him go. I sit up and reach for the folder. Along with the passport, the university papers, and the British Airways tickets, it contains a student identification card, a bank card, and two hundred pounds.

I take one of the pills that usually help me to sleep, but it has no effect. It's as though I've drunk a whole thermos of coffee. Lying on my back, fully dressed, with my shoes still tied, I stare at the ceiling, which a neon sign outside splashes with bloodred light. The traffic noise has diminished. Occasional vehicles pass with a muffled swish, taunting the silence that's taken hold of the city.

In the next room, Dr. Jalal's awake, too. I hear him walking in circles. His condition has worsened.

I wonder why I didn't mention the writer's visit to Shakir.

※ • ※

Shakir's here on time. He waits in the suite while I finish my shower. I get dressed and follow him to his car, which is parked in front of a large store. Despite a chilly breeze, the sky is clear. The sun ricochets off windows, as sharp as a razor blade.

Shakir doesn't drive into the clinic's inner courtyard. He goes around the building and down a ramp to a small underground parking area. We leave the car, enter a hidden door, and climb a few flights of stairs. Professor Ghany and Sayed meet us at the entrance to a large room that looks like a laboratory. The doors leading to the aboveground floors of the clinic are reinforced and padlocked. At the end of a corridor illuminated by a series of recessed ceiling lights, there's a gleaming room entirely covered with ceramic tiles. A large glass panel divides it in two. On the other side of the glass, I see a kind of dentist's office with an armchair under a sophisticated light projector. There are metal shelves loaded with chrome-plated containers all around the room.

The professor dismisses Shakir.

Sayed avoids looking at me. He feigns interest in the professor. Both of them are tense. I'm nervous, too. My calves are tingling. My pulse pounds in my temples. I feel like vomiting.

The professor reassures me. "Everything's fine," he says, pointing me to a chair.

Sayed sits beside me; that way, he doesn't have to turn away from me. His hands are red from kneading.

The professor remains on his feet. With his hands in the pockets of his lab coat, he informs me that the moment of truth has come. "We're going to proceed to the injection shortly," he says, his voice choked with emotion. "And I want to explain to you what's going to happen. Clinically, your body is fit to receive the . . . the *foreign* body. In the beginning, there will be some side effects, but nothing serious. Probably some dizziness in the first few hours, maybe a touch of nausea, but then everything will return to normal. I want to put your mind at rest immediately. Before today, with the help of volunteers, we've carried out several tests, and all along adjustments have been made as required, based on whatever complications arose. The . . . *vaccine* you're going to receive is a total success. You have nothing to worry about on that score. After the injection, we're going to keep you under observation all day—a simple security measure. When you leave the clinic, you'll be in perfect physical condition. Forget about all the medications I prescribed for you earlier—they're no longer necessary. I've replaced them with two different pills, each of which must be taken three times a day for a week. You leave for London tomorrow. A physician will assist you once you're there. In the course of the first week, things will go along normally. The incubation period won't cause you any major undesirable effects. It varies from ten to fifteen days. The first symptoms to appear will be a high fever and convulsions; your medicine will be at your side. After this phase, your urine will gradually turn red. From that moment, the contagion is operational. Your mission then will consist in riding the subway and going to train stations, stadiums, and supermarkets, with the goal of contaminating the maximum number of people. Particularly in train stations, so the epidemic will spread to the other regions of the kingdom. The phenomenon propagates with lightning speed. The people you contaminate will transmit the virus to others less than six hours before they themselves are struck down. It acts somewhat like the Spanish flu, but the catastrophe will have decimated a good part of the population before people realize that the two epidemics aren't really alike at all. This new one is unique, and we alone have the knowledge that will be required to stop its further spread. And our intervention will require compliance with certain conditions. This is an unstoppable mutating virus. A great revolution. It is *our* ultimate weapon. . . . The physician in London will explain whatever you'd like to know. You can confide in him; he's my closest collaborator. . . . After the onset, you'll have three to five days to visit all the most frequented public places."

Sayed takes out a handkerchief and pats his forehead and his temples. He's on the point of passing out.

"I'm ready, professor." I don't recognize my voice. I have the feeling I'm slipping into a trance. I pray for the strength to get up and walk without collapsing to the air lock that leads to the room behind the glass panel. My sight blurs for a few seconds. I breathe deeply, struggling for a little air. Then I come to my senses and heave myself to my feet. My calves are still tingling and my legs wobble, but the floor remains firm. The professor puts on a silver HAZMAT suit, complete with mask and gloves, so that he's entirely covered. Sayed helps me get my own suit on and then watches us go through the air lock to the other side of the glass panel.

I place myself in the chair, which immediately starts rising and reclining with a mechanical hiss. The professor opens a small aluminum box and extracts a futuristic syringe. I close my eyes and hold my breath. When the needle enters my flesh, every cell in my body, with a single unified movement, seems to rush to the perforated spot. I feel as though I've fallen through a crack in the surface of a frozen lake, which pulls me down into its depths.

※　●　※

Sayed invites me to dinner in a restaurant not far from my hotel. It's a farewell meal, with all that such an occasion entails for him in terms of embarrassment and awkwardness. You'd think he'd lost the power of speech. He can't bring himself to say a word or look me in the face.

He won't drive me to the airport tomorrow. Neither will Shakir. A taxi's going to pick me up at 4:00 P.M. sharp.

I spent the whole day in Professor Ghany's subterranean clinic. He came in to examine me with his stethoscope from time to time. His satisfaction grew with every visit. Then I had four uninterrupted hours of a deep, dreamless sleep, followed after I woke up by only two dizzy spells. I was as thirsty as a castaway on the sea. They brought me some soup and crudités, which I couldn't finish. I didn't feel sick, but I was groggy and pasty-mouthed, and I had an incessant hum in my ears. When I got out of bed, I staggered several times; then, little by little, I was able to coordinate my movements and walk properly.

Professor Ghany didn't come and bid me farewell. Since Shakir had been sent off duty, it was Sayed who stayed with me in the afternoon. After nightfall, we left the subterranean parking garage in a small rental car and drove away from the clinic. The city lights were at full blaze, illuminating even the surrounding hills. The streets were seething, like my veins.

We pick a table in the back of the dining room so we won't be disturbed. The restaurant's packed: families with lots of kids, groups of laughing friends, couples holding hands, shifty-eyed businessmen. The waiters are busy on all fronts, some of them balancing trays, others writing down the customers' orders in minuscule notebooks. Near the entrance, an enormous and rather odd fellow laughs hard enough to burst his carotid artery. The woman sharing his meal looks uneasy; she turns toward her neighbors and smiles wanly, as if asking them to excuse her companion's indecorous behavior.

Sayed reads and rereads the menu and remains undecided. I suspect that he regrets having invited me. I ask him, "Have you been back to Kafr Karam?"

He flinches but doesn't appear to understand my question. I restate it. This relaxes him a bit; he lowers the menu he's been using as a screen and looks at me. "No," he says. "I haven't been back to Kafr Karam. Baghdad gives me no time off. But I've remained in contact with our people. They often call up and tell me what's going on over there. The latest news is that a military camp has been established in the Haitems' orchards."

"I sent my twin sister a little money. I don't know whether she got it."

"Your money order arrived intact. I talked to Kadem on the phone two weeks ago. He was trying to reach you. I told him I didn't know where you were. Then he put Bahia on. She wanted to thank you and to find out how you were doing. I promised her to do everything possible to find you."

"Thanks."

Neither of us finds anything to add. We eat in silence, each of us lost in his own thoughts.

Sayed drops me off at my hotel. Before getting out of the car, I turn to him. He smiles at me so sadly that I don't dare shake his hand. We part without pats or embraces, like two rivulets spilling off a rock.

## 22

* • *

There's a message for me at the reception desk. An envelope, taped shut, no writing on it. Inside, a card with an abstract design on the front, and on the back, a line written with a felt-tipped pen: "I'm proud to have known you. Shakir."

I slip the note into the inside pocket of my jacket. In the lobby, a large family swarms around a low table. The children squabble and jump off the backs of chairs. Their mother tries to call them to order, while the father laughs, ostensibly having a conversation on his cell phone. Beyond them sits Dr. Jalal, exasperated by the kids' racket and deep in his cups.

I go up to my room. A brand-new leather traveling bag is sitting on my bed. Inside, there are two pairs of designer pants, underwear, socks, two shirts, a thick sweater, a jacket, a pair of shoes in a bag, a toilet kit, and four large volumes of literature in English. A piece of paper is pinned to a strap: "This is your baggage. You'll buy whatever else you need once you're in place." No signature.

Dr. Jalal comes in without knocking. He's drunk, and he has to keep clutching the doorknob to avoid falling. He says, "Going on a trip?"

"I intended to tell you good-bye tomorrow."

"I don't believe you."

He staggers and catches himself twice before he manages to close the door and lean back against it. Totally disheveled, with half his shirt hanging out of his pants and his fly wide open, he looks like a bum. The muddy blotch on his left pants leg is probably the result of a fall in the street. His face is ghastly, with swollen eyelids, wild eyes, and leaking nostrils.

His mouth, which he wipes on his sleeve, has gone soft, unable to articulate two consecutive words without drooling. "So, just like that, you're going away on tiptoe, like a prowler? I've been hanging around the lobby for hours because I didn't want to miss you. And what do you do? You pass me by without a word."

"I have to pack."

"Are you running me off?"

"It's not that. I need to be alone. I have to get my bags ready and put some things in order."

He squints, thrusts out his lips, sways, and then, with a deep breath, gathering all his remaining strength, he straightens himself and cries, "*Tozz!*"

Although it's a weak cry, it makes him reel. He clutches at the doorknob again. He says, "Can you tell me where you've been from morning till night?"

"I went to see some relatives."

"My ass! I know where you were holed up, my boy. You want me to tell you where you were holed up? You were in a clinic. Or maybe I should say a nuthouse. Son of a bitch! What's that like, the world of mental-defectives? Shit!"

I'm stunned. Paralyzed.

"You think I'm stupid? You think I couldn't figure it out? A transplant, for God's sake! You don't have any more scars on your body than brains in your skull. Damn it all, don't you realize what they've done to you in that shitty fucking clinic? You have to be stark raving mad, putting yourself in Professor Ghany's hands! He's completely fucked-up in the head. I know him. He could never even dissect a white mouse without cutting his finger."

He can't know, I tell myself. Nobody knows. He's bluffing. He's trying to trap me. "What are you talking about?" I say. "What clinic? And who's this professor of yours? I was with some relatives."

"You poor sap! You think I'm trying to fool you? That moron Ghany has lost it altogether. I don't know what he shot you up with, but it's surely a load of crap." He takes his head in his hands. "Good God! Where are we, in a Spielberg film? I'd heard about that nutcase doing creepy things to prisoners of war when he was with the Taliban. But this is going too far."

"Get out of my room."

"Not a chance! It's very serious, what you're going to do. Very, very, very serious. Unthinkable. Unimaginable. I know it won't work. Your shitty virus will eat *you* alive, just you, and that's all. But even so, I'm still worried. Suppose Ghany has succeeded, loser though he is? Have you thought about the extent of the disaster? We're not talking about terrorist attacks, a few little bombs here, a few little crashes there. We're talking about pestilence. About the apocalypse.

There'll be hundreds of thousands of dead, maybe millions. If this really is a revolutionary mutating virus, who's going to stop it? With what, and how? It's completely unacceptable."

"You yourself said that the West—"

"We're well past that point, you idiot. I've said a lot of stupid fucking things in my life, but I can't let you do this. Every war has its limits. But this—this is beyond all bounds. What do you hope for after the apocalypse? What's going to be left of the world, except for rotting corpses and plagues and chaos? God himself will tear out His hair. . . ." He jabs his finger at me. "Enough of this bullshit! Everything stops now! You're not going anywhere, and neither is the filth you're carrying. Teaching the West a lesson is one thing; massacring the fucking planet is something else. I'm not playing. Game over. You're going to turn yourself in to the police. Right away. With a little luck, maybe you can be cured. If not, you'll just have to croak all by yourself, and good riddance. You unspeakable fool!"

※　●　※

Shakir arrives at once, breathless, as if he has a pack of devils on his heels. When he bursts into my suite and sees Dr. Jalal on the carpet with a pool of blood like a halo around his head, Shakir puts his hand over his mouth and utters a curse. He glances over at me, slumped in the armchair, then kneels down next to the body lying on the floor and checks to see if the doctor's still breathing. His hand pauses on Jalal's neck. Furrowing his brow, Shakir slowly withdraws his hand and stands up. His voice cracks as he says, "Go into the next room. This is no longer your problem."

I can't pull myself out of my armchair. Shakir grabs me by the shoulders and hauls me into the living room. He helps me sit on the sofa and tries to yank the bloody ashtray out of my cramped hand. "Give me that," he says. "It's all over now."

I don't understand what the ashtray's doing in my hand or why my finger joints are skinned. Then it all comes back to me, and it's as if my mind has rejoined my body; a shiver passes through me, shocking me like electricity.

Shakir succeeds in loosening my grip and taking away the ashtray, which he slips into the pocket of his overcoat. He goes into the bedroom, and I hear him talking to someone on the telephone.

I get up and go to see what I've done to the doctor. Shakir blocks my path and escorts me—not roughly, but firmly—back into the living room.

About twenty minutes later, two medical technicians enter my suite, busy themselves around the doctor, put an oxygen mask over his face, shift him onto a stretcher, and carry him away. From the window, I see them push their patient into an ambulance and drive off with their siren wailing.

Having mopped up the blood from the carpet, Shakir's sitting on the edge of my bed with his chin in his hands; his eyes are fixed on the spot where the doctor lay. I ask him, "Is it very bad?"

"He'll make it," Shakir says without conviction.

"Do you think I'm going to have problems with the hospital?"

"Those med techs are ours. They're taking him to one of our clinics. Put it out of your mind."

"He knew about everything, Shakir. About the virus, the clinic, Professor Ghany, everything. How is that possible?"

"Everything's possible."

"No one was supposed to know."

Shakir lifts his head. His eyes have almost no more blue in them. He says, "It's no longer your problem. The doctor's in our hands. We'll be able to find out the truth. You should be thinking only about your trip. Do you have all your documents?"

"Yes."

"Do you need me for anything?"

"No."

"Do you want me to stay with you awhile?"

"No."

"You're sure?"

"I'm sure."

He stands up, walks to the door, and steps out into the corridor. Then he turns and says, "I'll be in the bar in case you should . . ." He closes the door. Without a word of farewell, without so much as a sign.

※　　●　　※

The desk clerk informs me that my taxi has arrived. I pick up my bag and take one last look at the bedroom, the living room, the sun-splashed window. What am I leaving here? What am I taking away? Will my ghosts follow me? Will my memories be able to manage without me? I lower my head and walk quickly down the corridor. A couple and their two little daughters are loading their luggage into the elevator. The woman struggles in vain to budge an enormous suitcase; her husband watches her contemptuously. It doesn't occur to him to give her a hand. I take the stairs.

The clerk's busy checking in two young people. I'm relieved that I don't have to tell him good-bye. I cross the lobby in a few long strides. The taxi's parked in front of the hotel entrance. I throw my bag into the backseat and jump in. The driver, an obese fellow wearing a gigantic T-shirt, eyes me in the rearview mirror. His hair cascades down his back in long black curls. I don't know why, but I find him ridiculous, him and his sunglasses. I say, "Airport."

He nods, puts the car in first gear, and then, with studied nonchalance, slowly drives off. Slipping between a microbus and a delivery truck, he merges with the traffic. It's hot for April. The recent downpours have washed the steaming streets clean. The rays of the sun ricochet off vehicles like bullets.

At a red light, the driver lights a cigarette and turns up the sound on his car radio. It's Fairuz, singing "Habbaytak Bissayf." Her voice catapults me through space and time. Like a meteorite, I land on the edge of the gap near my village where Kadem had me listen to some of his favorite songs. Kadem! I see myself in his house again, looking at the photograph of his first wife.

"Would you mind lowering the radio?"

The driver frowns. "It's Fairuz."

"Please."

He's irritated, probably even horrified. His fat neck

trembles like a mass of gelatin. He says, "I'll turn the radio off if you want."

"I'd like that."

He turns it off, offended but resigned.

I try not to think about what happened last night. Dr. Jalal's words resound like thunder inside my skull. I shift my eyes to the crowds on the sidewalks, the shop windows, the cars passing on both sides of the cab, and everywhere I look, I see only him, with his incoherent gestures, his thick tongue, his unstoppable words. The traffic flows onto the road to the airport. I lower my window to evacuate the driver's smoke. The wind whips my face but doesn't cool me off. My temples are burning and my stomach's in an uproar. I didn't sleep a wink last night. Didn't eat anything, either. I remained shut up inside my room, counting the hours and struggling against the urge to stick my head in the toilet and puke my guts out.

The ticket counters are thronged. The public-address announcer is a woman with a nasal voice. People are kissing one another, separating, meeting, searching the crowd. It looks like everybody's getting ready to leave Lebanon. I stand in line and wait my turn. I'm thirsty and my calves are aching. A young woman asks me to give her my passport and my tickets. She says something I don't understand. "Do you have any bags?" Why does she want to know if I have any bags? She looks at the one I'm carrying. "Are you holding on to that?" What's that supposed to mean? She rolls a label around one of the straps on my bag, shows me a number and a time on my boarding card, and then points me to the area where people are kissing one another before they part. I pick up my bag and head to another counter. A uniformed agent instructs me to place my bag on a conveyor belt. On the other side of a glass, a woman watches a screen. My bag disappears into a big black hole. The security agent hands me a little tray and tells me I'm to put on it all the metal objects I'm carrying. I obey. "Coins, too."

I step through a frame. A man intercepts me, runs a wand over me, lets me go. I recover my bag, my watch, my belt, and my coins and walk to the gate indicated on my boarding card. There's no one at the counter. I take a seat near a big picture window and watch the dance of the airplanes on the tarmac. On the runway, there's a steady turnover of flights landing and taking off. I'm nervous. It's the first time in my life I've ever set foot in an airport.

I believe I must have fallen asleep.

My watch reads 5:40 P.M. All the seats around me are taken. Two ladies are busy behind the counter; the illuminated screen above their heads has been turned on. I see my flight number, the word LONDON, and the British Airways logo. On my right, an old woman pulls her cell phone out of her purse, checks to see if she has any messages, and thrusts the phone back into her purse. Two minutes later, she yanks out the phone and consults it again. She's worried, waiting for a call that doesn't come. Behind us, a future father beams upon his wife, whose belly swells under her maternity dress. He attends to her every need, alert to the slightest sign from her, eager to show her how deeply he's enraptured; his joy shines in his eyes. A young European couple leans against a vending machine, their arms around each other and their golden hair covering their faces. The boy is tall, with a fluorescent orange T-shirt and ripped jeans. The girl, as blond as a bale of hay, has to rise up on her toes in order to reach her boyfriend's lips. Their embrace is passionate, beautiful, generous. What's that like, kissing someone on the mouth? I've never kissed a girl on the mouth. I don't remember ever even holding a girl cousin's hand or having anything resembling a romance. In Kafr Karam, I dreamed about girls from a distance, secretly, almost ashamed of my weakness. At the university, I knew by sight a girl named Nawal, a doe-eyed brunette. We greeted each other with our eyes; furtive looks were our farewells. I think each of us felt something for the other, but neither of us had the nerve to find out exactly what that was. She was in another class. We contrived to pass each other in the halls—our encounters lasted long enough for a couple of strides. A smile sufficed to make us happy; we basked in its memory throughout the ensuing lectures. After classes ended, my fantasy's father or older brother would wait for her at the university gates and spirit her away from me until the following day. Then the war came and gave my daydreams the coup de grâce.

An announcement comes over the public-address system: The flight for London is now boarding. Nervous bustling begins all around me. Already two lines of passengers have formed, one on each side of the counter. The elderly woman on my right doesn't stand up. For the umpteenth time, she pulls out her mobile phone and stares at it dolefully.

With a heavy heart, she places herself at the end of the line. A young woman checks her passport and hands her a piece of her ticket. She turns around one last time and then disappears into a corridor.

I'm the only one left.

The ladies behind the counter laugh as they exchange pleasantries with a gentleman. He leaves through a glass door and comes back a few minutes later. A last-minute passenger arrives on the run, amid the squealing of his wheeled suitcase. He apologizes effusively. The ladies smile upon him and show him the corridor; he hastens toward it.

With a look of annoyance, the gentleman at the counter checks his watch. One of his colleagues leans toward a microphone and makes a final call for a missing passenger. The passenger she's talking to is me. She repeats the call a few times over the course of the next several minutes. Finally, she shrugs, puts things in order behind the counter, and runs after her two colleagues, who have preceded her into the corridor.

My airplane rolls to the middle of the tarmac. I watch it turn slowly and reach the runway.

The screen above the counter goes black.

        ❊    ●    ❊

It's long past nightfall. Other passengers joined me in the seating area before disappearing into the corridor. Now another flight is announced, and the seats around me are occupied for the third time.

A small gentleman, highly excited, takes the seat beside me. "Are you going to Paris?" he asks.

"I beg your pardon?"

"Is this the flight to Paris?"

"Yes," someone says reassuringly.

The airbus for Paris takes off, majestic, impregnable. The great halls of the airport grow quiet and sleepy. Most of the waiting areas are empty. In one, however, there are about sixty passengers, patiently waiting in what seems like religious silence.

An airport security agent comes up to me, walkie-talkie in hand. He's already made two or three passes through this section, apparently intrigued by my presence. He plants himself in front of me and asks me if everything's all right.

"I missed my flight," I say.

"I thought as much. What was your destination?"

"London."

"There aren't any more flights for London tonight. Show me your tickets, please. . . . British Airways. All the offices are closed at this hour. There's nothing I can do for you. You're going to have to come back tomorrow and explain what happened to the company concerned. I warn you, they're pretty inflexible. I don't think they'll let you use to-day's ticket tomorrow. Do you have a place to stay? You're not allowed to spend the night here. In any case, you're going to have to talk to the airline. I'll show you where their office is. Come on, follow me."

*　　●　　*

I head for the exit. My mind's a blank, and I let my feet carry me. I have no choice. A great hush has fallen over the airport. There's nothing for me here. An airport worker pushes a long caterpillar of carts ahead of him. Another applies rags to the floor. A few shadows still haunt the remoter corners. The bars and shops are closed. I have to leave.

A car pulls up beside me as I wander away from the terminal in a daze. A door opens. The driver is Shakir. He says, "Get in." I sit in the passenger's seat. Shakir skirts a parking lot and comes to a halt at a stop sign before turning onto the road, which is lined with streetlights. We roll along for an eternity without speaking or looking at each other. Shakir doesn't head for Beirut; he takes an outer ring road. His labored breathing matches the rhythm of the car's engine.

"I was sure you were going to chicken out," he says in a colorless voice. There's no reproach in his words, but, rather, a distant joy, as when a person determines that he hasn't been wrong. "When I heard them announce your name, I understood." Suddenly, he strikes the steering wheel with his fist. "Why, for God's sake? Why put us through all this trouble, only to pull out at the last minute?"

He calms down and unclenches his fist; then he notices that he's driving like a madman and eases off the gas pedal. Below us, the city evokes a giant jewelry case, open to reveal its treasures. After a while, he asks, "What happened?"

"I have no idea."

"What do you mean, you have no idea?"

"I was at the gate. I watched the passengers boarding the plane and I didn't follow them."

"Why not?"

"I told you: I have no idea."

Shakir ponders this response for a moment before he loses patience. "That's just nuts!"

When we reach the top of a hill, I ask him to stop. I want to look at the lights of the city.

Shakir parks on the side of the road. He thinks I'm going to throw up and asks me not to do it on his floor. I tell him I want to get out, I need some fresh air. Mechanically, he moves his hand to his belt and grasps the butt of his handgun. "Don't try anything cute," he warns me. "I won't hesitate to shoot you down like a dog."

"Where do you think I'm going to go with this stinking virus inside me?"

I search in the darkness for a place to sit down, find a rock, and occupy it. The breeze makes me shiver. My teeth chatter, and gooseflesh rises on my arms. Very far off, on the horizon, some ocean liners traverse the pitch-black sea, like fireflies carried away on a flood. The sigh of the waves fills the silence of a hectic night. Lower down, set back from the shore to escape the marauding waves, Beirut counts its treasures under a waxing moon.

Shakir crouches down next to me, one arm between his legs. "I've called the boys. They're going to meet us at the farm, a little higher up from here. They are not at all happy, not at all."

I pull my jacket tight around me, hoping for warmth. "I'm not moving from this spot," I say.

"Don't force me to drag you away by your feet."

"You do what you want, Shakir. Me, I'm not moving from here."

"Very well. I'm going to tell them where we are."

He pulls out his mobile phone and calls "the boys," who, it turns out, are indeed in a rage. Shakir stays cool, explain-

ing that I categorically refuse to follow him. He rings off
and announces that *they're coming,* that *they're* going to be
here soon.

I gather myself around my thighs and, with my chin
wedged between my knees, I contemplate the city. My eyes
blur; my tears mutiny. I feel sad. Why? I couldn't say. My
anxieties merge with my memories. My whole life passes
through my mind: Kafr Karam, my family, my dead, my living, the people I miss, the ones who haunt me. . . . Nevertheless, of all my memories, the most recent are the most
distinct: that woman in the airport, hopefully examining
the screen of her cell phone; that father-to-be who was so
happy, he didn't know which way to turn; that young European couple kissing each other. . . . They deserved to live
for a thousand years. I have no right to challenge their
kisses, scuttle their dreams, dash their hopes. What have I
done with my own destiny? I'm only twenty-one years old,
and all I have is the certainty that I've wrecked my life
twenty-one times over.

"Nobody was forcing you," Shakir mutters. "What made
you change your mind?"

I don't answer him. It's useless.

The minutes pass. I'm getting colder. Behind me, Shakir
paces up and down; his coattail flaps noisily in the wind.
He stops abruptly and cries out, "Here they come."

Two sets of headlights have just turned off the highway
onto the road leading to where we are.

Contrary to all expectations, Shakir puts a compassionate hand on my shoulder. He says, "I'm sorry it's come to
this."

As the vehicles come closer, Shakir's fingers dig deeper

and deeper into my flesh, hurting me. "I'm going to tell you a little secret, my man. Keep it to yourself. I hate the West more than it's possible to say, but I've thought about it, and I think you were right not to get on that plane. It wasn't a good idea."

The crunching of tires on gravel fills the air around the rock. I hear car doors slam and approaching footsteps.

I say to Shakir, "Let them be quick. I don't hold it against them. In fact, I don't hold anything against anybody anymore."

I concentrate on the lights of the city, which I was never able to perceive through the anger of men.

THE ATTACK

Dr. Amin Jaafari is an Arab-Israeli surgeon at a hospital in Tel Aviv. As an admired and respected member of his community, he has carved a space for himself and his wife, Sihem, at the crossroads of two troubled societies. Jaafari's world is abruptly shattered when Sihem is killed in a suicide bombing. As evidence mounts that Sihem could have been responsible for the catastrophic bombing, Jaafari begins a tortured search for answers. Faced with the ultimate betrayal, he must find a way to reconcile his cherished memories of his wife with the growing realization that she may have had another life, one that was entirely removed from the comfortable, modern existence that they shared.

Fiction/Literature/978-0-307-27570-7

THE SWALLOWS OF KABUL

Set in Kabul under the rule of the Taliban, this novel takes readers into the lives of two couples: Mohsen, who comes from a family of wealthy shopkeepers whom the Taliban has destroyed; Zunaira, his wife, exceedingly beautiful, who was once a brilliant teacher, and is now no longer allowed to leave her home without an escort or covering her face. Intersecting their world is Atiq, a prison keeper, a man who has sincerely adopted the Taliban ideology and struggles to keep his faith, and his wife, Musarrat, who once rescued Atiq, and is now dying of sickness and despair. Khadra brings readers into the hot, dusty streets of Kabul and offers them unflinching but compassionate insight into a society that violence and hypocrisy have brought to the edge of despair.

Fiction/Literature/978-1-4000-3376-8

Printed in the United States
by Baker & Taylor Publisher Services